The Tantric Exorcist

The Tantric Exorcist

Ashwin Mudigonda

JUGGERNAUT BOOKS
C-I-128, First Floor, Sangam Vihar, Near Holi Chowk,
New Delhi 110080, India

First published by Juggernaut Books 2021

10 9 8 7 6 5 4 3 2 1

This is a work of fiction. Any resemblance to persons, living or dead, or to actual incidents is purely coincidental.

P-ISBN: 9789353450724
E-ISBN: 9789353450731

Typeset in Adobe Caslon Pro by R. Ajith Kumar, Noida

Printed at Thomson Press India Ltd

To my guru, Sadhguru Jaggi Vasudev,
who showed me the path
To Sri M.,
who illuminated it when needed
and
To my parents

1

'Vikram!' his mother yelled. 'Last time I'm telling you. Get up!' She beat his door. 'You're late for college!' She rapped harder. 'Dei Vikky! Get up! Sleeping late-late. Then not being able to get up.'

The doorbell rang and her muttering faded as she went to answer it.

Vikram squinted and then slowly opened his eyes. He didn't want to get up this morning, for today was one of the more difficult exams, which he was sure he wasn't going to pass. His heart sank at the thought of breaking the news to his parents when he'd receive his report card in a few weeks. How was he going to explain those abysmal marks to them? He wished the problem would just go away. He picked up his phone and checked the time. It was a quarter to seven.

'I'll sleep till seven,' he told himself and flopped back into the bed. Part of him was excited that once the mock exams were over he'd have six weeks of study holidays before the university exams began. The burst of excitement fizzled out when he remembered all the cramming that lay ahead, leave alone working out complex sums for hours on end.

Vikram sat up in a huff, sweat beading his forehead. He pushed his hair back. He was trying to grow it out and it was in a phase where he could neither tie it nor would it mind itself atop his head. He exhaled in frustration. The maidservant had entered his room, switched off the ceiling fan and was sweeping the floor. Vikram glared at her. She smiled. She was, no doubt, in cahoots with his mother.

Shanta, the maid, had worked in their household since Vikram was a child. She came in each morning, swept the house, washed the porch, drew a simple geometric kolam and then did the dishes before earning a meal and a cup of tea from his mother. She had seen him grow up, knew his likes and dislikes almost as a mother. She knew he liked samia payasam, especially with pistachios in it. And she knew he hated it when the fan in his room was switched off while he was still sleep.

'Get up, pa,' she said. 'You'll be late for kalej. If you don't, amma will come with a tumbler of water.'

Vikram irritably flung the bedsheet aside and leapt out of bed.

As he was about to head out of the house, his mother called out to him from the kitchen. A cooker whistled atonally to the background of sloka chants from a music player.

'Dei Vikky,' she said, walking out with one finger outstretched. Vikram noticed the sheen of ghee on her fingertip and bent his arm. Each time she cooked with the fat, she made sure to use every bit of it, and whatever remained she smeared and rubbed on to his elbow. 'I'm going to sell off all that old comic books to the recycling fellow. Do you want to keep something?'

Vikram's brow wrinkled. 'But why, ma? They're my favourite . . .'

'Nothing doing,' his mother snapped, her brow furrowing even more. 'From when I have been saying I'll give I'll give and you say you'll sort them and donate to the library.' She waved her palm about. 'That library has got sold and now there are flats there. Enough! No space in this house only. I'll sell this afternoon when that paper fellow comes.'

She walked away and Vikram hurried to the storeroom where boxes of all sizes hibernated like reptiles in winter. It was dimly lit, the air laden with the odour of raw rice, sun-dried vadams and pickling mangoes.

As a child he had found the tiny room magical. Packed with snacks and sweets in tins, he'd steal in to pilfer a bite when hungry. On afternoons he was bored, he'd slip into the room and rummage through the cylindrical aluminium dabbas, hoping to find something interesting. Even the sun didn't fill this space up like the rest of the house, gently filtering in through a gauzy curtain, casting a golden glow on all the shiny metal repositories. A hoary metal trunk sat in one corner, filled with blankets, sweaters and other useless woollens along with old books.

He squatted and pulled out a few comics from it. They were musty, redolent of fading ink and the smells of nostalgia. He picked up a couple of issues of *Tinkle* and smiled. He flicked a few pages and chuckled at *Kalia the Crow*, *Suppandi* and other stories. They had kept him company during the long train rides in summer vacations past. But he had outgrown the comics now, preferring the adventures of *Asterix* and *Tintin* these days and the occasional slice of American life through the world of *Archie*. A few issues of *Phantom*, *Tarzan* and a stack of *Amar Chitra Katha*s lay underneath. He rifled through those too. He stuck his hand further down, all the way to the bottom of the box, and fished out a pile of *Chandamama* periodicals. His eyes lit up. *Chandamama* had coddled him with intriguing folk tales and mythological stories along with titbits of trivia. He picked up a couple of issues, planning to read them on the train ride to his college. If he was going to fail the exam, he might as well not bother wasting time studying for it.

Before leaving the house he stopped by his grandfather who was sitting in an enormous wicker reclining chair with one leg over the other. An old transistor radio in his lap played a Carnatic violin solo to which he wagged his foot. He tapped his knee to the rhythm of the percussion with one hand, holding the daily newspaper in the other.

'Thatha!' Vikram said. 'I'm going to college. I'll be back later.'

'Dei Vikram!' his grandfather said, carefully folding the newspaper and clipping his ink pen on to it. His grandfather was the only person besides his friend Tony who could solve the daily cryptic crossword in the newspaper. The solutions were neatly penned into the boxes in crisp capital letters. 'Come here,' he beckoned, and cracked his favourite joke: 'You are leaving the thathosphere and entering the atmosphere, is it?'

Vikram glanced at his watch and then approached the old man with a big grin. He squatted beside the chair and started pressing the old man's calves. 'Yes, thatha? How's the weather in the thathosphere?'

'Sunny with hundred per cent chance of crossword. Did you pray?'

'I . . .'

His grandfather gestured eating with his right hand. 'Did you pray to the one million gods? You know what I'm talking about?'

'Yes, thatha. Rice.'

The old man slapped his thigh and guffawed. 'Rice is the only true god – boiled, fried, or spiced.' He licked his lips. 'When you come in the evening, no, get me some bajjis from that Murugan Bajji Palace.'

'Sure! You want the green chilli one too?'

His grandfather slowly leaned forward and reached for his wallet on the table nearby. He fished out two coins and gave them to Vikram. 'Here. Two rupees.'

Vikram fingered the coins. 'Thatha, it's more than . . .'

'Back in my day,' his grandfather said, easing back into his chair and folding his arms across his chest, 'one packet was six annas. And the oil was fresh daily. And he used fresh vegetables. There was a Shiva temple right next door to him. Cha! Cha! What am I saying? The bajji stand was next to the temple. And what a beautiful temple it was! So vibrant with large kolam by the entrance and the bell could be heard for miles.' He tapped the armrest. 'Even till here. Your granny kept the time by the evening arthi bells.'

Vikram looked at his watch again and stood up. 'Okay, thatha! I'll get us a packet.'

'Make sure the bugger does not use the Carnatic events page to wrap the bajjis. Those people didn't become pandits to end up as wrappers for oil-soaked bajjis. People have no respect for music these days. Vikky! What's that in your hand?'

'This-aa?' Vikram said, holding up the *Chandamama* comics.

'It's *Chandamama*!' his grandfather said in a cheery voice, leaning forward. 'You know what it means? Means uncle of the moon in Telugu.'

'Oh! I didn't know that,' Vikram said slowly.

'I was joking! It means the moon. It's the bible for folk stories, Vikky.' The old man raised his finger for emphasis. 'Bible!'

'Thatha, I am getting late.'

'Don't forget the bajji, okay?' He sank into his chair and softly said, 'Tonight, in the thathosphere . . . calm winds, clear skies with a chance of bajji showers . . .'

Vikram stuffed the book in his satchel. Just as he reached the door his mother approached him with a handkerchief and a copper plate which had a smouldering piece of camphor and a splotch of sacred ash on it. 'Vikky!' she said, pocketing the handkerchief. 'Put veebudhi on your forehead and let me take off your dhrishti.'

Vikram shot another glance at his watch. 'I'm late, ma! I'll miss the train.'

His mother stood at the doorstep, frowning. 'It's inauspicious to leave home like that. At least go to the Vinayagar temple and apply veebudhi from there . . .' Watching his head bob to the music he was listening to through his earphones, she sighed and turned around. 'Bad things will happen,' she mumbled.

2

Vikram drove by the temple down the street. For a moment he contemplated stopping and entering the sanctum. He would circumambulate the idol, accept a flower from the priest, drop a coin in the donation box and mark his forehead with vibhuti. Instead, he zipped ahead on his Scooty, navigating the morning traffic with the left earphone dangling out and the other blaring film songs from the local FM station into his right ear. He reached the railway station, parked and locked his vehicle. He still had a little more than ten minutes before his train arrived. Even though it was early in the day, the Chennai heat was already harassing its denizens. Mopping his forehead with his handkerchief, he sauntered to the metal shack near the station gates underneath a large and shady tree. A crow cawed solemnly from above.

'Mohan,' he said, knocking on the steel and yanking out the earphone. 'Two Wills. Fast! Train is coming.'

Mohan quickly ripped the plastic off the cigarette pack and whisked out two smokes. Vikram handed him the cash. 'No change,' Mohan replied and slammed two Halls mints on the metal lid of a candy jar. With a flick of his wrist, he produced a box of matches.

Vikram lit the cigarette and let it dangle from the corner of his mouth. Checking his phone, he said, 'When only you'll have change, Mohan? For all the Halls you have given me, I could have bought a proper motorbike instead of this Scooty. Which girl is going to give me a second look when I drive by on it.'

Mohan laughed and brushed his moustache with his nails. 'Oho! So with a bike you can get any girl to finally fall for you, is it?'

Vikram grinned and saluted him. 'See you tomorrow.'

'Eat a Halls before you go home,' Mohan yelled as Vikram left. 'Or else your mom will know!'

Just as Vikram made it to the platform the engine blasted its horn and the train lurched forward. Running along with it, he waited for the doorway to appear and then hopped into a carriage.

A couple of his friends hopped on at the Chromepet stop. 'I'm going to fail today,' Tony said. 'Guarantee.' He reached for the crucifix around his neck and toyed with it.

Tony, one of his close friends, was shorter than Vikram and so thin that Vikram had once asked him if he had any thyroid issues. Tony had hung his head and confessed that he did. 'I have to . . .' Tony's voice had dropped in embarrassment. 'I have to take an injection daily . . . myself.' When he had opened his satchel to reveal a set of vials and a syringe, Vikram had decided he would protect this frail friend whose name didn't fit in with the stereotypical Tamil names in their classrooms. With each passing day they had grown closer, sharing the train journeys to and from college and many evenings afterwards. Despite his diminutive stature, Tony was an excellent footballer. The days when their friends didn't show up at the grounds, Tony and Vikram shot penalty goals at each other. That same height, Vikram theorized once, must give his blood a shorter distance to travel, making his brain more oxygenated. There could be no other explanation for why he was so sharp at mathematics. Or how he could rearrange anagrams to solve a cryptic crossword clue which, to Vikram, made no sense.

Tony was a wizard at solving the cryptic crossword. He carried the paper in his back pocket the entire day, having folded it in a way that only the crossword was visible. He would often bite the blue cap of the Reynolds pen and ask Vikram something like, 'Viks, seven letters for excess. Starts with *s* and ends with *t*.' Vikram would give his best effort and start spewing words at random. 'Socialist! Excessive! Seagull!' Perhaps Vikram's solutions dislodged the boulders in Tony's mind, for his eyes would invariably light up and he'd neatly fill in the actual solution to which Vikram would say, 'Surfeit? Such a word exists?'

Once, after an evening of playing Frisbee on the beach and constructing intricate tunnels by the shore, they lay on the sand and stared at the sky, trying to identify constellations. 'Who came up with this dumb idea of Orion and Ursa Major Minor,' Vikram said, amused. 'I can make it up too. Henceforth, I declare that any two stars form a Vikram constellation.' Tony quipped, 'I declare any star to be a Tony constellation.' And the two friends broke into fits of laughter.

Now Tony's lack of confidence in his preparations made Vikram happy. 'Pffft . . . Not sure why I'm going to write the test. Might as well prepare for the arrears and the vacation,' Vikram said and turned to his other friend. 'Sukku, what about you, da?'

Shivakumar was a portly chap with a porcine face. He had wide-set eyes and a bulbous nose. He wore thick glasses and was almost always buried in his notes. He was a smart guy who hadn't managed to get into the prestigious IIT, which he had taken as a personal insult. He swore to himself that he'd pass out of college with the best marks possible and land either a cushy job or a scholarship to study abroad. And to achieve this goal he cracked a coconut each morning at his neighbourhood Ganesha temple, held his earlobes and performed squats in front of the idol, while mentally repeating formulas, for they were the only slokas that would lead him to engineering heaven.

'You are the same every time,' Vikram said, whacking Sukku on his head. He dramatically clutched his chest. 'Machan, I'm going to fail, da. Surely fail! And then when the results come, you'll get something in the nineties and say, "Machan! This teacher is an idiot. Cut five marks for not showing steps."'

Not one to be left out, Tony added, 'If not, I would have got ninety-six.'

'While we all failed,' Vikram completed for his friend.

Shivakumar slapped Vikram's hand. 'Don't say such impure things before an exam. It's bad omen.' I'm going to revise. Don't disturb me.' And then he delved into his thick thermodynamics textbook.

Vikram noticed Tony massaging his knee. 'How's it? Your knee.' he asked.

Tony shrugged. 'It'll be fine.'

'What happened?' Sukku asked.

'Idiot was boarding the train,' Vikram said. 'Running as usual because he thinks it's cool. He twisted his knee and fell. Almost fell on to the tracks.'

'And then?'

'Then he rolled away and escaped but missed the train. Hurt his knee really badly.'

'Go to the doctor, no.' Sukku suggested, always the pragmatic one.

Tony scoffed. 'It'll heal. Ligament must have torn slightly. It'll go away.'

Sukku stared at the duo, shook his head disapprovingly and went back to his notes, muttering, 'Why didn't you study medical?'

Vikram and Tony exchanged smug grins.

'Oh, by the way,' Vikram said, reaching into his bag. 'I found some old *Chandamama* comics.' He handed Tony an issue and flipped through another himself. 'Remember this from back in the day?'

Tony put his finger on the pages and ran them over the print. The train jerked and they grabbed the leather hand straps. 'So many stories from Mahabharata,' he said. 'And all these silly titbits . . . check this out . . .' He held a page out for Vikram to see. 'An ad for Forhan's toothpaste. Do you remember Forhan's? I vaguely remember it from my childhood.' Vikram shook his head but held up his own copy, saying, 'Oh, and remember this? Vikram and Betal.'

'Ha! Yeah, I do. That thing always had me on edge. I thought Betal was a ghost or something.'

'Sometimes I'd take two issues and compare the image of the king carrying the corpse to see if there were any differences.'

Tony laughed. 'I'd never thought of that.' His face grew serious. 'Actually, you know, I have seen the original book at my uncle's place in Kottayam.'

'What book?' Vikram asked.

'Hey guys,' Sukku moaned from behind. 'Come and study. Sums are going to be hard.'

'You study, Sukku,' Vikram said. 'And pass the paper.' He turned back to Tony. 'Yeah, what book?'

'Original Vikram and Betal, man. You think *Chandamama* people made that story up? It's been there forever.'

'Oh! I didn't know that. How was it?'

'Like those old and well-worn books in lawyers' offices. Very British. Hardbound in that shit-brown colour. Weird font. And the pages smell old and familiar.'

Vikram nodded. 'Yeah, yeah. I get it.' His phone buzzed with an incoming message. 'Guys at the college are saying that the paper is going to be tough.'

Tony shrugged nonchalantly. 'We do our best and still fail. The system is broken. Who cares. What matters is the university exam.'

'Well, that's in six weeks.'

'So we have time. We'll finish the syllabus in the study holidays after the trip. Okay, listen, I was not done with the Vikram–Betal thing.'

'Yeah, what?'

'The original was in Sanskrit and my uncle said that it's kept at the Theosophical Society's library. You know that place in Adyar?'

'Yeah, near Aavin Circle. I've been there to see the banyan tree.' Vikram snapped his fingers. 'Why don't we go check it out?'

'What now-aa?' Tony asked incredulously.

Vikram threw his head back. 'Fuck this exam, man! Anyway we'll flunk it. Might as well cut it, no?'

Tony was not sure. 'But report card . . .'

'We'll worry about that later, da. I know how to fix the numbers. There's a guy at a Xerox shop who does this for a small fee.' He turned to Shivakumar who was nose deep in the textbook. 'Sukku,' Vikram said, 'Tony and I are going to cut college.' He walked up to his friend and drew his palms around his head and then cracked his knuckles on his own forehead. 'There! I have taken away your dhrishti. No evil eye will bother you. You do well in your exams, okay?'

Shivakumar looked up, nervous. 'Where . . . where are you guys going?'

The train was slowing down at the Meenambakkam stop. Vikram and Tony hopped off and waved him goodbye.

'Dei . . . don't cut college,' he said, adjusting his glasses. The duo had already begun to walk towards the exit. 'Bad things will happen . . .' he finished, but they were gone.

Little did he know how prescient his words would turn out.

3

Vikram and Tony boarded the train going back and got off at the Saidapet stop. Mohan's shack was teeming with people. Vikram elbowed his way through to the front.

'Wills?' Mohan asked in a businesslike tone, and before Vikram could respond, whisked out two cigarettes and a couple of packets of Halls. He then moved on to the next customer.

Vikram paid and carried the cigarettes to Tony. 'Here,' he said. 'It's only Wills.'

Tony waved him off. 'Gold Flake is no better.' They lit their cigarettes, hopped on to Vikram's Scooty and took off.

Vikram zipped through the Chennai traffic, weaving through stalled cars and avoiding pedestrians. Tony checked his phone and said, 'Sukku messaged.'

Vikram exhaled smoke with the cigarette still in his mouth. An autorickshaw in front of them belched blue smoke in response. 'What did he say?'

'Says there is a strike in college. No one is allowed inside.'

Vikram narrowly escaped a cow that was casually ambling along the road. 'Strike-aa?' He spat out the cigarette.

Tony put a hand on his friend's shoulder. 'Yeah, some issue

with the neighbouring college guys. They suspended a few people and now it's got out of hand.'

Vikram laughed and clapped his hands. 'I guess the study hols started early!'

'Dei!' Tony yelled. 'Hold on to the bike!'

Vikram gripped the handlebars again. 'Why are you fretting? You are the guy who used to hold my shoulder while sitting on a bicycle and ask me to go as fast as I could.'

Tony's grip tightened. 'Teenage follies, man. What only I was thinking those days! One slip and I would have been smashed like a good-luck pumpkin you guys use.'

Vikram laughed harder. 'Good-luck pumpkin!'

Tony grinned. 'Vicks, want a clue?'

'Shoot.'

'To New York with my best friend. Four letters.'

Vikram thought for a moment. 'New York. NY. My pal.' He turned his head to one side and exclaimed. 'PayPal!'

Tony slapped the back of his friend's head. 'How on earth is that four letters, you idiot!'

'What is it?'

Tony stuck his right hand out and waved it about. 'Take this right, Vicks. Shortcut. It'll put us right near the Theosophical Society. Tony da. My name.'

Vikram shook his head. 'Yeah, I know. What about it?'

'Dei! The answer to my clue.' He gave an exasperated sight. 'New York is NY, you got that right. To . . . the first word. To plus NY equals Tony.'

Vikram was confused. 'But how are you your own best friend?'

Tony squeezed Vikram's shoulder lightly. 'I mean . . . yeah . . . the clue was for you. So I thought you'd interpret it as your best friend, but you're right. It needs work.'

Vikram grinned as the Scooty coasted and came to a halt. 'Come! We're there.'

The Theosophical Society was a verdant campus situated by the Bay of Bengal. Inside, old and shady trees stood like ancient guardians of a sacred place. They shook their boughs in the sea breeze and spoke in leafy whispers, throwing shadow puppets on the ground for all to enjoy. Many decades ago the Society had allowed a road to be built through its premises, so anyone driving on it felt like they were going through a forest.

'It's so much cooler here,' Tony remarked as they reached the gate. 'It's like AC.'

'Gets even cooler as we go inside,' Vikram said.

The old watchman dressed in loose-fitting khakis rose from his foldable metal chair and beat his lathi once to get their attention. 'What do you boys want?'

Vikram glanced at the white board that stipulated the timings to visit the banyan tree. It was believed that the banyan tree inside was the oldest in the world and, in a fashion, a local attraction. 'We came to see the tree,' he said.

'Go straight. Don't take any other roads. See the tree and come back. Okay?' The watchman directed them in.

They nodded and walked in.

The air did grow cooler and the din of traffic was replaced with the sounds of birds and insects. The banyan tree was enclosed by a rusty chain link fence as if it were an animal at the Guindy Zoo. A metal plaque with lettering in English,

Hindi and Tamil explained its significance, how old it was, how diverse its mini-ecosystem was, and how a century ago it was considered a deity capable of bestowing boons.

'Cool!' Tony exclaimed and gazed up at the tree. It looked like yet another banyan tree with its snaky overhead roots that criss-crossed its various branches like an aerial roadway. It formed a splendid canopy and the air was noticeably even cooler around it. Little birds hopped and tweeted as a murder of crows eyed the boys carefully, their heads tilted to one side.

Vikram turned around and snapped a picture of himself against the tree. 'I think the library is that way. Come.'

They walked on the gravel road past old British era bungalows which were painted a staid grey. Massive arches bloomed from the foundation, many chipped from their time spent in the unforgiving monsoon and heat. Most houses had ornate gardens teeming with tropical plants and iridescent flowers. Ancient ceiling fans with leaf-shaped blades lazily wobbled and spun in the large and airy verandas. Plants hung and overflowed from pots along the sides of the houses, snagging and dragging one to surrender oneself into their perfumed silence. Colourful birds, some rarely seen in the city, flitted from tree to tree, sounding alien to ears accustomed to the drab caws of crows.

Now they reached a simple concrete building. A small sign indicated it was the Theosophical Society Library.

'This way,' Vikram said, walking straighter. 'Act like you belong.'

Tony opened his lab notebook, pinched his chin and tapped on the page studiously.

Vikram smiled and walked briskly. The library was an unassuming place with many tables in the middle of the room. Along the walls, scores of books rested on glass-covered shelves. Large windows allowed for ample light and the garden smells wafted in. An array of urgently spinning ceiling fans rifled the edges of the pages as if an impatient ghost was searching for something in those books. Motionless geckos clung to the pale walls, staring at the world with their distant gazes. There were a few people there, immersed in their books, although none of them were as young as them.

'What are they reading, da?' Vikram asked.

'Arrears, machan,' Tony said. 'Once you fail, you have to keep writing forever.'

Vikram elbowed his friend. 'Shut up, man. I had just forgotten about that stupid paper.'

'Who cares. It'll be cancelled surely.'

'Vikram!' a shrill voice called out.

He turned to face the corpulent lady in oversized glasses. 'Uma aunty?'

The lady smiled. 'How are you?' She looked at Tony. 'Your friend?'

'College friend, aunty . . . Tony.'

'Anthony.'

Vikram shot him a surprised look. 'That's your name?' He snapped his head back towards the lady. 'Uh . . . what are you doing here, aunty?'

'I work here, pa. Amma never told you or what? And your hair has grown so long!'

Vikram scratched his head and tried to smooth his hair. 'Oh ya! Amma used to tell me that Uma aunty worked in the banyan tree library. I thought you worked in a treehouse when I was a kid.'

Uma laughed. 'You did have a wild imagination. Anyway, what are you boys doing here?' Suddenly her voice dropped. 'Shouldn't you be in college?'

'Uh . . . thing is,' Vikram began, 'we had an exam–'

'Example to demonstrate Betal,' Tony finished and looked on blankly.

Uma knitted her brows. 'What?'

Vikram quickly cut in. 'That is, we . . . we had this philosophy . . . introduction to philosophy course, no? For that we had to . . . uh . . . demonstrate by giving examples.' Now his voice grew confident. 'And Sir was asking us to give examples of ancient Greek philosophers, but I thought' – Tony kicked his foot – 'we thought that we could use Indian examples. So, we decided to research Vikram and Betal.'

Uma's face underwent a series of contortions before settling on a smile. 'I'm proud of you boys. This library, you know, has the largest collection of occult books in the world.' She beamed at them. 'In the world, Vikky! Do you want to see the original copy or the first English translation?'

The boys' eyes lit up. 'That would be awesome, aunty,' Tony said.

'Can we see both?' Vikram asked eagerly.

'Come, come. This way.' She adjusted her spectacles and led the boys to a corner. A table with a glass box stood by itself, containing parchments and strips of bamboo with writings on them. Uma carefully opened the glass cover, retrieved one of the parchments and placed it on a nearby table. She then picked up leather-bound book.

'Here,' she said and tapped Vikram on the shoulder. 'Be very careful. Okay? The book is more than a hundred years old.'

The boys nodded in unison. 'And this . . . cloth?' Vikram asked, placing a finger on the parchment.

Uma shrugged. 'No one knows. I'll be back in twenty minutes.'

The cover said in cursive Gothic font *Vikram and the Vampire, or, Tales of Hindu Devilry*. The words were limber and inked in gold. Age had worn the leather down and left it looking dull. Vikram carefully opened the cover. It smelt exactly how an old book would – slightly dank yet evocative of quiet libraries where bibliophiles hovered. 'Works of Captain Sir Richard F. Burton,' he whispered. He reached for his cellphone and took a picture of the cover.

'Some cricket captain?' Tony enquired and tittered.

'I doubt it,' Vikram said, putting his phone away. 'Remember cricket came from gilli-danda and we had to yet give it to the angrez.'

Tony nodded and slowly flipped the pages. He stopped at the first illustration. It showed two bearded men, dressed in soldiers' livery, looking up at winged creatures with fear. Four impish beasts hovered over the petrified men. They had hooked beaks, large leathery bat-like wings and sharp claws.

They grinned from ear to ear as if about to throw balloons filled with coloured water on the hapless soldiers.

'So cool,' Vikram whispered as he turned the pages.

A faint aroma of ink emanated from the pages. Some of them stuck together and many had worn-out edges. An illustration appeared every other page or so. 'Look here,' he said, *The Baital Pachisi*, or the twenty-five tales of a vetal, is the history of a huge bat, a vampire, or evil spirit that inhabited and animated dead bodies.' He glanced at his friend.

'Fuck, man,' Tony said. 'This is already giving me the creeps. *Chandamama* made it sound like a fairy tale my grandma would tell me. This looks like that crazy chick from *The Exorcist* will appear in the corner of the room if I read it aloud.'

They flipped through the pages some more and gave up. 'I don't remember any of these stories and this English is too stiff,' Tony complained. "Love is like the drunkard's cup . . . delicious is the first drink, palling are the draughts that succeed it." He looked at Vikram. 'What the fuck does that mean?'

Vikram shrugged and turned a chunk of pages. He cleared his throat and said, 'And now a love poem.' He spoke in an ersatz British accent. "She was to me the pearl that clings / To sands all hid from mortal sight / Yet fit for diadems of kings / The pure and lovely light."

'Wah! Wah!' Tony said and started showering imaginary currency notes on Vikram. 'You'll crack the GRE for sure.' As soon as he said this, his phone started crowing like a rooster.

He jumped and took it out of his pocket, which made the crowing louder. Other readers shot him disparaging glances. Fumbling, he silenced it finally. Uma came up to them and put her hands on her hips.

'Sorry . . . aunt . . . m'am,' Tony said. 'I . . . I have to take an injection twice a day and this is my reminder.' Seeing that she didn't believe him, he showed her the syringe and medicine packet.

'Thyroid issue,' Vikram said and pursed his lips.

Uma's nostrils flared as she sighed loudly. 'Put it on silent.'

Vikram quickly went back to the book as Tony lifted his shirt and stabbed himself near his waist with the syringe. 'Bugger!' he said. 'Silence it, man. One day it's going to ring in some exam or some important place and you'll be in deep shit.'

Tony was unperturbed. 'If I don't hear the alarm, I won't remember.'

'Anyway, this book . . . it's got the poetry to rhyme and all. I didn't know the stories were written in sloka form.'

'Hey, you know Sanskrit, right?' Tony said, pressing his fingers on his hip.

Vikram shrugged. 'A little. Studied it in school. It came naturally to me, but it's a bloody hard language to learn. Everything has one of three genders.'

'Three-aa?'

'Masculine, feminine and neutral.'

'It was hard enough learning French with its two genders,' Tony said. 'How do you handle three?'

'I don't remember. As soon as I finished ninth standard,

I didn't have to study it any more and forgot everything I had learnt.' He traced his fingernail along the verses and said, 'Man! These Britishers were really serious about this translation.'

'Then imagine the original,' Tony said and moved his attention to the parchment. It was rolled up tightly.

'What do you think this is,' Vikram said, running his finger along the rough surface. 'Cow?'

Tony leaned in and sniffed. 'I don't know. Maybe.' He glanced around and whispered. 'What if it's human?' He carefully undid the black thread binding it and tenderly unfurled the many scrolls that were layered on top of each other. The duo hunched over the table and brought their faces close to the scrolls. The writing was small and in Sanskrit. There were no pictures of the vampire or spirits and if someone had handed it to Vikram he'd have guessed it was just an older version of the *Vishnu sahasranamam* – the thousand names of Lord Vishnu – composed as slokas. The only illustration was a carefully drawn tree on the last scroll, its dangling roots resembling serpents.

'It's a banyan tree,' Vikram said.

Tony's pocket made a buzzing sound. He read the message and said, 'The strike has got out of hand, Sukku says. I have to go.'

Vikram shot an annoyed glanced at his watch. 'It's only afternoon.'

'No, I have a contact who said he could leak the question paper if the exam were to be cancelled.'

'Oh! So the exam has been cancelled today?'

'Exams. Sss. Plural. All of them are cut until the strike is resolved.'

Vikram looked at the parchment. 'I want to read this, then.' He grinned. 'Now that we have holidays.' Tony picked up his satchel and walked out, gesturing to Vikram to message him later. He waved at Uma and slipped out.

Vikram's mother had decided that he would learn Sanskrit instead of French as his third language at school. Vikram wanted to learn French, like Tony. But his mother was firm. 'A Brahmin boy must know how to recite the Vedas,' she said. 'It will come useful in your life.' And so, she had unknowingly set a malfeasant ball rolling.

At first the language had confused him. The script was Devanagari, the same as Hindi, which he had studied all his school life. He could read the language but didn't understand a word of it. The Sanskrit teacher was a crotchety lady named Seethalakshmi, with a penchant for smacking the boys with her wooden ruler if they didn't perform well. Most classes, Vikram zoned out, befuddled by the number of ways a word could be conjugated before it subjugated him. By the ninth standard, he had got a passing grade and was glad to be done with the arcane language, though his mother remarked that his enunciation of the slokas had become much better. Even the priest who had performed his sacred thread ceremony praised his recitation of the sacred mantras and urged him to come to the temple each evening so that he could learn to recite the Vedas. But Vikram had chosen not to indulge him.

The original stories of the Betal intrigued him. Outside, the sun had sunk behind the clouds and a cool breeze rose from the sea, a daily phenomenon at this time of the day. It drifted in through the windows, bringing with it the smells of the vegetation outside. A gravid scent of jasmine lingered in the air. He brought his nose closer to the parchment and inhaled the organic smell of hide.

'Are you okay, Vikram?' Uma asked. 'What are you doing so close to the scroll?'

'Oh . . . aunty . . . reading it. Handwriting is hard to read.'

'Oho! You can read Sanskrit, is it? Read me a line.'

'It's . . . small print, aunty.'

'Arre! Read something, no? I only speak English and Tamil and always wanted to hear the Sanskrit written in these ancient scrolls. You know there are parchments from thousands of years ago, written on lambskin and papyrus.'

'I see.' Vikram looked at the scroll, placed a finger on a line and slowly said, '*aham griham gacchami . . . twam . . .*' He looked up, hoping that she didn't figure out that he had just said, 'I am going home.' Uma was smiling. '*Twam griham kim* . . . uh I can't make out this word. I think it's . . .' He struggled and spat out the first one that sounded like Sanskrit. 'Calcium.'

'Calcium-aa?' Uma looked at him quizzically. 'It says calcium there?'

'No, no. Not calcium, aunty. *Kal* means tomorrow. It . . . it means about tomorrow . . . uh . . . I, Betal, will go home.'

Uma nodded slowly. 'Interesting. Did you get all the material you needed for your research? Where is your friend?'

Vikram pulled a notebook out of his bag. 'Actually, aunty, if I could get some more time. I want to take some notes. Tony has gone to the . . . uh . . . Xerox shop.'

Uma checked her watch. 'Library closes at two, pa. Do it quick.'

'Aunty, please. I live so far away. It'll be hard to come during the daytime from college.'

Uma took a deep breath, clearly in two minds. 'Okay. Make it fast. I don't want someone checking your library card and all.'

'Okay. I'll be quick.' Vikram smiled at her.

He spent the next hour studying the scrolls. Many words he didn't understand, but some he did, and even with the sparse information, he figured that a tale was being told. This ancient story of a vampire written in a dead language thrilled him. He felt like he was privy to an ancient secret. Every few minutes, he flipped to the last scroll and stared at the banyan tree. Drawn with a dark ink, it grew more beautiful every time he looked at it. The fifth or sixth time he noticed something in the tree. Peering closer he saw the distinct shape of a man hanging from the tree. He sat up straight. He was sure he had not seen it the first few times. He looked around. There were only a couple of patrons in the large room. The fans continued to spin noisily overhead. He reached for his phone, stood up so that he had a clear shot of the scroll, and took a few pictures. He checked the image for quality and zoomed in on the tree to make sure the words were sharp. Satisfied, he got up and headed out.

'Bye Vikram,' Uma said, adjusting her spectacles. 'Tell your mom I asked after her.'

'Okay, aunty,' he said and hurried out.

There was a canteen nearby. It was a sorry, boxy space, barely furnished. A refrigerator wheezed in a corner. A few bags of chips and snacks hung from a basket. There were glass cases with biscuits. A Nescafé coffee machine, all old and banged up, perched quietly atop a stained table. Next to it was a tray of samosas on which flies buzzed.

Vikram got a plate of samosas and a cup of instant coffee. The samosas were hot and spicy, the coffee too sugary and milky. He downed the food anyway, suddenly ravenous. He bought a packet of Parle-G biscuits and ate them quickly one after the other, unable to make sense of this sudden hunger.

He absently started walking. The distant sounds of the engines and horns formed a monolithic hum that was at once human and alien. But, here, inside the lush greenery, Vikram felt as if he was walking inside a powerful force field that repelled the alien sound. He found himself in front of the banyan tree. Crows hopped and cawed from its branches, which were caked with their excrement. What if, he thought, the story had some roots here in Chennai, in Adyar? What if the Betal haunted its gnarly roots, swung from the branches at night?

He drew out his phone and his hanky fell out. He picked it up and carefully mopped his forehead. The crows wouldn't stop cawing. He waved the hanky at them, but they barely flinched. Instead, they craned their tiny necks towards him and cawed harder. Ignoring them, he pulled up the image of the scroll and zoomed into the Sanskrit words. The image was dim and unclear. He opened the photo editor and began to adjust the brightness and contrast when he accidentally tapped the flip button. Just as he was about to hit the undo button, he noticed that the words were still legible.

He read them slowly, making sure to pronounce the words and the aspirated sounds correctly. There were eight lines and he read them in one go. After he did so, he frowned. The lines started with vetal and ended with the same word – samarpayaami. This, he knew, meant: I offer. What was vetala, he wondered. His brain instinctively began to play with the word and for a moment he felt like Tony as he hewed and minced words. Then it occurred to him that vetala must be the same word as betal. Perhaps, it was the original word for the entity before it morphed into the one found in the old *Chandamama.* As he was mulling over what it was that he had offered he heard a voice, 'What are you doing?'

It was the watchman. 'Still here?' he asked in an angry tone. 'How long to see the tree? Were you boys smoking ganja?'

'What? No! I . . . I was just reading a sloka,' Vikram shot back.

'For what? A tree? Mad or what? Get out of here. Enough sightseeing for one day.' The watchman beat his lathi on the ground.

The raucous crows had suddenly gone quiet. Vikram checked his pocket to ensure that his keys were still there and headed towards his bike not realizing that he had dropped his handkerchief in the process.

4

Professor Ranganathan was a mild-mannered, short-statured, Atlas bicycle-riding Sanskrit professor at the Madras Sanskrit College. In his own mind he was a legend, a rock star, afforded the same encomiums given to luminaries in their fields. A Bharat Ratna, no less, with all the Padma awards thrown in for good measure, ought to have been his by now. It was, he reasoned, only a matter of time before the people would recognize his brilliance and shower him with the attention he so deserved.

He had a strong command over the Sanskrit language from childhood when he recited the Vedas with aplomb, winning prizes and accolades at recitation competitions in temples across Mylapore and Triplicane at first and then all over Chennai. Not only were his diction and pronunciation impeccable, but he also had a brilliant grasp on grammar and understood how the language smashed and minted neologisms on a whim. Elderly bearded purohits with their shaved heads flecked with tiny white hairs and wearing grey-black rattails closed their eyes in rapture when young Ranganathan reached for the mic and started reciting.

'The Sanskrit alphabet,' he liked to start his first-year lectures, 'is arranged so that the first sound – *ka* – starts at the base of the throat and then ends with *ma* where? Here. At the tip of the mouth. The language was designed for the human vocal cavity.' He'd look at the handful of bright-eyed aspirants, some of whom were foreigners, and feel a sense of pride at having imparted one of the most key details of the language before reaching for his well-thumbed textbook.

There were no viable career opportunites for a Sanskrit graduate, except teaching at the Madras Sanskrit College. And teaching Sanskrit was a thankless job. The pay was barely enough and life monotonous. All he did was hold classes, correct exam papers and look forward to the afternoon coffee and bajjis from Murugan's Bajji shop down the street. The one thing he eagerly awaited was the annual travel to Allahabad University where he was garlanded, welcomed as a distinguished lecturer and where he officiated as an examiner. He relished conversing in the purest Hindi with pandits, something the Tamil-obsessed Chennai could not grant him. In those long train rides, he'd dream of going back in time and visiting Nalanda University and not only lecturing the students, but also conversing with other teachers in Sanskrit.

To add some excitement to his life, he dabbled in naming babies. The ancient scriptures stated that every human form had a specific sound associated with it such that when given a name with that sound, the person inhabiting that body would be successful in life. People invited him to their homes to assess the newborn and take his recommendations for the sounds the name ought to contain. He was well reputed among the superstitious Brahmins of Mylapore. A lad stood first in his third standard monthly test. A little girl's Carnatic abilities were being heralded in the neighbourhood. And yet another girl was proving to be a budding chess champion. The parents attributed their children's success to the professor's divining art and new parents slowly trickled in.

But even this began to take on a certain dullness in Ranganathan's life and soon he was performing them as a chore, unable to avoid the temporary stardom, and mainly for the quick money that let him go to the movies or get new clothes tailored.

It was in this state of despondency that he decided to go to the Besant Nagar beach one morning in the hope that the mystique of dawn, so revered in the scriptures, could imbue some vigour and purpose in his life. He trudged to the seashore and stood there, basking in the infinite glory of the sunrise and relishing the way his feet slowly sank into the sand as the waves retreated. Growing up he had been told that the nexus of night and day – dawn – was a sacred time of the day and if one was to sit down and hold one's breath in a certain way, it would do wonders for the body. But no one had shown him how to sit and hold his breath in that certain way, and, thus, wondrous things had eluded him.

The sun thrust its fiery self over the Bay of Bengal and began roasting him with its warm embrace. Figuring he ought to do something resembling exercise, Ranganathan started jogging on the spot.

Within a few seconds he was panting, his Brahmanical

diet of rice and vegetables, sambar and yogurt, pickled vegetables and stews having made his insides pliable and his outside rotund and inflexible. He spent the next few minutes attempting aerobics to the best of his knowledge before running out of steam. It was at this moment, as he was massaging his already sore yogurt–rice-powered legs that he heard a cluck. It was a sharp sound and shot at him like a bullet. 'Exercising or what?' the voice said.

He turned away from the water and noticed an old man standing beside him. In a sea of neatly barbered men with clean-shaven faces, this individual stood out like a cotton ball in a sack of coal. Clearly many years older than him, the stranger exuded a sense of vitality that he only dreamed of possessing. The man looked like he could run from the beach till Mylapore without breaking into a sweat. He stood with perfect posture, his back ramrod straight and his shoulders pushed back. He had long flowing white hair and an equally long flowing salt-and-pepper beard, both of which billowed in the gentle seabreeze like the sails of a strong ship. He carried a walking stick, but it didn't appear that he needed it. The crabs didn't hesitate around him. Instead, they edged towards him and assembled around his feet as if prostrating in front of a massive deity.

Ranganathan unrolled his pants with his feet and grinned. 'Something like that,' he said.

The old man pinned him with an unblinking gaze, one that seemed to bore right into him, scanning his insides like an X-ray. He stood so still that he could have been mistaken for a statue at night. Finally, he smiled and said, 'For a Sanskrit speaker you don't seem too cheery.' He walked towards Ranganathan. 'It's a dead language and yet, here you are, one of the few who can speak it.'

Ranganathan's eyes widened. 'How . . . how . . .'

'Name is Vasi,' the man said, reaching out his arm, 'Chaturvasi. Call me Vasi.'

'Vasi?' Ranganathan repeated. The reverberations of the sound and the person were so in sync he began to feel his breath flutter for no reason. 'Ra-Ra-Ranganathan, sir,' and he quickly added, 'please call me Ranga.'

Chaturvasi smiled and it was a beatific one. It leapt from his face, zapped across the saline air and instantly washed over Ranganathan like a cold waterfall after a long trek on a sweltering day. 'You are looking for excitement in your life, but you don't realize that life itself is in a constant state of excitement. You are just not tuned to it.'

Ranganathan's eyebrows rose. 'Sir?' He couldn't bring himself to address the man by name. He seemed to be a human reservoir of knowledge, almost omniscient, and Ranganathan couldn't debase him by calling him Vasi.

Chaturvasi held up his hand and Ranganathan observed a tiny crab perched on it. 'See this tiny crab,' Chaturvasi said, 'you and everything else is a manifestation of creation. What you eat becomes your body, isn't it? And everything anything consumes comes from the earth. Have you ever stopped to think what causes a small piece of the earth to turn into the crab or a Sanskrit speaker like yourself?'

Ranganathan shook his head.

'No matter.' Chaturvasi tapped his walking stick into

the sand and played with it. He looked up and said, 'Your problem, Ranga, and everyone's' – he lifted his stick and spun it around – 'is that you are all trapped inside the cage of your mind and body.'

'How, sir?'

With a speed normally exhibited by big cats in the savannah, Chaturvasi leapt forward and caught one of Ranganathan's pant sleeves. And before the latter could react, he tugged at the seam and ripped it open, making Ranganathan fall down. 'Sir . . . what . . . you tore my . . . it's the college pant . . . it's . . .' He stood up, angry and confused. 'Why, sir? Why? I only have two nice pants and my mother got this stitched for me last Deepavali and . . .' Ranganathan's words tapered off when he saw Chaturvasi's serene smile.

'Tearing your pants caused you physical distress?'

'Yes . . . yes, sir.'

Chaturvasi clucked. It sounded like a marble being thrown on the ground. 'Why, Ranga? Are the pants part of your body? Did you grow them on your skin?' he asked with mock concern.

'I . . .' Ranganathan looked down as his toes slowly sank into the thick sand.

'You associate yourself with something beyond you. In your case your clothes and in someone else's case, his car and in some other case, her child. Something inside you yearns to expand far beyond its boundaries, but it doesn't know how. So it goes for whatever is physically available.'

Ranganathan looked at his torn pants and slowly saw them

as a piece of fabric that, despite its state of disrepair, was still admirably doing its job.

'You think your body is you, but even that is wrong,' Chaturvasi said. 'If you can put a gap between the *you* inside and your body and mind, Ranga, you will suddenly find life to be positively explosive. Look, a human being breathes twelve to fifteen times per minute. If your breath eases to twelve, you shall glean the ways of the earth's atmosphere and the weather. You can know if a storm is approaching or even if it will snow. If it reduces to nine, you will be able to communicate with all the creatures on the planet.' Ranganathan's eyes widened. 'If it reduces to six, you will know the very language of this planet. If it reduces to three, you will become aware of the language of the very source of all this wonderful creation.' He spread his arms wide. 'And while exploring that, I think I will have some need for your skills as a Sanskrit speaker. Help me and I will help you. You will have all the trousers you desire if you still choose to want them.'

Ranganathan scratched the back of his head. His torn pants flapped in the breeze like a wounded crow trying to fly again. 'How . . . Vasi sir?

Chaturvasi laughed. 'I will show you how, but first let's get some coconut water.'

That day onwards, Chaturvasi inducted Ranganathan into the ancient and esoteric practice of tantra. He explained to him the various psychoenergetic points in the body – the chakras – which Westerners were increasingly falling in love with and figuring out a way to commoditize. He explained to him how the endocrine glands, if they came under one's control, could be used to make the ordinary body superhuman. He taught him that the breath oscillated between the two nostrils and that if he were to simply pay attention to it as he would when studying a new Sanskrit text, he would notice the subtle shift in the way his body felt and the strange pulsating that slowly coursed through him. He opened his mind to the fact that the word yoga did not mean to simply contort and hold his body in jalebi-like positions, but to merge the drop of superconsciousness within every individual with the universe so that one realized that the universe was within one and one was within the universe.

This didn't make much sense to Ranganathan at first, but he dutifully woke up before dawn, poured a bucket of cold water over himself, wiped himself down with a thin cotton towel, sat facing east in his tiny flat, performed various asanas until he felt his body and joints warm up and turn pliant, and then sat in a precise posture, pinched his nostrils at the exact point and inhaled and exhaled in the prescribed manner.

Within weeks he could feel a slow, but noticeable, transformation within himself. The days no longer dragged endlessly. His jitteriness reduced and he noticed that he made no unnecessary movements. He stopped shaking his legs and drumming the desk. He lost his tic of rolling his tongue along the edge of his teeth and his constant need to rub the tip of his nose disappeared. In fact, he found that he was suffused with more energy than he had ever known. And like his cell phone data plan, the energy rolled over to the next day. Soon, he found himself sleeping fewer hours and waking up more refreshed than before, eager to recharge himself with yoga.

He found a new sense of enthusiasm in doing simple things. He waved to people on his way to work and chatted with the other teachers cheerily in the staffroom. He surprised everyone by declaring he had given up coffee and confounded his mother and sister when he announced he had stopped eating brinjal. 'My rudraksha,' he told them one day over dinner, 'is my metre.' He unbuttoned the top of his shirt and fished out the necklace made of a hundred and eight rudraksha seeds. 'It's from the Himalayas,' he told his befuddled family. 'From a small family that harvests these specific seeds and makes these malas.'

'What's so special?' his sister asked in a sceptical tone.

'Watch,' he said. He looked around, picked up an apple and placed it in front of him. He clutched the mala over it and waited.

'What?' his sister said.

'Shh! Watch.'

Within seconds the mala started swirling in a clockwise direction around the apple. His mother and sister stared at it agog. He picked up a pod of garlic and repeated the experiment and they saw with astonishment as the mala spun counterclockwise. He wore the necklace and leaned back with a grin. 'No garlic. No brinjal.'

His mother sighed. 'What else can I not use for cooking?'

Ranganathan got up and grabbed his bicycle keys. 'Why look at it like that, ma? See all the things you can cook with. Ash gourd, ginger, pumpkin . . .' He looked at his watch and ran to the door. 'It's amavasya tonight. I must perform my practice before midnight.'

As the months went by, his practices grew intense under Chaturvasi's guidance. When he visited Chaturvasi, the latter checked on his progress and fixed any issues he was facing. It was during these meetings that Ranganathan learned that Chaturvasi was a dentist; that he had lost his daughter, Shruti, twelve years ago in an accident; that he had been devastated for a few months and blamed himself for her death; and that he was responsible for his wife's decision to hold her silence forever.

It wasn't just the death of their child that had muted his wife, Chaturvasi once told him. It was that when they managed to extinguish the flames of the burning car and retrieved the tiny body, it was headless. Chaturvasi didn't say any more and Ranganathan didn't ask.

During their time together, Chaturvasi would ask Ranganathan to do mundane chores like count the grains of rice in a cup or draw a kolam with a bowl of rice flour, and Ranganathan executed them without questioning because by now he knew that when Chaturvasi uttered a word it was not without careful deliberation and a lot of forethought. The elder would recommend dietary changes or special practices on certain days and Ranganathan would adopt them immediately. Once Chaturvasi told him when mahashivratri, the longest night of the year, would fall and instructed him to start performing a new set of practices. Ranganathan had got so used to these sudden prescriptions that he didn't bat an eyelid. On the way out Chaturvasi said, 'And one more thing, Ranga. You must beg for your food seven times between now and mahashivratri, okay? See you soon.'

'Beg-aa?' Ranganathan froze midway through putting on his slippers.

'Yes! Yes!' Chaturvasi said, his eyes sparkling. 'Bhikshan dehi.' He made a bowl with his hands. 'Beg! Go. Figure it out.'

Ranganathan agonized over the instruction for days. When the prescribed day to begin the new practices dawned, he bathed, ate a small ball of neem paste and turmeric, tied a black band around his right arm, nervously went through the yoga exercises and went to work. He figured that if he didn't buy more food and ate what he had at home, he could write it off as begging. After all, begging was simply to get food he didn't have, but if he didn't eat at all, why would he have to beg.

A few days later he ran out of all provisions and his tiny pantry was empty. There wasn't a grain of rice or lentil in any of the dabbas, no fruits in the basket and no groundnuts and simple snacks on the top shelf. He briefly considered begging for food at his family's place, but knew that Chaturvasi would not approve of it. Famished and gaunt, he ambled on to the streets and sat outside a nearby hotel with his head on his knees.

All he had to do now was wait another fifteen days for mahashivratri. Then he'd be free. He dreamt of eating vadas soaked in the spiciest sambars, of balls of puliogare oozing sesame oil and browned peanuts, of oily appalams the size of Frisbees when he felt someone shake him. He blinked rapidly and realized it was the owner of the restaurant. The man had rushed out when he saw Ranganathan slumped by the lam ppost and, recognizing him, he quickly told a waiter to bring a cup of water and asked Ranganathan if he had eaten.

'Please come in and eat,' the man said, helping Ranganathan to his feet.

The Sanskrit lecturer stood up and then painfully stared at the yeoman. 'I cannot pay you,' he said, but felt like a liar, for he could pay the man if he wanted to. With his new-found energy he was naming names, translating books from Sanskrit to English, all of which were paying handsomely. He felt embarrassed as the restaurant owner studied him briefly and then smiled. 'No matter,' he said. 'You will be able to repay me some other time.'

After he had eaten and thanked the man, Ranganathan went home and performed his practices, after which he felt a dull sense of fullness, something that he couldn't explain. He felt something chip inside his mind and fall off a steep ledge, and something else, something radiant and pure, revealed itself in the process. The next day, without any thought, he stripped out of his shirt and pants, donned a thin orange dhoti and sat outside the railway station with a small bag in front of him.

He plaintively begged people for food. Many walked by without giving him a second glance. A few stopped and regarded him curiously, wondering why this clean-shaven, nice-haired man was begging for food when he looked like he was running a few minutes late for his ten o'clock meeting. Some dropped change into his bag. Someone placed a bunch of bananas. Yet another offered him a partially eaten railway dinner and by the end of the day he had eaten three square meals. When he had begged for the seventh time, he didn't know if he was Ranganathan or some other entity in the Sanskrit lecturer's bag of flesh and bones.

~

It was the day after mahashivaratri. Ranganathan had been up the previous night with Chaturvasi, his wife and a few other aspirants. At sunrise they broke their fast on Chaturvasi's terrace with a bowl of soaked peanuts and a cup of kanji.

Even though his body was beginning to feel tired, Ranganathan's mind was alert. Chaturvasi was barely fazed by lack of sleep, his eyes electric and his discourse filled with zingers. Chaturvasi took Ranganathan aside and said to him in an urgent voice, 'I need your help, Ranga.'

'My help?'

'It is a bit ugly,' Chaturvasi warned. 'And you may not be able to stomach it, but I still need you to see the . . . the scene for yourself.'

'What scene? What is ugly?'

Chaturvasi rolled up the sleeves of his white kurta and tied his hair into a bun. 'Meet me here at six sharp tomorrow evening.' When Ranga pushed for more information Chaturvasi simply said, 'It's best I don't cloud your judgement.'

~

As they were approaching the Guindy Zoo the next day, Chaturvasi went quiet, but in a way that Ranganathan had not seen before. The old man's eyes were darting across the insides of their autorickshaw, his lips moving silently. His fingers twitched as his wild hair and beard flapped like ghosts trying to flee a tomb. Ranganathan felt a sense of dread enshroud him. A thought began to form in his head, but before he could explore it, Chaturvasi turned to him and said, 'Yes, Ranga. The accident happened here. Shruti . . . she was made to exit her body there.' He pointed behind him, sighed and shook his head. 'It's all in the past now.' Ranganathan could not imagine the pain his teacher must have gone through after losing a young child, but knew that if anybody, it was the wild-haired dentist who could deal with the tragedy without letting emotions overwhelm him. 'Twelve years after her death . . . about a year from now, a sequence of events will be set in motion.'

'What events, Vasi sir?' Ranganathan's curiosity was now driving him insane.

'When the time comes, Ranga,' Chaturvasi said, placing his hand on the other's shoulder, 'I will need your assistance.'

'Anything, sir. Anything!'

'A mudra,' he began, 'is when you hold your fingers in a certain way. They form a seal. For example, when you bring your palms together to greet someone, it's called anjali mudra. It connects the energy circuits between the left and right sides of your brain and . . . well, makes you a whole person.' Ranganathan nodded his head.

'Mudras are powerful, extremely powerful if you know how to use them.'

'I see.'

'Hold your hands like this,' Chaturvasi demonstrated, placing his palms together. His right thumb rested on his left wrist. His right index finger touched the tip of his left thumb, and the tip of his right little finger rested on his left index finger.

Ranganathan cocked his head like an attentive puppy and then mirrored the finger placement. 'What to do now?'

'This is the kurma mudra, Ranga, the tortoise seal. When coupled with pranayama it enables you to draw from a bottomless reservoir of courage to face any difficulty.'

'What is it I am about to face?' Their autorickshaw stopped outside the government hospital in Egmore. Ranganathan was puzzled. 'Sir . . . government hospital-aa?'

'Come,' Chaturvasi said, stepping out of the autorickshaw.

'But, Vasi sir . . .' Ranganathan trailed behind the old man like a recalcitrant child on his first day of school. 'This is a hospital.' Then he saw a police inspector hurrying towards them. 'And the police?'

'It's a small matter,' Chaturvasi said. 'Hurry!'

The small matter took the duo along with the cop down a grubby set of stairs with wheezing and sickly patients, past a long tube-lit corridor with doctors, nurses, men in ill-fitting white uniforms pushing patients in wheelchairs, past the X-ray room, past paan-stained walls down another set of stairs into an empty corridor which smelt of phenyl, past a series of swinging doors, and finally into a cold room.

Just as Ranganathan mumbled 'Vasi sir, what is this smell . . .' the policeman turned on the lights. 'Sir! Body! Dead body,' Ranga yelped.

'Calm down, Ranga, this is the morgue.' Chaturvasi placed a soothing hand on his arm. He turned to the policeman and said, 'Give us ten minutes, Venkat. We'll come up. Go, get some coffee.'

Venkat took a deep breath and removed his khaki cap which was laced with a black ring of sweat. He mopped his brow with the back of his palm. 'Vasi sir, please help us. This is the fourth murder . . .'

'Murder-aa?' Ranganathan exclaimed. The all-nighter followed by the morning practices the previous day had sent his mind and body into high gear. He had been coasting on the giddiness until this moment. Now his mind decided it wanted to break free and take off on its own.

Venkat viewed him with uncertainty. 'Sir, is this fellow okay here?'

Chaturvasi gently closed his eyes and nodded once. 'Venkat, go.' The inspector exited, eager to leave the morbid room.

Without opening his eyes, Chaturvasi said, 'Ranga, go out. There is a bench there. Sit with your legs crossed. Form the kurma mudra and watch your breath. Come back when you're centred.' Ranganathan exited the morgue. He removed his footwear and sat on the cold bench with his fingers forming the mudra. As he focused on his breath, he felt his thoughts leave him. Eventually, he sank into a bed of white vapour where he floated for what felt like an eternity, his fears condensing and disappearing like black snowflakes on the ground. When he was rid of all fears he sighed and slowly opened his eyes. A tear had trickled out of his right eye. As he quickly wiped it away he heard a terse knock from inside the morgue.

Ranganathan walked in calmer and dispassionately observed the scene in front of him: the dry air, the steady thrum of a fan, many empty gurneys, a corpse on one. Chaturvasi was standing next to it. Venkat was back in the room, scrolling away on his phone in a corner.

'Ah Ranga! Come! This is the fourth in a series of murders,' Chaturvasi said without looking up. 'Venkat is a policeman, but also a tantric student and practitioner like yourself.' The disclosure didn't surprise Ranganathan. 'Sometimes he approaches me to see if I can find clues that elude ordinary human perception.' Looking up, he added, 'Venkat helped me at the time of Shruti's . . . Shruti's accident.' He paused for a moment. 'Come closer, Ranga.'

Ranganathan stood next to the corpse which was covered with a sheet. There were splotches of blood on the face and chest areas and a lump on the throat. He focused on his breathing and steadied himself.

'Remember,' Chaturvasi said, placing a hand on the shroud, 'the earth loans us this body and claims the debt without interest once we are done with our time here. There is nothing to be afraid of.' He gently peeled back the shroud. 'It is part of the earth.'

Ranganathan stepped back with a gasp. When alive, he would have been just another Chennai inhabitant, probably an accountant or a shopkeeper, someone who had a small family, an ordinary two-bedroom home, someone who liked to eat rice and had grown a pot belly, someone who shaved regularly but kept a moustache.

In short, he was just another man.

Here he appeared quite a monster. His eyes had been gouged out and the hollows filled with wax from which two black burnt-out wicks stuck out. Chaturvasi unfurled the shroud more and revealed lips sutured shut with white twine. He walked around and pulled back the entire cloth, revealing the naked corpse in its entirety. 'Post-mortem,' Chaturvasi explained matter-of-factly.

Ranganathan expected to find a regular body underneath the cloth, stiff with eyes closed, like he had seen in movies. What he saw was beyond his imagination. The mutilated lips and eyes had already disturbed him, but the tattoos on the corpse left him numb. The man's head had been tonsured and a detailed lotus with hundreds of petals was inked on it with a circle at the crown. A two-petalled lotus with the word *om* was tattooed between his eyebrows. On his throat was a sixteen-petalled lotus with the Sanskrit letter *hum* in the middle. On his sternum, right below his ribcage was a twelve-petalled lotus with the word *yum* in the middle.

'They are bheejaksharas,' Chaturvasi offered, gazing placidly at the corpse. 'Seed sounds from which all mantras are assembled. Someone has desecrated his body . . .'

'Desecrated?'

'Well, set it up to invite a malevolent entity. Someone desecrated it with full knowledge of what they were doing.'

'I see,' Ranganathan replied in a distant voice.

The belly button had a ten-petalled lotus with *rum* inscribed in the middle. Holding his breath, Ranganathan walked around and looked between the legs. On the genitals was a six-petalled lotus that spanned the abdomen and the inside of its thighs. In the middle it said *vum*. Right around the anus was a four-petalled lotus with *lum* tattooed crudely around it. When he bent down and inspected the belly button, he noticed that each petal had a finely tattooed consonant in it. He stepped back, overwhelmed.

After a few moments he inched closer to observe the corpse again. Its skin was pale and he could see a hint of blue on the back and thighs. He reached for his handkerchief and placed it over its face, unable to stare into the blackened eye sockets. He circled the corpse, studying the lotuses, his mind poring over all the texts that he had ever studied. Now he donned a pair of gloves he found nearby and walked to the head. Bending forward, he examined the multi-petalled lotus closely. Chaturvasi, having read his mind, confirmed what he was thinking. 'It's clearly the work of a tantric, one who has decided to engage in the occult. But we have no clue who he could be.'

'Or she,' Ranganathan said absently.

Chaturvasi frowned. 'Hmm . . . that never occurred to me. It's possible, but exceedingly rare for women to indulge in such rituals.'

Ranganathan moved towards the corpse's feet. 'There is something here,' he pointed out.

'The coroner checked,' Chaturvasi answered. 'He said it was a birthmark.'

'Vasi sir, I don't think it's a birthmark,' Ranganathan insisted, gingerly touching it. The mark was small, about fingernail-sized, and had fuzz on it, which, when parted, revealed a red triangle. 'This man was possessed by a succubus.'

'What?' Chaturvasi walked over to him. After peering at the crude triangle within the peachy fuzz on the man's sole, he smacked his fist into his palm. 'I should have guessed it, but this . . . this work is unknown to me. Ranga, how do you know it?'

'Sir, I teach a course on devas and rakshasas. We learn about the spirits and entities that inhabit the various realms.' Ranganathan brought his palms together. 'Surely, you must know about it.'

Chaturvasi guffawed. 'Clearly not all of it.'

'I have a textbook . . . it's an ancient book. It's called *Obscure Religious Cults As Background of Bengali Literature*,' Ranganathan said, now in professor mode. 'Shashibusan Dasgupta. Interesting theories he proposed in it. I borrowed it from the Theosophical Society and photocopied it. I use it to teach and there is a page on succubi that I remember reading.'

He peeled the gloves off and tossed them into the dustbin. 'I will send you the information once I get home.'

'Venkat,' Chaturvasi called out. The inspector looked up from his phone. 'Take out your notebook. Ranga, close your eyes. And simply be. Just be with me.' Ranganathan hesitated for a second and then complied. 'In your mind, walk to the bookshelf in your room and locate the textbook.'

The professor closed his eyes and tried to concentrate. 'Don't force it, Ranga,' Chaturvasi instructed. He made a gesture at Venkat to be ready. The inspector flipped through the pages and uncapped his pen. Chaturvasi closed his eyes and stood straight. 'I see the symbol. Venkat. Write this. Take equal quantities of . . . chi . . . chi . . . chikana. *Hedysarum lagopodiodes*. Of kosht. *Costus specicosus*. Of vekhand. *Orris root*. Are you getting this, Venkat?'

'Sir! Yes sir!' Venkat replied, his pen moving fast to keep up with Chaturvasi's words. Ranganathan was breathing harder now.

'Almost there, Ranga. You are doing an excellent job. Stay focused. Venkat . . . Of gajapimpali. *Pothos officinalis*. Of askhand. *Physalis flexuosa*. Pound and mix in butter. Apply to the male member and after forty-eight minutes it will assume an equine magnitude.'

Chaturvasi opened raised his hands to shield his face rubbed his temples. 'Sir, what was that? How did . . .'

Chaturvasi turned to Venkat. 'Those are the herbs that went into making a potion that the tantric used to invoke the succubus. She appears to have made the potion and' – he glanced at the corpse, gently covering it with the shroud – 'applied it to his genitals before the succubus took over and killed him.'

'Okay sir,' Venkat said. 'What should I do?'

'Find a botanist or an ayurvedic doctor. Go to Guindy College. Or IIT. Show him or her these roots and find out where they grow. The potion must have been made fresh. That will give you a geographical clue where to search.'

Venkat slammed his feet together and saluted the duo. 'Sir, this is the best lead we have gotten in months. I should have come to you earlier.'

Chaturvasi laughed and looked at Ranganathan who was still in a daze. 'The student was not ready yet. Oh! And Venkat?'

'Sir?'

'Find that ayurvedic doctor. A good one. He can help.'

'Okay sir!'

The information turned out to be critical in apprehending a tantric priestess. Venkat reached out to an ayurvedic practitioner and discovered that the plant most likely grew near Nellore. This narrowed their search perimeter and with the help of other clues they found the priestess, who lived a cushy life infecting rich men with succubi, making them give away their wealth before executing them ritualistically.

The experience changed Ranganathan's outlook on life. Chennai's underbelly, it appeared, was teeming with occult criminals and he was elated to be a part of the tantric force required to neutralize them. Every now and then he'd ask Chaturvasi if there were any more cases to crack, to which the former always replied, 'Do your practices, Ranga. When the time is right, you will help me crack the hardest puzzle I have ever encountered.'

5

It was close to sunset and as he walked through the Theosophical Society's gates, Vikram popped a Halls mint into his mouth and texted Tony to ask about the question paper but received no response. Throughout the drive back home he felt light-headed and a bit woozy, which he attributed to his hunger. There was a soreness in his throat and he wondered if he was coming down with a cold.

Vikram zipped between the lumbering cars like a nimble gazelle. When he finally got on to Mount Road, he relaxed a bit as the breeze ventilated his clothes. He felt a dull sense of separation from his body.

He drove by a family of four on a motorcycle, the father driving assiduously, a small boy perched on the petrol tank like a bobsled racer, the wife sitting behind him with both legs on one side, her sari flapping like a flag as she held an infant with one hand and her husband with the other. He shook his head in annoyance and then astonished himself by growling. Just then, a Cielo overtook him, missing him narrowly, and he jammed on his horn. Its tinny sound barely registered in the cacophony of horns and he smacked his rear-view mirror in anger. He readjusted it and almost let go of the handlebar, for he noticed a black shape with a hooked nose sitting in the pillion seat, baring its teeth at him.

Vikram swerved but regained control immediately. When he looked in the mirror again, there was nothing. He glanced back in panic and found the pillion empty. Confused, he slowed down and lifted the visor of his helmet.

What was that? It'd been an inky blob with gleaming yellow slits for eyes. The four years of engineering studies had taught him to be logical and methodical in his reasoning, but what he had just witnessed made no sense. He concluded that he had either imagined the creature, or something had briefly hitched a ride with him. Not really convinced by either explanation, he drummed the side of his helmet as he drove.

Soon he realized his senses were becoming numb. The traffic sounds and smells felt distant. His memories began to unravel. Even the vision from a few seconds ago was fading from his mind. His body drove the Scooty on autopilot as his mind powered down.

There was a sudden splotch of black on his right. He looked askance and saw a crow flying beside him. He regained control over himself, remembering a documentary called *Winged Migration* where the moviemaker flew alongside migratory birds and filmed a unique perspective of their flight. In this moment he felt like that documentarian as the crow flapped its wings furiously and flew closer to him. Seconds later, a pang of panic shot through him as the bird turned its head and fixed him with a penetrating and hypnotizing gaze. That was not how a crow was supposed to look. Unable to break the eye contact he steered through the traffic almost unconsciously.

Another crow appeared from behind him and flew to his left, so close that he could see the gauzy grey feathers around its face move ever so gently in the wind and its tiny legs tucked beneath its body. He noticed the scales on its legs and even a smattering of white shit on one of its claws. Within moments a dozen more crows dropped from the sky and surrounded him like jets scrambling to escort an enemy plane out of their territory.

The first crow began to caw, followed by the rest. Vikram was getting disoriented. Did the people around him not see the crows? No one stopped and gasped or pointed in his direction. The crows began to close in like black drops of blood, assuming the formation of one giant crow, its wings beating in mesmerizing slowness.

The Scooty began to wobble and Vikram tried to pull over to the side of the road. The massive crow with gargantuan wings darted up in the air like a missile. When he looked up it dived straight at him.

He screamed and raised his hands to shield his face, finding the helmet instead. His knees hit the ground, but he was oblivious to the physical pain, his panic-stricken eyes still locked with the unblinking yellow gaze of the crow as it ploughed through the air and streaked his mouth like a jet of velvet ink.

6

Most people who encountered Chaturvasi at the beach each morning found him to be a grouchy old man with a salt-and-pepper ponytail and flowing beard. He swung his wooden walking stick energetically as he passed the early morning walkers and joggers, his white canvas shoes looking out of place with his dhoti which was itself a mismatch with his baggy T-shirt with giant horizontal white stripes.

A disciplined man, Chaturvasi structured his day precisely. Waking up a couple of hours before dawn, he trekked to a secluded spot on the beach. Once there he dug a shallow hole and fashioned the sand around the hole so that it resembled an igloo. He carefully placed an oil lamp inside the cavity, lit it and brought his palms together in veneration. Then he undid his hair, cleared his throat, hawked and spat into the sea. Using a copper lota with a spout, he sent a stream of water up one nostril which trickled out of the other and then cleansed the other one similarly. After that, he spent ten minutes slowly swallowing a ten-metre-long ribbon his wife had made by stitching together dozens of smaller ribbons. Forcing himself not to gag, he stared at the sea and patiently consumed the cloth until he held the bright yellow one, the last one, Shruti's favourite.

After a short pause, and then with the speed and aplomb of a magician doing a stage trick, he yanked it all out, a lightness descending on him as his digestive tract was cleansed of any matter. He then consumed a litre of boiled tap water from a copper bottle in which it had to have been stored for at least six hours. He drank the water in big gulps, forcing himself to keep it down. After he was done, he stuck two fingers into the back of his throat and emptied his stomach of its liquid contents. At this point, precisely twenty minutes before sunrise, he contorted himself into various yogic poses before sitting down on the sand with his eyes tightly shut, looking, to a fascinated observer, like a lifelike statue with a flickering lamp beside it.

When he got up later, dusted the sand off his back and walked away, a passer-by would wonder why the sand had scorched and turned into glass. The watchman, Muthu, who stared at him on some days as he went through his purification ritual, wondered what made an educated doctor with a fashionable ponytail perform these actions when he could be lying in his bed and asking his wife to bring him the daily newspaper and coffee. Chaturvasi knew the celestial arrangement at any time of the day and any day of the month the way one knew when one's shoelaces were undone. He was aware of which nostril was inhaling more air. When he had to slip into deep meditative states, he could ensure he was breathing evenly through both nostrils.

After his morning walk Chaturvasi picked up milk packets

from the sleepy vendor at the head of the street. Back home he read the newspaper closely. A herbal potion made with ginger, pepper, honey, coriander and a mélange of roots and shoots with unpronounceable names would be waiting for him on the table. This he downed in a gulp before heading to the prayer room to sit on his wooden stool and offer flowers and holy water while chanting slokas.

When she heard the rapid tinkling of the bell and the trumpeting notes of the conch, his wife dropped whatever she was doing, found a fresh towel and hovered outside the puja room. Chaturvasi then exited his sanctum, took the towel and headed to the bathroom while routinely whining about how living in a flat was not conducive for a yogi these days, what with the lack of a nearby river, ample greenery and potent temples consecrated by yogis in the past. Afterwards, and before sitting down for breakfast, he made five boluses of rice loaded with ghee and placed them outside the window. Appearing beside him his wife watched pensively as a couple of crows cawed and alighted outside, cautiously regarding them with their corvine eyes before devouring the offering. This was a ritual he always performed before eating his first meal of the day, and no matter where he was, or what time of the day it was, the crows always arrived and they always fed. Then, and only then, would Chaturvasi turn to his wife and ask, 'What's for breakfast today?'

As a dentist Chaturvasi was a local legend. He pulled out teeth, inserted new ones, cured gum diseases, installed braces, pored over X-rays and scribbled prescriptions.

Certain patients he stared at for minutes on end, sometimes tears forming and running down his cheeks, much to the confusion of the patient. Then, shaking his head and smiling in an undentist-like fashion, he placed his hand on their heads, his lips moving silently. He gave them a packet of vibhuti or a flower, or told them that their dental issues were the least of their concerns and that they should go to a specific temple and perform certain rituals. The ones who followed his advice returned with overwhelming gratitude and continued to visit him even when he'd ordered them not to. They brought him fruits and offerings, invited him to their weddings and functions and sang his praises.

His compounder and receptionist knew better than to invoke his dark mood, for he was known to mutter under his breath with unblinking eyes and sometimes cause the electricity to go off when he snapped his fingers or cause the hairs along their spine to stand. When he was not in the office, they discussed if he was in fact a tantric, one with supernatural powers. At the sight of him briskly marching into the building, they quickly got back to their seats. Where he went for an hour during lunch they didn't know, but each day precisely at eleven-thirty he locked his office and left. He returned looking like he had been injected with caffeine, his eyes twinkling and his fingers twitching.

When it was close to sunset, he headed back to the secluded spot on the beach, which lay beyond the open toilet used by the fishermen who lived nearby, beyond the Temple of Eight Lakshmis (in front of which he brought his palms together to offer obeisance to the granite idol of Vishnu and his eight consorts within), beyond more thatch huts. It was the backyard of wealthy people, one of whom he had guided in their spiritual quests, who, in turn, had given him access to the pristine beach behind his sprawling home in the upscale Kalakshetra Colony neighbourhod.

After nodding at Muthu and lighting a lamp inside a mud igloo, he sat cross-legged and sank into a deep trance, probing the gaps between his thoughts. As he meditated, the bored watchman, while trying to decode the motivations of this mysterious man, ensured no one bothered him during his sojourns to the spiritual realm.

Back home, he settled on the sofa after dinner to watch and discuss with his wife the antics of the actress Raadhika (the extra *a* in her name, he always observed, was what had turned her life around) as she played a double role in the serial *Vaani Rani*, which progressed lethargically but kept them hooked with its daily cliffhangers. He spent a few more minutes doing puja before going to bed where he slept like a classic vampire with his hands crossed across his chest, and unlike one, looking forward to sunrise.

~

This day started like any other. After his morning practices and walk, he headed home, feeling a strange sense of unease which grew stronger as the day went on. However, it was a rare day with respect to planetary alignment, and he felt it in his core and in every cell. While people consulted almanacs and pored over flimsy tear-away calendars, Chaturvasi experienced within himself the interplay between Saturn, the moon and the earth. Wherever he looked he saw pools of energy. Harnessing even one of those vortices could make a person's life vibrant for weeks. That certainly wasn't the source of his unease and failing to identify what was made him anxious.

He performed a couple of root canal surgeries, tightened the braces of a teenage girl (and told her to get rid of the plastic doll she had found on the beach), referred a middle-aged man who had come for a regular check-up to a cardiologist (he saw the beginnings of the man's heart disease in his aura as flecks of black blobs, but told him that the plaque build-up on his enamel was a sign of a failing heart) before stopping for lunch. Even on a regular day, he barely ate, preferring to keep his stomach empty. But today, he simply poked at the ash gourd sambar and rice that his wife had packed for him. He glanced at the balls of rice he had placed outside his office window. They remained untouched like strange snow globes.

He washed his hands and left his tiffin outside the window, hoping a feast instead of the usual fare would entice the crows. The he lit an oil lamp, sat down on a mat and closed his eyes, his mind expanding outwards like tendrils probing for the anomaly that was disturbing him.

When he centred himself back in his physical form, he slowly opened his eyes. Shapes swam on the periphery of his vision and he brought his palms together in supplication. Still unclear why the universe was not unfurling in the way it should, he cleared his head and opened the door, gesturing the receptionist to start sending him his patients. As the afternoon unwound, he found himself gazing into the void of a patient's mouth and finding slow-moving vortices of energy swirling in the small blackness of her throat. When the woman tapped his wrist and tossed her head back as if to ask if everything was okay, he took a deep breath and smiled. 'Gingivitis,' he said absently. 'No need for any medicine. Just rinse your mouth with saltwater three times a day and avoid all sweets until Deepavali.' When the woman tried to pay him, Chaturvasi waved her away, his mind now buzzing again.

Now he emptied an ice tray into a bucket of water in the toilet. He then called Sowmya, the receptionist, and told her that he was not going to see any more patients. She looked puzzled, for Chaturvasi had never left early in the many years that she had worked for him.

'Sir, if they ask . . .' she began but stopped when she met the dentist's burning glare. 'Yes sir. Clove oil,' she mumbled to herself, adjusted her dupatta and hurried out of the door, turning the sign around so that it read 'Doctor is out'.

Chaturvasi spent the next half-hour buried in books that looked like they would come apart with a mere blow. When he was done, he stepped into the bathroom, poured the bucket of icy water on himself, towelled himself dry and sat cross-legged on a deerskin that he kept in a Godrej almirah. He took off his shirt and smeared lines of ash on his forehead, throat, chest and abdomen. His doctor's handbag which, in case of a dental emergency, had just a few vials of clove oil, was full of other paraphernalia. He rummaged through it until he found a rosary made of a hundred and eight rudraksha seeds. He carefully arranged the other items in front him: a red oleander, a twig of the ashvattha tree and blades of kusha grass. He closed his eyes and visualized the glorious form of his guru and chanted verses.

The body, his guru had told him before initiating him, was a piece of the world and the world was a piece of the body. Only when he understood the body would he realize what he was seeking: divinity.

~

As a youth, he had found himself questioning the point of existence during his commute to college. What had begun as an interesting foray into logic and philosophy slowly began to consume him. After reading many books and conversing with learned men, he had deduced that existence was pointless for the simple reason that one didn't have a choice in being born. He was becoming a star dentist, but he felt as empty inside as his patients' mouths. Academics and ordinary life were losing their appeal. In his mid-twenties, a strong calling had made him quit his fledgling practice and set off to the Himalayas, thirsty for a guide.

While desperately seeking a guru, Chaturvasi had commingled with the Aghoris, a sect of tantrics known for their extreme unconventionality. He had spent many months at cremation grounds where, clothed only in the ashes from funeral pyres, he had pursued his solitary meditations, sometimes atop charred corpses. He had drunk water and arrack from the skull he carried around in his cloth bag along with a few other meagre possessions. He had listened to scrawny yogis whose bodies were smeared with human ash and who had matted hair like giant beehives, reddened eyes and squeaky white grins. They smoked chillums in the dead of the night and taught him the ancient ways of using the dead to embellish his life, the only other sounds being the howls of hungry strays. But he had found all this hollow and unrewarding.

Their practices were austere and intensified with time. His mentor would often ask him to make a sojourn to a certain village or a temple and meet someone specific as part of his training.

Once, he had met a yogi who had never sat down and didn't plan to until his last breath, spending all his time meditating, leaning on a set of ropes when he needed to rest. His legs were swollen with veins crawling along his calves like giant worms. Another time he met a baba who had his left arm stretched out vertically for sixteen years. The arm had shrivelled and turned into something resembling a twig, and the fingers all curled up as if from severe arthritis. Despite all this these men were radiant and bubbly, making Chaturvasi wonder if he could endure such travails in his quest to decode his life. If joy, and probably the meaning of life, came from such self-abnegation then he didn't want it.

When his frustration had reached boiling point, he had decided to end his life by jumping into the ice-cold river, figuring that maybe in his next birth he may get clarity. It was then that a man, dressed in orange clothes, with matted hair and exhuding radiance had appeared before him and smiled. Chaturvasi had run to him and fallen at his feet. 'I will never leave you,' he had said, weeping, confident that he had found his guru. 'We'll see about that,' the other had said.

A few years later, he had returned to Chennai a transformed man not just spiritually, but also physically. His voice had changed as had the intensity of his gaze. His eyes had sunk and his face seemed to have become more symmetric. When he laughed, his entire body bounced as if it were resting on a spring. And his body was bereft of any odour.

~

His guru had shown him the dimensions beyond the ordinary and transmitted to him practices that required nothing more than a small patch of the earth and an oil lamp. Now, bringing his palms together, he half closed his eyes and slipped into a trance, starting the invocation ritual to appease and invite beings from other realms to come to his protection. He had asked his compounder and receptionist to go home early and lock the doors. He did not want them to hear the cawing, barking, grunting sounds accompanied by flashes of light punctuated by rapid thuds and heavy footsteps from behind the frosted door.

At sunset, the nexus between the realm of the sun and the moon, a period of the day considered powerful enough for the ancients to prescribe people to sit cross-legged and breathe in a certain fashion to harness the energy, Chaturvasi's eyes opened wide. His body trembled, not in the typical way it did when it was suffused with energy. The last time he had experienced terror it had been moments after his car had lost control and landed on its roof, after a good Samaritan had broken the window and hauled him out, after he had tried to go back in to save Shruti, after he had collapsed watching the vehicle explode and after he had rushed to it when the flames were under control and saw his child's headless charred corpse.

The days, and especially the nights, that followed the incident were a blur. His wife retreated within herself and he was once again disoriented and confused, having stopped his daily practices. He felt rage at his guru for sending him back to the plains and commanding him to start a family. He felt guilty for not taking Shruti's nightmares seriously when she had clung to him in the mornings, begging him to check if her skull was still attached.

'Why, Shruti kuti?' he had asked the third time that had happened. He had put on his stethoscope, placed it on her chest and then gravely told her that her skull was indeed still attached to her torso and if she didn't clean the inside of it regularly, he might have to pull out some bones from it.

But she hadn't found it funny. 'I dreamt, appa, that a black man was cutting my head off with a big axe.' He had prescribed her a sugar pill after placing it between his forehead and muttering some Sanskrit words. After her passing, he hadn't been able to forgive himself for being so callous about interpreting her dreams.

One-third of his family was dead and another third had become mute. Nothing made sense any more and the mountains called to him once again. But this time he couldn't abandon everything and disappear. The running river also beckoned him feebly, but now he knew what the sin of taking one's life would do to his soul in the afterlife. He had reached out to his guru, who had kept his silence.

With a heavy heart, and a part of him completely wiped out, he had returned to his daily yogic practices and his dentistry. He had tried to feed the crows and when the first one landed on the air-conditioner and pecked at the rice ball, something had moved within him, something tender and palliative. While he had bootstrapped the subtle bobs in his emotion and bounced back, his wife had spun a cocoon and numbed herself, sifting through Shruti's belongings like a living ghost.

With surgical precision he had excised all negative emotions and cast them aside, while she carefully tended and pickled them before storing them in neat rows inside her. A few years later, he had penetrated the sheath of misery that had befallen him and emerged from it a positive being while she had slowly withered into a gauzy creature, always dressed in widow whites, her presence barely noticeable. It wasn't that he had forgotten and buried Shruti in the tombs of his mind, no! Instead, he had enshrined her and taped her to the tip of his nose so that every moment was a meditation about her.

Over time, clues had began to emerge and Chaturvasi slowly began to see what had really happened.

His body trembled not with the usual unbridled energy, but from a deep sense of fear. He was whisked back to the moment when he was restrained by strangers as he watched his daughter burn and he experienced a jolt of terror.

A menacing entity had slipped into the mortal realm.

Outside, the airconditioner shuddered to life and he noticed the food he had left out remained untouched.

7

Parvati emerged from the recess in her kitchen where she kept and prayed to various idols. It was a small alcove that also doubled as a pantry. Aluminium dabbas containing rice, lentils, sun-dried vadams, packets of dry spices were neatly placed in rows on the shelves. Maggi packets perched between these storage cans like bright yellow fruit. A powerful bulb hung from the ceiling dispelling the darkness that liked to roost in the space when the main kitchen light was off. A couple of Tamil calendars and various framed photos of gods hung from nails on the walls. All of them were garlanded and some gods had a red vermilion dot between their painted eyes.

Vikram's strange behaviour over the past few days was worrying her. A couple of nights ago she heard voices in the house. First she checked on her father-in-law. He was peacefully snoring in his bed. With a big sigh, she slowly closed his door and walked to Vikram's room.

She hovered outside for a few seconds, straining to make sense of the sounds coming from the room. She initially thought Vikram was talking to himself, but could not make out the language. As far as she knew Vikram spoke only Tamil and English. This sounded like neither. Just as she was about to knock on his door, a loud spine-chilling laugh rang through the room. It didn't sound like her mild-mannered teenage boy. In fact, the sound wasn't human at all. She scurried back to her bedroom where her husband, Gopal, dressed in a banian and veshti, was reading a book in bed.

'What, Paru?' he said, removing his bifocals. 'What happened?'

'It's . . . Vikram,' she sputtered. They never referred to their son by his full name unless they were at a function or at a parent–teacher meeting in school.

Figuring that it was yet another one of her anxiety attacks about her son, he flipped a page and asked, 'What happened now? Caught him reading *Archie* comics again? Or was it a bad magazine?'

She collapsed on the bed next to him. 'Something is not right. There are voices coming from his room.'

'Voices-aa? He's on the phone?'

'No. Talking to someone.'

'Who?'

'I . . . I don't know. And I'm scared to open his door. The voice . . . it was like some big and powerful . . . thing.'

'What nonsense.' Gopal said, tossing the book on the bed and standing up. Retying his veshti before slipping into the Bata chappals, he marched out of the door mumbling, 'What someone big and powerful . . .'

Parvati followed him, her tremulous hand holding on to his shoulder.

They could hear the growling as they approached their son's room. It was a haunting sound, as if coming from the depths of the earth. Turning to Parvati, Gopal asked, his voice laced with uncertainty, 'Is he watching a movie? What's that sound?'

'That is what I am telling you. There is . . . there is someone . . .' She joined her palms before at Lord Murugan on the calendar smiling beatifically with a vel in his hand, oblivious to the commotion in the room he was supposed to keep an eye on.

Laughter echoed from inside, followed by cawing. Brows pinched, Gopal bent his finger to knock when the door slowly opened.

'Come in, appa.'

The couple entered the room after exchanging hesitant glances. Parvati clasped her mouth with her sari the moment they were inside. Gopal coughed and covered his mouth with his hand. A strong musky stench hung in the air, something distantly sulphurous and caustic.

'Vikky!' Parvati exclaimed.

Vikram was squatting on the ledge of the window, holding a cigarette between his thumb and forefinger like a coolie on a platform. He took a deep drag from it. Outside, the bougainvillea vine, which normally looked so inviting and peaceful, loomed like black haze. A few birdlike shapes were perched on it, staring into the room.

'Vikram! Badava! Rascal!' Gopal thundered as Parvati gripped his shoulder harder. 'What are you doing?'

Vikram smiled and looked at the cigarette before offering it to his father. 'Smoking, pa. What does it look like to you? Don't tell me you didn't try it in college.'

Gopal was livid. Words formed and died on his lips. Parvati stepped forward and asked, 'What was that voice here earlier?' Taking in the room she noticed how messy it was – clothes and books strewn everywhere. He normally kept his room in a mess, but never had it looked like it had been ravaged by a cyclone.

'There were no voices, ma,' Vikram answered, flicking the cigarette out. 'It's all in your head.' When he hopped in he seemed taller. Gopal stepped back and Parvati clung on to the door handle. Advancing towards them, Vikram said with a malicious grin, 'Go on. Go to your room. Make me a brother or a sister.'

'Vikram!' Gopal roared and raised his hand.

Vikram caught his father's hand and squeezed it, turning his wrist a dull shade of red. 'What?' Vikram said coldly. There was a crow scuttling on his desk, its talons clicking as it pushed stationery about. It let out a low guttural caw and then studied Gopal with intelligent eyes.

Gopal had to wiggle his hand out of Vikram's grasp. A harried Parvati whispered to her husband, 'Please! Let's go. He's not himself. Come! Your hand is swelling up.'

Watching his parents hurry out of his room, Vikram threw his head back and laughed.

The next day, Parvati bathed and wrapped her hair in a gauzy white cotton towel before entering her alcove in the kitchen. She played the suprabhatam tape, lit incense and refreshed the flowers and vermilion for all the idols. She joined her palms and prayed furiously before going about making breakfast. Each time the tape ended, she rewound and replayed it as if the soothing sounds of M.S. Subbulakshmi entreating Lord Rama to wake up would also ensure that Vikram woke up as his normal self.

She tried to actively forget the previous night's episode, blaming it on the demands of college. She had heard from her friends that engineering was quite stressful and got to even the best students in school as they waded through the coursework. Convinced that it was just a one-off incident, she had made his favourite breakfast – bread upma. She hoped and prayed that her husband would leave for work before Vikram woke up so that there was no more drama in the house. Upon hearing a chair being dragged and her father-in-law addressing Vikram, she heaped the contents of the pan on to a steel plate, picked up the tumbler of filter coffee and rushed out. She was relieved to find that Gopal had left.

'Slept well?' Parvati asked Vikram, unable to think of anything else to say. She placed the plate in front of her son and slid the tumbler towards him. Vikram was cheery as he chatted with his grandfather. He looked well rested, even though his hair seemed to have grown longer. She noticed that his T-shirt stretched at his shoulders and was riding higher. Had he grown taller? How was that even possible?

'It's good, ma,' Vikram responded, grabbing the plate and the tumbler. He began pecking away on his phone and Parvati had to hold back from chiding him for it.

'Where's the bajji?' his grandfather asked. He was breaking

off sections of a banana and tossing them into his mouth. 'I waited forever last night until your mother put food on the table. Then I knew no hope for bajji today.' He then he glanced up and pronounced, 'Forecast dry. Thathosphere is facing a bajji drought.' With a quick smile and no further response Vikram went back to his phone. 'No college?' his grandfather enquired.

'Let him stay,' was Parvati's instinctive response. 'If you want to take rest . . .' she continued, her eyes wandering all over her son's face, probing and fishing for signs that something was wrong. There were a couple – acne on his cheeks (something he had never had) and a nervous tic which had him moving his upper lip every few seconds. His hair seemed oilier than usual and clung to his temples like worms crawling out from the ground.

'No college, thatha,' Vikram informed his grandfather. 'Strike.'

'I'll apply sesame oil on your head,' Parvati offered, having already diagnosed that stress was causing an imbalance in his internal composition. The heat had been rising now that it was almost peak summer. All that heat coupled with his erratic lifestyle must have disoriented her otherwise well-mannered boy. 'Take a head-bath and stay at home. It will pull out all the heat from inside. I'll make cooling food. Cucumber salad and buttermilk rice.' Picking up the plate and tumbler she said to her son, 'Rest,' and to her father-in-law, 'Don't disturb him.'

'Me-aa?' the old man guffawed, folding the newspaper. 'What will I do? I'm going to meet my friends.'

'Good,' Parvati said. 'Vikram! Go sit in the bathroom. I'll bring the oil.'

Vikram stood up with a groan. Parvati was sure he had grown in height. Unable to digest that, she darted to the kitchen to heat a cup of oil.

Despite her trepidation, the day unfolded normally. As she applied the oil to his scalp and torso, she exclaimed, 'See! How it is all disappearing. The heat is too much inside you.' After the oil massage Vikram scrubbed the oil off with chickpea flour. He had a heavy meal, retreated to his room and slumbered for a couple of hours with the fan on full speed. When he walked out later with a fat book in his hand, Parvati at once knew that that book, whatever higher order math or physics it dealt with, was the reason her son had been tormented lately. It was a numerical djinn that had possessed him, one that carried away many young boys and girls in its arithmetic grip and deposited them extremely far from normalcy. She had seen those children, slaves to their guidebooks and exams, having forgotten what life was, snarling and snapping at anyone who tried to lure them out of their academic cage. While giving him a cup of coffee she said, 'Don't study too hard, Vikky,' instantly breaking the mould of the stereotypical fastidious Tamilian mother.

When Gopal returned, she rushed to the veranda to greet him and entreated him not to bring up the happenings of the previous night.

'He has been studying so hard. I can see it in his face. It's all–' she dabbed her cheeks – 'like this like this. Poor boy. He is stressed.'

Gopal let out a groan while undoing his laces. 'That is not the way to talk to his parents. What nonsense he was saying, Paru. You heard him. Smoking in my house? How dare he!'

She tried to placate him, saying, 'Slowly! Just leave it, please. College boys do such things. It's just a phase.'

Later, over dinner, they made small talk as Parvati fussed about, serving food and playing mediator between father and son, deftly changing topics and asking irrelevant questions so that the conversation never veered towards the incident. Though the pent-up tension in Gopal was thick and palpable. After the meal Vikram picked up his phone, brushed his hair back and sauntered to his room.

When Parvati heard a caw from Vikram's room her stomach lurched, but she instantly dismissed it as just another nocturnal aberration. There was always a dog howling, a cow mooing, or a crow cawing during the day, she reasoned. However, besides the occasional territorial fights among the strays, the other animals minded their business and held their silence through the night.

After clearing up the kitchen and ensuring her father-in-law's water bottle was filled, Parvati checked the padlocks and slipped into the kitchen to offer prayers to all the gods. It was unnatural to be in front of the gods at this time of day, for she thought the gods really slept; if not, why did they play the suprabhatam to wake them up each day? But her mind had been restless and prayer brought respite. Touching the feet of all the slumbering gods in their glass palaces, she tiptoed to the bedroom, pausing briefly in front of Vikram's room. She could see shadows move back and forth from under the door and assumed Vikram was pacing as he studied for his exams.

'Vikram is . . .' Gopal began to say as she stepped into the room.

'I think something is wrong with him,' she cut him off instead, while nervously removing her earrings and placing them on the dressing table. She peeled off her bindi and stuck it in the corner of the mirror. 'He's acting strangely.'

'I know,' Gopal shot back in an irate tone.

She sat down on the bed and grabbed his hand. 'It's not normal.'

Gopal studied his wife for a second. He had always trusted her instinct when it came to Vikram, but now it seemed the boy had outgrown the fawning and was beginning to show signs of an impetuous adult. 'I'll straighten him out.'

'Please . . .'

'Now, go to sleep, Paru. It's late. I have to take appa to the doctor tomorrow.'

'I think it's best appa stays with Mahesh for a while.'

'Mahesh-aa? Why?'

Parvati applied a dab of Fair & Lovely on her face and spread it with her fingers. 'I don't know. I just feel he should be away.'

Sleep cocooned Parvati like fog rolling over a placid lake in the cold of the night. It was late and the house was silent, except for the usual nocturnal sounds – the whirr of the ceiling fan, the tapping of the Gurkha's cane outside as he made his nightly rounds and the snores of the house's denizens.

A crashing sound from the kitchen jolted Parvati out of her sleep, but when she saw Gopal sound asleep next to her, she assumed it was a nightmare.

She crept out of her bed with the intention of checking on Vikram, but her feet would not take her out of her room. The umbilical connection she had always felt with Vikram was severed now. Something else was dangling on the other end. She returned to the bed, draped the sheets over her head and fell asleep.

When she heard the cawing, she thought it was dawn already and her eyes struggled to open. It was unlike her to sleep past sunrise. Parvati remembered that she was sheltered inside her cloth coffin and lifted the edge of the sheet, and saw Gopal's face. His brows were furrowed as if he was angry. Then she heard someone breathing heavily and a steady stream of whispers and soft chuckles.

She lay petrified under the sheets. The breathing was more forceful and drawing closer. She heard an almost growl-like caw from outside the room and held her breath. How did the crow get into the house? She slowly turned under the sheet like a pupa inside its cotton chrysalis and caught sight of a hulking shape beside her. She exhaled sharply, her brain racing.

'Gopal,' she moaned. But her husband didn't respond. She wanted to poke him but trembled at the thought of exposing her hand. The figure gradually rose next to her, bones cracking as it gained height. She bit her pallu and stared through the gauzy sheet at the thing that looked like her son, but also wore the cloak of something inhuman. It was Vikram, but his eyes were a dull yellow and he rocked back and forth on his heels, staring down at her. In the dim light coming in from the street, she saw a toothy grin appear on his face. Mother and son held each other's gaze for what seemed like hours. Parvati forgot that she possessed a body as she lay ramrod straight, paralysed by the animal eyes. When she finally mustered some courage, she whispered, 'Vikram,' and the figure began to rock faster. He shook his head like he was entranced by his music, his limp hair flying around his face like a rocker on stage. After a few minutes he stopped and his smile faded. Parvati felt her fear evaporate, and just as she was about to emerge from her cocoon, there was a sharp thud of something falling to the ground.

Parvati threw away the sheet and exclaimed, 'Vikram! Are you okay?'

Gopal, who was awake now, darted out of bed and stared at the knife on the floor and then at his son. Holding his hand like he was a schoolboy, he dragged him out of their room, down the hallway and pushed him into his room. 'Don't make me call the police,' he yelled so loud that Parvati started crying.

The boy grinning at her in the dark had not been her son, but the terror-stricken face when Gopal woke up was definitely Vikram's. She knew then that her son was slipping away from them.

8

Professor Ranganathan studied Tony carefully. He didn't look like a Tony. The *na* consonant was what he felt must have been embedded in his name, but it was being forced to contort into the *nee* sound. This was not resonating with the boy's slim build, piercing eyes and ugly bushy moustache. Ideally, it should have been a *ma*, he deduced. Maybe a Matthew, or, if he had had a say, definitely a Mahesh. Many years ago, Tony's Christianity would have gotten the professor's defences up.

Raised in an orthodox Brahmanical family, a Mylapore one at that, he had been groomed to steer clear of non-Brahmins. But the time spent under Chaturvasi's tutelage had broken down these rigid constructs. 'The same life that animates you,' Chaturvasi had said, 'also does so to everything on this planet. You may not be able to perceive it, but there is life even within a rock and the sands of the beach. Do your practices regularly and you may become attuned to it.' Now he viewed people as walking bags of life, their religion invisible.

Despite himself, Ranganathan couldn't help asking, 'How, uh, how did you find out about me?' He expected Tony to tell him that he was some sort of unknown celebrity, his sleuthing with Chaturvasi having earned him a sobriquet like the Sanskrit Sherlock. But the answer turned out to be something more prosaic.

'Sir, Vikram said he had read Sanskrit lines,' Tony said. 'I figured I'd come to the only place in the city I know where Sanskrit teachers . . .'

'Professor.'

' . . . Sanskrit professors teach. I saw your name on the board outside and came to your room.'

Ranganathan was a little disappointed. He leaned back in his creaky old chair and reached for his notepad. Tony was looking at him anxiously, his phone in hand. The boy claimed that his friend, Vikram, had been possessed by Betal, the vampire that haunted the imaginations of children, especially after they had managed to come across the *Chandamama* comics. He thought Vikram had summoned the vampire by reading Sanskrit lines from an ancient palm leaf at the Theosophical Society.

Ranganathan had a lot of respect for the venerable library by the Adyar backwaters, which seemed as ancient as the banyan tree that grew there. The boy hastily explained to him what had happened. Ranganathan inspected the images on the phone and studied the verses. A part of his brain – the one that came alive when Chaturvasi asked if he had time to meet Venkat, or when he had to figure out the right vowel in a name – lit up.

'What . . . what will happen?' Tony asked.

'Betal is not his name,' Ranganathan said. 'He is *a* betal.'

Tony looked confused. 'Sir?'

'A betal, or vetal as is the correct pronunciation.' He raised a professorial finger at Tony. His irritation at the way the Tamilians butchered Sanskrit was legendary. Lacking the aspirated emphasis on consonants, Tamil didn't distinguish between the soft *pa* or the harder *pha*. In fact, it even scooped the innocent *ba* and *bha* into the linguistic van and sped away. He made a mental note to posit this 'Is it betal or vetal?' question in his next grammar class. 'It is a type of entity,' he continued. 'Tal and vetal are the two types of magic. One good, the other bad. Your friend got mixed up with the bad kind.'

Tony squirmed in his seat. He cracked his knuckles rapidly. 'Vikram is in danger, sir.'

'I know.'

'I saw him yesterday in his house. His mother had asked me to visit. She was very scared.' He proceeded to tell the professor about the incidents Vikram's mother had narrated to him earlier.

Ranganathan leaned forward. 'And? How is he?'

'Sir, he looked different,' Tony said.

'Different? Different how?' Ranganathan drummed his fingers on the table. 'I'll need all the facts. But what happened to your leg?'

Tony stopped massaging his knee, something he didn't realize he was doing until now. 'Injury. Anyway, Vikram seemed to have grown taller and his hair was stringy and . . . he has always had long hair, but earlier it was nice. Now it looks oily and limp.' He dragged his fingers through his hair. 'It's like he is hiding behind his hair. And there was a strong smell of . . . of . . . I can't explain, but it was hard to breathe in his room. He looked at me from the corner of his eye and his gaze bore right through me.'

'I see.'

'And it was frightening to look at him. When I walked into the room, I felt like there was another . . . thing . . . present, watching me. Vikram had a grin on his face and he was murmuring constantly as long as I was there. He didn't call me by my name. Just stood and rocked back and forth in a corner. He was acting like a mental patient.'

Ranganathan leaned back in the chair. Above them, a ceiling fan spun furiously. 'You see, Tony, there are many worlds between this earth and hell.'

'Really?

'Seven to be precise. Each world has its own set of entities. In the worlds nearer to the earth, the creatures are simply mischievous. But as you go further away, you encounter malicious beings who actively slip into our world only to cause misery. Some of them are summoned by black magicians, trapped and then made to do their bidding. I don't know what type your friend has attracted, but he has caught something. The signs are not good. This . . . this thing that is tunnelling its way into Vikram is starting its work by dismantling his relationship with his parents. That is the biggest hurdle for a being. Once it can create distrust and even disgust in the victim's own parents, it can then make the body do anything.'

'And that's what Vikram . . .'

Ranganathan stared outside. The sun was still up, hazing the city with its white heat. A few crows perched on a telephone wire stared back at him. He wondered if the crows could understand Sanskrit. They seemed like such intelligent birds that it wouldn't be too far-fetched to expect them to respond to the ancient language. He made a mental note to try it out.

'Sir, please sir,' Tony pleaded as if Ranganathan had some sort of magical spell or counter slokas to undo the deed. Sounds were important, people didn't seem to realize that. All of creation, Chaturvasi said, was just a sound. Even the Bible opened with the words: 'In the beginning was the Word'. During one of his sermons, Chaturvasi had explained how there was an esoteric meaning to that enigmatic sentence, and it had to do with sound. Mix the right sounds in an interview or with a paramour and one will reap success. But if one were to mix sounds in a certain way, then dimensions hidden to the senses begin to manifest, and, in a case such as Vikram's, open portals and invite unwanted beings.

'I'll have to do some research.' He looked around, took a question paper out of a stack and asked for Tony's phone number. He scribbled it down, feeling like a doctor prescribing critical medication for an extremely sick patient. 'I'll be in touch.'

Tony got up. 'Sir, let me know as soon as you find something.'

Ranganathan watched the boy cross himself on his way out. He scoffed. If the vetal decided to possess Tony, the cross would not help the boy repel it. And neither would it help Vikram shed the spirit from his life.

That would require an exorcist.

9

Chaturvasi checked his watch. It was almost six. The sun had risen and was bestowing its energy on all mortals, including the lazy joggers who were just pouring on to the beach. The predawn coolness would soon be vaporized.

He had been on edge lately. He hadn't slept the past two nights, knowing that whatever disturbance he had sensed would manifest itself eventually. For the past twelve years he had been preparing for this episode and now he knew it was upon him. In a way he was giddy with anticipation.

He clucked at the sight of a middle-aged man wearing fancy shoes, sunglasses, trackpants, tugging at a Pomeranian's leash. 'All show,' he grumbled and rapped his walking stick. A sleeping stray woke up with a start and stretched. Crossing the road he made his way to the milk vendor, annoyed at the plastic and trash all around. 'How this beach used to be,' he said to a man who was listening to music and walking beside him.

'Huh?' the man said.

Chaturvasi gestured to him to remove his earphones, miffed that he had to vocalize the obvious. The man plucked the earphones out not knowing why he did it, for Chaturvasi's tone commanded people, and sometimes other entities, to pay attention.

'This beach,' Chaturvasi yelled.

'I'm not hard of hearing,' the other replied, now getting annoyed at having his walk interrupted.

Chaturvasi charged on, briefly turning around to point at the beach. 'Beach was a nice place. Quiet. Clean.'

The other man nodded. 'Yes, I remember. My wife would bring our son in a pram and feed him curd rice right there where the exercise bars used to be.' He smiled.

'All rusted now,' Chaturvasi said. 'Kids will get tetanus if they play there.' The other man slowly nodded and began to place his earphones back when Chaturvasi said, 'Curd rice? You must provide the body the right nourishment so that it can perform in the best possible manner. You see, the world is not a mere illusion.' He rapped his walking stick rapidly on to the road. 'It is a manifestation of the supreme reality. If the universe is real, the body must be real as well, yes or no?'

The other nodded.

'If the universe is a divine creation, so must be the body, no? The body is a piece of the universe and the universe is a piece of the body.' His voice became softer. 'When we truly understand the body, we discover that it is the universe, which in essence is the divine.'

'I . . . I am a Christian,' the man said, exasperated.

Chaturvasi slapped his forehead and marched on. 'Bloody fool. No hope at all.'

He then terrorized the milkman, yelling at him for sleeping so much and missing out on the joy of watching the sun rise. 'You know what the Buddha said?' he asked.

The milk vendor shook his head.

Chaturvasi started counting by touching the middle phalanx of his right ring finger with his thumb. 'Birth is suffering.' He touched the bottom phalanx. 'Life is suffering.' He touched the bottom phalanx of the little finger. 'Death is suffering.' He moved to the middle phalanx of the little finger. 'Everything is suffering.' He clapped his hands. 'For you, bloody fellow, getting up in the morning is suffering.'

'Sir, I work two jobs,' the milkman said, scratching his neck.

'Don't work hard, work smart. Find something better to do if you plan on sending your kids to school.' He wagged his finger at him. 'And you should send them to school. You gave them life without their permission. Now make their lives worth it. Their minds and bodies must be stimulated. And if you want, send them to me once a week. I'll teach them the Vedas and how to perform rituals to improve their health.' He leaned in towards him. 'They are very powerful.' His voice softened now. 'Come to me if you need a loan.' He picked up the packets of milk and walked away.

Swinging his walking stick, Chaturvasi walked back to his building, expecting the watchman to be asleep. Instead he found him chatting with a friend.

'Ada! Ranga! How are you?' he said, glancing at his watch.

'I'm fine, Vasi,' Ranganathan said. He kicked the stand on his bicycle and retrieved the bright yellow cloth bag which had been transported under the carrier's spring-loaded catch like a trapped animal.

The watchman walked up to Chaturvasi and bowed. He handed him a three-tier tiffin carrier. 'Sir, a man gave this dabba.'

Chaturvasi inspected the dabba and brought it to his chest. A second later he smiled and looked up at Ranganathan. 'To what do I owe this' – he checked his watch again – 'this sudden trip? Getting married finally?'

Ranganathan looked down at his shoes with a grin. His mother and sister kept harping on about him getting married and settling down, but the Sanskrit professor felt that he had still not achieved much in his life to impress a woman. Without waiting for the other's response, Chaturvasi turned serious. 'How are your practices? Are you able to hold the locks?'

'The neck lock is still giving me issues. And sometimes when I exhale I am not able to keep the other locks in place,' Ranganathan answered.

Chaturvasi inched closer and peered at his friend and student. 'Hmm . . . you need to practise hatha yoga, Ranga. Those muscles need to be limber.'

'Vasi, the thing is . . .'

'And make it fast. I have to perform my puja.'

'Of course. Of course.' Ranganathan cleared his throat. 'Yesterday, a boy came to me. Tony . . .'

'Tony-aa?'

'Tony. Christian lad,' Ranganathan said absently and then quickly came to the point. 'He told me an incredible story.

He and his friend – a boy named Vikram – had gone to the Theosophical Society and found the original . . .'

Chaturvasi stopped tapping his foot and raised his eyebrows. 'Original what?'

'Vetalapanchavinsati.' The syllables rolled off his tongue like gentle waves on a moonlit night.

'The five . . . you are the Sanskrit expert. What's it?'

'Twenty-five.'

'Twenty-five tales of the vetal?'

'Yes. Except he read it by the old banyan and . . .'

Chaturvasi held up his hand as the epiphany struck him like a blinding bright light. The unease he had felt the other day was tied to this. 'I know what happened.' He closed his eyes and pinched the bridge of his nose. After a while, he said softly, 'Ugra.'

Ranganathan drew a sharp breath. 'He . . . he did this?'

Chaturvasi placed his hands on Ranganathan's shoulders. 'Ranga, I have been telling you for years about needing your help . . .'

Ranganathan's back straightened and tensed. 'Whatever you need. If I have to take leave from college . . .'

Chaturvasi patted his shoulders. 'Not yet. I don't know how this will unfold.' He crossed his arms behind his back and paced. 'Ugra has been in hiding for twelve years and I think he has made his move now.'

'But you said Ugra was your shishya and that . . .'

'I said all that so that your opinions were not clouded. When the time comes – as it has now – you must act with the facts in hand.'

'So, what has he done now?' Ranganathan still didn't understand the gravity of the issue. Once, and only once, had Chaturvasi explained his theory since Shruti's passing. Ugra, one of his best disciples, who had increasingly demanded that Chaturvasi show him the occult powers, had reached a crescendo where he had become too persuasive. Chaturvasi had banished him from his school. However, having initiated him, he was intimately tied to Ugra and knew what he was up to at every instant. One day, when the umbilical went silent, Chaturvasi knew that Ugra was too far gone down the left-hand path and had accepted another guru. He told Ranganathan all this and added, 'He will come for me. He took Shruti's head. Now he's come for mine.'

'That place . . . that Theosophical Society was an old cremation ground many hundred years ago before Blavatsky and Annie Besant founded their headquarters there. It was infamous for the vetals that inhabited the corpses.'

'I am confused, Vasi sir. What has Ugra got to do with the vetal?'

'He has been initiated into the Kapalika sect.'

'Kapala . . .' Ranganathan mumbled. 'Skull . . .' And then realization dawned on him. He cupped his mouth.

'Ranga, I don't have time. I will explain in detail later, but Ugra is behind this vetal possession. He is using this poor boy Vikram as a bait.'

'How?'

'You are here, aren't you? I know how to exorcize the vetal, but this is simply a bait to draw me to him.'

'But . . . if you exorcize the vetal then . . . then it's over, no? What bait?'

'Vasi,' Ranganathan said. 'I think it's best I investigate this at the Theosophical Society.' Chaturvasi stood with his eyes closed. Ranganathan noticed the bulge behind the eyelids moving rapidly. 'Vasi?' he said gently.

Chaturvasi's eyes shot open. 'Yes, Ranga. Find out all you can about the document. There might be something else that could hint towards the name of the vetal. If what I suspect is correct, the vetal is slowly coiling around that boy right now and nudging his essence out. It'll be sporadic possession at first as it samples and savours its new body, but if it likes what it can do, it will make a permanent home in him and then . . . who knows what else it has planned.'

Ranganathan was kicking his bicycle off the stand when Chaturvasi said, 'Wait, Ranga! Wait!' He dashed into the entryway of his building, the steel tiffin carrier clanging against its handle like the bell around a goat's neck. 'I'll be back.' Minutes later he returned with a black thread. 'Show me your right hand,' Chaturvasi said and tied the thread around Ranganathan's wrist. 'It's best to be careful. Keep me posted on what you discover.'

Ranganathan nodded and pedalled off, excitement tingling through his body.

That afternoon during lunch Professor Ranganathan placed his books on the staffroom shelf. He cancelled his grammar class and informed the principal that he had an urgent family matter to attend to. Figuring that he had to make haste, he decided to take the bus to Adyar.

He got off the PTC bus and walked towards the Theosophical Society, crumpling the ticket and tossing it aside. He waited outside the gate, checking his watch periodically, taking in the strong smell of brine that hung in the air. A few minutes later Tony drove in on his TVS Champ. 'Sorry sir,' he said. 'Got late. Traffic was not moving only.'

Ranganathan nodded curtly and walked through the gates. Tony followed.

'Sanskrit professor,' he announced to the half-asleep old watchman. 'I'm going to the library,' he added authoritatively. The watchman waved him in. He turned to Tony and said, 'They respect me here because it's not every day they see a Sanskrit speaker amidst them.' Tony nodded sagaciously.

Ranganathan felt important here, for inside the walls of the campus had been a library of utmost value and it was almost as if it was created for people like him. There were ancient Sanskrit scriptures and tomes enshrined here, the sanctity of which was lost on the average person. He, and only he, knew their worth. He knew how important some of those writings on lambskin and palm leaves were, how they had been carefully preserved for centuries in temples, caves, monasteries, how they had survived fires, marauders and how their greedy, or indigent owners had sold them for a song.

Chaturvasi had said that the banyan stood on an ancient burial ground. It could be possible that this compound, so verdant and anomalous in the stark city, might have once harboured a consecrated temple, or even a shrine.

He scanned the area for signs of one, but spotted none. He wished he had full mastery over his senses like Chaturvasi. No doubt he would have closed his eyes and moved his head around like an antenna before taking off in a mad fury to find a tiny shrine or even a worn-out stone, and said, 'This, right here, is charged!'

As he walked into the cool, shady confines of the Society he puffed his chest out. He glanced superciliously at the small army of sweepers chatting and raking leaves. He knew Sanskrit, the language of the gods, and by extension was a sort of god himself.

'Sir,' Tony said. 'Have you spoken to your friend? The one you said could help?'

'I have,' Ranganathan replied. 'That's why we are here. He . . . I suggested that I study the texts myself to see if there was anything that could help us.'

'I see. And did he say anything about Vikram?'

'What's there to say yet? Hmm? The doctor must see the patient first to make a diagnosis. Right now we are doing the X-ray and blood tests.'

As he ascended the library steps, Ranganathan mused: there was a young botanist at the Guindy University by the name of Cyrus Treewallah. He was a Parsi, and one with a serendipitous last name that accurately described his profession. Ranganathan wondered if Parsis changed their last names after they found their jobs, or if their family names were passed on to the next generation, like everyone else. If it was the latter, this Cyrus chap was either blessed with the most apt last name, or his parents had decided his career at birth. At any rate, this Treewallah had been making news lately for his discoveries with regard to the soma plant. It rankled Ranganathan's nerves – as he entered the cool, cavernous library room – that the botanist had used an English translation of some of the ancient texts to narrow down his search for the mythical soma plant. Had he known

Sanskrit or someone who knew the language, such as the yet-to-become-famous Professor Ranganathan of Madras Sanskrit College, he would have unearthed more facts about the plant. His paper titled 'The Botany and Chemistry of Soma' had been accepted at a cryptobotanical conference in Bonn, Germany, and the Parsiman was being flown first class by the government to present his findings there.

As he stood at the information desk and spoke with a Mrs Uma, Ranganathan wondered if he too could get a paper out of this vetal. Maybe there were conferences on apparitions and paranormal phenomena where he could present his findings. America had a lot of scope for such things. The thought of flying first class to a conference excited him. He leaned forward, drummed his fingers on the desk and raised his eyebrows. 'I'm not looking for the English translation . . . looking for the original Sanskrit scrolls.'

'Tony?' Uma said, 'what are you doing here . . . with him?'

Uma studied the short man with the off-centre tie, its knot too big. She saw the bright vermilion namam that shot from the bridge of his nose high into his receding hairline like a sunbeam in a dark forest.

'Aunty, it's that . . . I . . .'

'Thing is,' Ranganathan said glibly, 'the students presented me with a good essay. I did not believe that they managed to track down the original document. You see, it's been missing for centuries. So, when they showed me their paper, I had to verify the source. I think they made it up.' He glared at Tony, who shrank. Then he smiled at Uma. 'I'd like to see the original, please.'

She sighed and stood up. 'Please follow me.'

As they were walking she asked, 'What is this sudden interest in Vikram and Betal stories?'

'Vetal,' Ranganathan corrected her absently.

'What?'

'No, no. Sorry,' he said quickly. 'Why do you ask?'

She casually waved her hand as she made her way around the ancient furniture. 'Oh nothing. Just a few days ago a friend's son came here with Tony. They said they were doing some college project and were looking for the same scroll.'

'Ah yes! Project assignment.' He looked at Tony, who nodded. 'I am a professor, you see.'

Uma regarded him with equal parts seriousness and confusion. 'Something!' She carefully retrieved the parchment and kept it on the smudged glass. 'Here,' she said.

Ranganathan's fingers trembled at the sight of the parchment. Tony peered from behind him.

'Do you have gloves?' Ranganathan asked Uma. 'I don't want to do any damage.'

Uma handed him a pair of sterile gloves that the library stored for people like Professor Ranganathan. He donned them, fished out his magnifying lens and gently unfurled the parchment. Satisfied that she had left the document in careful hands, Uma retreated to her desk.

Ranganathan spent the next couple of hours poring over the text line by line, making notes as he went. He asked Tony to record him on his phone as he spoke. While most of the paragraphs were stories told by the vetal to the king, the last set appeared to be an invocation. Having been schooled by Chaturvasi to always start his yogic practices with an invocation, he thought it was interesting to see those lines here. He fretted over the meaning of the lines, but it didn't seem to be out of the ordinary. Just a generic invocation for a divine spirit to manifest to the reader and guide him on his journey.

When he reached the end of the parchment he squinted at the little drawing on the side.

'What's that, sir?' Tony asked, coming closer.

It was a winged creature hanging from a banyan tree. Ranganathan trained his eyes on the drawing. The creature hung from the branch like a large bat, its wings outspread and a smile on its face as crooked and bent as its nose. He observed its hands. One was pointing at the text and the other at the reader. He didn't notice anything strange in the text. It was mostly just stories that the vetal had told King Vikramaditya. But something about its hands bothered Ranganathan.

'Why aren't its hands both pointing down?' he mumbled. It seemed to be an effort for the creature to raise its hands while hanging upside down. He glanced at the text again, re-reading the lines near the creature's hands. One of the words, asavah, which meant life, looked funny. He studied it under the magnifying lens. The penmanship was impeccable with the words curling and spaced perfectly, albeit in a style that was not used frequently. One thing particularly caught his attention: a horizontal line – the shirorekha – on top of the letters connected to form the words. However, in this script, there were lines underneath the words too. The more he stared at that word and the other words around it, he realized they contained more than what met the eye.

On a hunch, he picked up the parchment and turned it upside down. His eyes slowly began to widen. The Sanskrit words were now laterally inverted. His breath quickened. He couldn't decode the words. He raced to the nearby window and held the parchment up against the bright afternoon light. He cupped his mouth with one hand as he stared at a whole new set of words that appeared before him.

He ran back to Uma, unable to contain his excitement. 'Do you have a backlight?' he asked. 'Please! It's urgent.' He had the demeanour of a surgeon at the side of a dying patient.

Uma stood up and placed her spectacles on the desk. 'Yes. We have one in the microfiche room.' She edged her chair back and stood up. 'Follow me.'

Ranganathan thanked Uma for the light and hurried out of the microfiche room. Tony was at his heels, hastily stuffing his phone in his pocket.

'Is Vikram okay?' Uma asked, concerned.

Ranganathan nodded hastily, refusing to vocalize the seriousness of the issue.

Tony chipped in. 'He's doing fine, aunty. We did a group study yesterday.'

The duo walked briskly down the stairway and stood in front of the building. Lush plants threw their shade everywhere. But Ranganathan was visibly unsettled.

'What is it, sir?' Tony asked. 'What did you read in that room?'

'The verses . . .' Ranganathan started pacing. 'The verses were harmless when read from the front.' His face soured now. 'If it's paining so much, your knee, go to the doctor, no?'

'It's fine, sir.'

'The verses . . . they were just a simple invocation . . .'

'Invocation? Means?'

Ranganathan scowled at Tony for having to explain it to him, but the thought faded as quickly as it formed. The boy was ignorant of the ways of the yogis just as he had been until Chaturvasi had shown him.

He relaxed and sighed. 'An invocation is a few lines that are chanted before a ritual or even eating to invite the appropriate deity to grace the space.'

'Eating-aa?'

'Of course. Doesn't the food you eat transform into your body? Or does your body simply grow from magic? So it's the most important thing you are allowing to enter into your body. You must be respectful.'

'I see. And Vikram's chanting of the invocation when seen from the other side of the parchment was . . .'

'An invocation to a vetal, not a benign entity. Vikram somehow read it backwards.'

'I must check with Vasi sir.' He looked Tony in the eye. 'He invited a vetal named Kakasura to this world.'

Tony slowly shook his head while his eyes ballooned. 'Kakasura?' Now Tony started to pace. 'When I visited him yesterday I heard a clicking sound. At first I ignored it. I thought it was from his PC or something, but the sound came again.'

'And how was he? Was he conversing normally?'

'Oh yes. He seemed different physically . . . like his hair is all grown and his shoulders seemed broader, but he was cracking jokes and stuff. Dirty jokes, but he normally does that. However, I couldn't look at him. Every time I did, he seemed to come closer to me and he didn't blink. Each time I looked up he was staring at me with an intense gaze. I . . . I just couldn't look at him.'

'Hmm . . .'

'But that's not it. That clicking sound . . . when I looked around I saw a crow sitting outside his window, pecking on it.'

'A crow?'

'Yeah! It was a big bird and it was pecking on his window.'

'That is not a good sign,' Ranganathan said, beginning to walk towards the gate. 'We must go meet my teacher. He'll know what to do next. Hurry, if we can catch the next bus . . .'

'Sir, I have a moped,' Tony said, trying to keep pace with him. 'We can go on that.'

Ranganathan and Tony sat on a small wooden bench outside Chaturvasi's flat. A sign above them read – *In case of any emergency, apply clove oil and come to the clinic tomorrow.*

There wasn't a board stating the name of the resident anywhere. Instead, a garland of yellow flowers snaked along the door. The bottoms of the door jambs were painted yellow with red dots. In front of the threshold, on the landing where they sat, was a white kolam. The design was simple, yet beautifully executed, clearly the work of an experienced artist. Stacked neatly around the kolam was footwear.

From the adjacent flat came the sounds of a family spending the evening together. Children fought, parents yelled while the TV supplied unending cricket commentary.

'India–Sri Lanka,' Tony said, leaning towards Ranganathan. 'Third match. If we win this, we will win the series.'

Ranganathan nodded. Playing or watching sport had never been of interest to him. He found his hand–eye coordination to be unfit for any game involving a ball and his patience too short for cerebral games such as chess. He took a deep breath and formed the kurma mudra with his hands.

'What are you doing?' Tony asked, intrigued by Ranganathan's lattice of fingers.

'Placing a mudra. It's a seal. Helps . . . uh . . . it helps in calming oneself. Anyway, what course are you studying?'

'Electrical engineering.'

'Why? You didn't get into computer science?'

'Actually, I got upgraded in my second year to CS.'

'Wow! You must be smart then.'

'I don't know, sir, but I insisted that they give me back electrical. I chose it on my own. I like it. I always wanted to study it. I have no interest in computer science.'

Ranganathan saw a fierce determination in Tony's eyes. If only, he thought, if only he could nudge a syllable or two out of his name and replace them with something else, the lad would shine through life. Just then the door to Chaturvasi's flat opened, letting out a file of men with tonsured heads, wearing white veshtis.

'Chris,' Ranganathan said softly. One of the men flinched for a second, but looked down immediately. Ranganathan understood and joined his palms together. He nudged Tony who followed suit. The others too looked down as they put on their footwear and, without greeting the duo, slipped away silently. The last one had tears rolling down his cheeks, though he did not look distressed. If anything, he had a look of bliss. Chaturvasi appeared behind them and beckoned Ranganathan inside.

'Brahmacharis,' Chaturvasi said, glancing at the door. He sat down on a mat on the floor. Next to him was a metal bowl in which a fire crackled and danced. He poked it with a stick and then tossed the stick into it. The flat smelled sacred, of frankincense and camphor. His words were heavy and floated over the diaphanous smoke like the voice of a god. 'Their practices are getting more intense. They have been observing silence for weeks now.'

'Weeks?' Ranganathan asked, sitting down on one of the floor cushions. Tony followed suit, uncomfortably folding his legs under him.

Chaturvasi clucked. It sounded like a knock on the door. Tony rose to open it but sat down when he figured out the source. 'It is needed,' Chaturvasi said. 'In time, everything will manifest. And it is almost time.' From inside the house they heard the faint sounds of a bell ringing. 'Anyway, what did you learn today? Wait.' He held up his hand. 'What's your name?'

'Tony . . . sir.'

'Tony,' he said softly and studied him for a moment. 'Does your knee hurt too much?'

Tony's jaw dropped. He reached for his knee absently. 'How . . . but . . .' He turned to Ranganathan who shrugged. 'It does a bit.'

'You met this boy Vikram recently, yes?'

'Yes.' And he proceeded to update him on the happenings of the past few days.

'Kakasura, Vasi sir,' Ranganathan said, showing him his phone. 'Here, I took the picture of the parchment lit from behind. You can see how the words make sense even from that side. It's a marvellous work of calligraphy. I feel it could be the work of the Madhavacharya.'

'Who?' Chaturvasi said, peering into the phone. 'That famous Karnataka Sanskrit poet?' He leaned back and closed his eyes, his fingers finding the edge of his beard and caressing it. After a couple of minutes, he opened his eyes and said, 'It's too late.'

Ranganathan leaned forward. 'What? What do you mean?'

'Kakasura is a higher order vetal. It won't possess a live body. It only makes a corpse its home, but the signs of possession are evident. That means the boy is now in the clutches of another vetal.'

'Sir,' Tony said, his voice low. 'How . . . how do we know that this is a ghost or a spirit? I mean, how can they exist? He could just be having a mental breakdown or something.' Ranganathan nudged him and he went quiet.

Chaturvasi's wife emerged from behind a gauzy red curtain. Ranganathan brought his palms together and bowed his head.

Tony could not help but stare.

The woman was pale, inhumanly pale, like a leaf that had been left in a dark room. She wore a loose white skirt and a white top, with a white duppatta draped around her torso. She adjusted it as she slowly walked with a copper plate in hand. A piece of camphor burnt in it, spewing black aromatic fumes. Her eyes were large and liquid. They drooped ever so slightly as did the corners of her mouth. A bright red kumguvam mark travelled from between her eyes and disappeared into her hairline. She didn't look at anyone as she walked, cupping the flame, consumed in her own melancholy. She approached Chaturvasi first who placed his palms over the fire and brought them to his face. She slowly inched towards the other two before bowing and disappearing behind the curtain like an actor exiting the stage.

A zephyr slipped in from the balcony door, disturbing the flame a bit. A grandfather clock ticked on the wall, counting seconds in the sacred silence. Finally, Chaturvasi cleared his throat. 'There are a lot of things, Tony,' he said, 'that can't be known by simply reading books, young man. There isn't a physical ghost like you see in the movies, haunting your friend's house. No. Everything is sound . . .'

'Everything is sound,' Ranganathan repeated softly.

'What do you mean?' Tony asked. 'Everything?'

'Everything is sound, Tony,' Chaturvasi repeated calmly. 'For life to exist, it must have energy and that energy sets things into motion. Whether you hear it or not, there is a sound associated with every form. You, me, Ranga, this newspaper, that paperweight . . . it all has a sound. Just as you cannot hear the bat's echoes, you cannot necessarily hear the sound of a body. The organs of perception that we possess are crude and incapable of discerning the finer aspects of existence.'

'Thus implying there are other organs of perception that we possess that are not crude and are capable of discerning the . . . the finer aspects?' Tony asked, incredulous.

On seeing a smile on Chaturvasi's face, he leaned back, his mind cranking. 'That doesn't make much sense. We only have five senses. Any child who has studied eighth standard science will tell you that.'

'It won't make sense because you are being logical and you don't have the right tools. It's like if you have never seen an elephant before, and are trying to study it by standing very close to it. You will have a blurry idea, but never the full truth.'

'Okay. I'll go with that assumption. There is a sound associated with everything. Then it can influence . . . it can affect anything . . . Or get affected. Sounds are waves. And they can be constructive or destructive. That's the property of a wave.'

Chaturvasi nodded slowly, the smile never leaving his lips.

'I mean . . . I mean,' Tony said, 'by the properties of sound, one can have more decibels and another can have a higher frequency. You mean someone is operating at a higher pitch than another person?'

Ranganathan snapped his fingers. 'Isn't that the case with people too? Some are more . . . more intense. Their presence is felt.' He turned to Chaturvasi and then back to Tony. 'You're catching on with the basics of tantra, Tony. I'm impressed.'

Tony shook his head. 'I'm not sure about this tantra thing.'

'You have only heard myths about it,' Chaturvasi said, his voice now serious. 'When the time to exit this earthly dimension arrives, one simply deposits the body that one has loaned from the earth and leaves with the sound that remains. Inaudible to most, but the faintest of sounds is all that leaves this dimension. But in this case, a vetal, this Kakasura – this name given because of the way its life energy sound – has merged with the sound of your friend.'

'It's like the superposition principle,' Tony said. 'It's . . . it's a theory in electrical engineering that states that if you have two or more . . . never mind. I think I understand what you are trying to say.'

'No, you don't.' Chaturvasi got to his feet. 'There are five sheaths to human existence – the food body, the mind body, the energy body, the information body and the bliss body. The body is the hardware. The mind is the software, but to power them both, you need energy.'

'And the other two?'

'Not relevant for now. Most people live their lives unaware of its existence or its influence on their bodies. Do you know the symbol for infinity since you are a science student?'

'Of course,' Tony made loops in the air with his finger.

'That is precisely how the energy system moves in one who has stilled his mind and merged his consciousness with that of the universe.'

'How does it flow in yours?' Tony asked, earning a kick on the foot from a glowering Ranganathan.

Chaturvasi guffawed, his body shaking as if he were riding on a bumpy road. 'When this is all over, if, come and see me.

You are probably one to follow the path of gnana, that is' – he tapped his temple – 'using one's logic to come to the ultimate. Anyway, there are seventy-two thousand points in the body called nadis. The energy flows through these nadis in a specific pattern. When the energy changes, the body feels it. When the body changes, the energies reflect that. When you utter a sound, a certain nadi is affected. That is why Sanskrit' – he brought his palms together and looked at Ranganathan – 'is considered the language of the gods, because it was created with this in mind. When Vikram uttered those slokas his energies moved in a way to allow an entity to merge with him.' Tony nodded slowly, absorbing the information. 'We'll go to the boy's house tonight. Ugra has summoned one of the most horrid demons from the netherworld. And I must respond. If it is a bait, so be it.'

'Who is Ugra?' Tony asked. Ranganathan nudged him and held up his palm, hinting that he'd explain later.

'I need to see the vetal at its peak,' Chaturvasi said. 'Twenty minutes before midnight.' He checked his watch. 'You have time. Go home, change, eat. I have to prepare.' He walked towards his puja room and paused. 'Tony, you meet us at Vikram's house.'

'Sir . . .' Tony said, looking guilty. 'I am not sure if I should.'

'Don't be scared,' Ranganathan assured him. 'Vasi sir will be there.'

'I feel like his mother will blame me for . . . his condition. I think she already does. She's quite protective of him.'

'Tony,' Chaturvasi said, 'you were the last person to mix

your energies with Vikram's . . . someone he trusted. You must come. Will you be able to? With your knee and all?'

He waved his hand. 'Knee is okay. I'll be there.'

'Ranga will be in touch as to when.' He brought his palms together and then closed the door.

10

A mantra, his guru had taught him after his initiation, was a powerful weapon when used in the right way. 'You can repeat a mantra a trillion times, like the idiots down south who pinch their nostrils and chant the gayatri mantra, and it would have zero effect. But if you know how to charge it first, then even a single repetition can be powerful,' he had said.

'How do I charge a mantra, guruji?' Chaturvasi had asked. They were in a cave atop a hill deep inside a forest near Rishikesh. A little fire burnt near them, crackling and hissing, and from the vantage point, the lush greenery rolled out like a celestial carpet. Near them a burbling brook meandered through the foliage. When the humans observed silence, sometimes for weeks at a stretch, there was only the melody of nature. Bears, tigers and other creatures roamed the forest, their roars and howls punctuating the twitter of birds.

'From the infinite reservoir of energy,' his guru had explained, 'comes the subtlest sound, dhvani. Out of the dhvani comes a more vibrant sound, the nada. And from it comes the vibratory source. A point. Bindu. And this is the source of all the letters and words.'

Chaturvasi had gaped at his guru in awe. He was a radiant being, slender and well proportioned. His hair was matted and tied up in a beehive bun on his head. At this point, a couple of years into his apprenticeship, Chaturvasi's hair had also grown long and matted. His mind tingled with the realization that his guru's words – which were sounds themselves – were explaining the mystery behind sounds.

'And from this vibratory source spring forth mantras,' his guru had continued, adding a stick into the fire. 'They are a manifestation of the divine energy, Vasi. If you arrange the sounds in the right way, you can channel Brahma himself into your life.'

'How do I charge a mantra, guruji?' Chaturvasi had asked eagerly.

'At first you should repeat it thousands of times,' the guru had elaborated, causing Chaturvasi's face to fall. 'Every mantra has a deity associated with it. Repetition of a mantra is like priming the pump. Without it, there is no potency. And it won't matter how many times you prime the pump if the mantra wasn't received from a guru.' The fire cycled through a hue of colours. 'Now find a tree by the river and recite the mantra I gave you. First aloud, then silently with your lips moving and finally in your mind. Return after you have gained command over it.'

And so, he had gone upstream to a remote location and sought out a tree by the Ganga. He had sat under it for weeks, reciting the mantra and meditating until it was the only thing on his mind. Even when he wasn't chanting it, the sounds reverberated through his body like the sound of a gong moments after it had been struck. He had returned to the ashram months later, with a longer beard and dreadlocks, and prostrated at his guru's feet. The guru had asked him to rise and searched his eyes. 'Tomorrow at dawn,' he had said, smiling, 'I'll instruct you how to make the mantra potent.'

Chaturvasi had been so excited about his next lesson that he barely slept that night, preferring to sit under the moon and gaze at the stars, wondering about the primordial sound that bathed the entire universe. At dawn, after performing the necessary ablutions and consecration rites, he had sat next to his guru who raised his finger and pontificated: 'First identify the mantra's constituent syllable from the alphabet. Then recite the syllable separately with the sound *aum* prefixed to it. Write the mantra down and sprinkle each syllable of it with water while reciting the seed syllable for air.'

'*Yam*?' Chaturvasi had said.

'Yes. That is called hammering. Now you must awaken it. You touch each written syllable with a red oleander flower while reciting the seed syllable for fire.'

'*Ram*.'

'Yes, *ram*. Once the mantra is awakened, it must be consecrated.' Here the guru had brought his palms together. Chaturvasi had mirrored him. 'Sprinkle each written syllable with water using a twig of the ashvattha tree. After awakened, it must be purified. And you do this by visualizing its impurities being burnt by reciting *omhraum*.'

'The mantra for light.'

'Yes. At this point it is starting to get potent, but you can strengthen it even more by sprinkling each written syllable with water from the tip of the kusha grass. Offer light and water to it and conceal it forever. It is meant for you and only you. If you reveal it to anyone it will lose its potency, or even turn around and harm you, but when it emerges from your being it will be omnipotent.'

~

Night slipped into Chennai unannounced.

Chaturvasi opened his eyes close to eleven and exhaled deeply. He shuddered for a few seconds as if someone had poured icy water down his back. Then he leapt up, got dressed and grabbed his bag.

His wife appeared beside him as he was strapping on his sandals. He dropped the bag and held her face in his palms, gently resting his forehead against hers. They stood that way for a while before he leaned away and whispered, 'Thank you. Please rest now.' And then she slipped away without a word.

After Shruti's death she had demanded that he teach her the esoteric ways of tantra. At first he had demurred, thinking she wouldn't be able to handle the energy once she uncorked it. But her determination over the months softened him and eventually he had shown her the basics of breath control and yoga. She had proved to be a quick study and soon they were on to more advanced practices, ones that were not time-consuming but required weeks of preparation.

He had altered her diet. Stimulants and depressants had gone out of the door. No more chai in the morning or warm milk at night. Food had become sustenance intended for the body, not for the tongue. He had taught her how to look deep inside herself until she experienced the five basic elements – wind, water, fire, earth and ether – and how to purify the elements so that her energies became malleable, slowly coming into her conscious control. He had her fast the day before and after ekadasi and perform austere practices on other critical days of the year.

Over time she had exhibited marked changes. While he still sensed her internal angst over Shruti's passing, externally she was transformed into a stone Buddha, placid and stoic. Nothing moved her any more. The young Carnatic singers with their freshly broken-in voices, the subtle chill of the breeze at dawn, the neighbour's kitten that cocked its head and snaked between her legs – none of it moved her soul, and neither did the barrage of bad news in the papers nor the hungry mendicant wasting away beside the temple gates, or the little boy with a tennis ball–sized tumour on his forehead who walked meekly holding his mother's hand each day to school.

Her assiduousness with her practices had begun to pay off. Sometimes Chaturvasi felt recharged by simply being around her and at other times her cool touch on his forehead would send ripples down his spine. He was concerned that her grieving had added a seriousness to her spiritual path and that at this rate she may begin to have out-of-body experiences – a few momentary ones at first, until the day she would be able to leave her physical form for good. He urged her to wear brass anklets. It was the one thing he insisted that she absolutely do without explaining why.

Ranganathan was waiting outside next to an autorickshaw. He had showered, consecrated and smeared himself with vibhuti as Chaturvasi had requested, after which he had sat and studied the slokas from an old sheepskin-covered book titled *Tripura Rahasya.*

Upon seeing Chaturvasi, he rushed towards him. 'Vasi, is everything okay?'

'Better than okay,' the other replied. 'Fully alive.' He hopped into the vehicle. 'Let's go. The vetal's power peaks at midnight. We must get there before that. Did you tell Tony to be there?'

Ranganathan nodded and asked the autorickshaw driver to get going. The man turned around and said, 'Could you give me twenty rupees above the meter reading?'

'We agreed . . .' Ranganathan began.

'It's so late,' the driver complained. 'And we waited for such a long time. My house is in Kodambakkam.'

'Shut up.' Chaturvasi clutched the metal rod in front of him. 'I'll pay hundred rupees more if you just start driving.' He leaned back, his face rigid.

The driver's eyes lit up. He started the vehicle, turned to start the meter and howled as his elbow grazed the rod. 'This thing is burning.'

'Drive,' ordered Chaturvasi.

And they sped off like bats into the night.

The traffic was minimal at this hour and the driver, salivating over the tip he was about to receive, zipped through the Theosophical Society, spun around Aavin Circle and shot out like a comet. He sped by the IIT campus, hurried past Guindy Zoo and tore into Saidapet.

Throughout the ride Chaturvasi sat straight, his lips moving silently, his gaze unblinking. Ranganathan shot furtive glances at his teacher. He felt like he was sitting next to a radiator, one that was not only putting out a lot of energy, but also sapping away his thoughts and coherence. He recognized the bag that was slung from the exorcist's shoulder. It was the yantra – a box with a small lingam inside that held immense value for Chaturvasi. Chaturvasi brought his palms together near his chest and then raised them to his forehead.

Ranganathan squirmed in his seat and probed the flimsy panelling. 'What has possessed Vikram?' he asked. 'Is Kakasura really an entity?'

'Show me your left hand.'

Ranganathan held his hand out. Chaturvasi fished inside his shirt pocket and retrieved a red thread with a piece of metal. He tied it around Ranganathan's wrist. 'We must be guarded going forward and until we close this case.'

Ranganathan pulled on the thread and adjusted it. He was used to receiving amulets and rings from his teacher, but lately he felt he was turning into some sort of bangle seller's stand with his hands filled with different charms.

'About Kakasura . . .' Chaturvasi said, placing a hand on the professor's shoulder. 'It is for me to diagnose. Fear not. There are seven realms beneath us from where trouble arises, but there are seven realms above us from where help can be sought. I've got friends in high places.' Saying that he closed his eyes.

Ranganathan leaned back in the Rexine seat and stared at the tarpaulin roof of the auto, wondering where the next heavenly realm began and who or what else was sharing this expensive auto ride to visit a possessed boy.

The auto turned into a side street and drove by a temple. Chaturvasi instinctively felt that the area had been consecrated for Lord Ganesha. He offered a prayer to the deity. Soon they halted outside Vikram's house. Tony was sitting on his moped, smoking a cigarette, which he flicked away as soon as he saw the auto.

Ranganathan reached into his pocket, but Chaturvasi stopped him. 'Don't worry,' he said and handed three hundred rupees to the driver. The man's tired eyes suddenly filled with life. 'Sir, you said only hundred. You gave two hundred?'

'And I'll give you another hundred on top of your return fare if you just stay here until we get back.' He glanced at his watch. 'Can't say how long we'll be gone.'

The driver nodded. 'I'll sleep in the auto only, sir. Take your time. This is your private auto for tonight.'

'Let's hurry,' Chaturvasi said and walked to the house.

Vikram's parents stepped out to greet them. They looked wrecked.

'This is . . .' Ranganathan began.

'Chaturvasi. I can help.'

'Please,' Vikram's father begged, his voice cracking. He had deep scratches on his cheeks and forehead as if he had been mauled by an animal. 'I'm Gopal and this is Vikram's mother, Parvati. Please help our boy. He came back a few days ago from college . . .'

'And he has been acting strangely,' Parvati said and then bit the end of her sari. 'He tried . . . he tried to . . . with a knife . . . that's not Vikram in there.'

'It's okay,' Chaturvasi responded in a calm tone, the one he used when informing patients that all their teeth were rotten and had to be pulled out, but once that was done they would feel immense relief. 'I will fix it.'

'Please come in,' Gopal said, pushing open the door. 'Thank you for coming so late.' Then he addressed Tony who was standing behind the two men, 'Tony, you have also come-aa? Come in.'

'It's not late,' Chaturvasi said, slipping out of his sandals. 'It's the right time to' – he studied the distraught parents and took a deep breath – 'right time to see what's going on. Before we go in, please show me your right hand, Gopal. Parvati, your left hand.'

Gopal and Parvati looked at him, confused. Chaturvasi tied black threads coated with lamp soot around their wrists. 'Tony, you too. Right hand. What we are dealing with is beyond religion.' He noticed the crucifix in the boy's hands and shook his head. 'That won't help. It has not been consecrated. Please, now show me your right hand.'

Chaturvasi stepped into the living room and paused to see the framed family photos atop the TV. He recognized his patient for the evening, Vikram, in one of them.

It was a photo of Vikram as a young teenager, his face chubby and a whisper of a moustache sprouting on his upper lip. His hair was neatly cut and he had an awkward smile. He stood behind Gopal and Parvati, his arms around their shoulders. In one corner of the room Chaturvasi noticed a slightly ajar door. Inside was an old man sleeping on his bed with a ventilator strapped around his face.

'My father,' Gopal explained. 'He had a mild stroke yesterday after . . . after the incident with Vikram. Nothing serious, but the doctors advised that he be on oxygen. I will transfer him to my cousin's place tomorrow.'

'I see. Now tell me,' Chaturvasi enquired in the tone he used when meeting a patient for the first time, 'what were the symptoms you observed in Vikram?'

Parvati wrung the end of her pallu and Gopal took off his glasses. They both sighed at the same time.

'He went to college a couple of days ago and came back a different person . . .' Parvati said and then looked at Tony. 'Tony, you were with him.'

'Who knows where all he really went.' Gopal said.

'Tony,' Parvati said, stepping forward. 'Where did you both go, hmm?' Ranganathan placed a reassuring palm on Tony's shoulder and squeezed it.

Tony looked at Vikram's parents with fear. He then glanced at Chaturvasi whose face remained placid, his eyes half closed and the tips of his whiskers slowly twitching with each breath. Seeing how calm he was Tony felt a tranquillity wash over him. He took a deep breath and narrated that day's events.

'Why did you leave Vikky alone in that library?' Parvati shrieked, her eyes red.

'Madam, how could he possibly know?' Ranganathan said.

'It was your fault . . .' Parvati began when Gopal cut his wife off. 'Not now, Paru. He only led us to Ranganathan. What do you think we could have done on our own? Asked Murthy to come and do a homam and crack a few coconuts? You've seen Vikram. Prayer alone won't suffice.' He turned to Chaturvasi. 'Arun and I – Arun is my cousin brother – we had to tie him down to the bed after last night.'

'You said he came back different,' Chaturvasi interjected. 'How? And please, we don't have much time.' He noticed Ranganathan intently staring at the couple.

'His chest was broader,' Parvati said. 'And he had grown taller. His chin became flatter and small bumps had formed on the side of his head. His hair had grown out so much. I always used to chide him to cut his hair, but so much hair . . . how can it grow in a few days? Shetty doctor said it's a medical condition . . .'

'So he changed physically is what you're saying?' Chaturvasi confirmed in his calm voice.

'His voice was deeper,' Gopal added, 'and he was scratching himself all over. Dr Shetty said it could be stress-induced psoriasis.'

'Shetty is an idiot,' retorted Chaturvasi.

'I asked him if he got allergy from something,' Parvati took over. 'When he was a kid we went to Kodaikanal and he ate egg and he got itching all over. Daily, I rubbed cream until it went away. But his was like this . . .' She puffed out her cheeks. 'So I asked if he ate eggs . . . and . . . and . . .' She wiped her eyes with her pallu.

'And?' Chaturvasi nudged her on.

A voice roared from inside one of the rooms. 'And I told the bitch to shut her mouth.' This was followed by the murmur of multiple low voices.

The couple exchanged panicked glances. 'And that night,' Parvati said, 'it became serious.' She quickly relayed what had transpired the previous few nights. Chaturvasi nodded solemnly, his eyes focused and his expression barely changing. He listened without a hint of motion in his body, his occasional blinks being the only sign that he wasn't in some trance.

'I called my cousin Arun to help us out today,' Gopal said. 'He came this evening . . .'

'Around which time Vikram must be getting agitated?' Chaturvasi said.

'Yes!' Parvati exclaimed. 'Right around . . .'

'Moonrise.'

'Oh,' Gopal said. 'Well, right around evening, he started pacing and talking to himself. He was smashing the wall and then suddenly crying. When Arun came he actually looked at me and said, 'Appa, help,' before growling at me.' Parvati began to weep again. Gopal hugged her and continued, 'Together, we tied him to the bed, but . . . but . . . it's too much. We can hear whispering and laughter in every corner of the house.'

'He's strong,' Chaturvasi said. 'That is not a human you are dealing with any more.'

'What happened?' Ranganathan asked, not sure he wanted to hear the rest.

'We were in bed,' Gopal said, 'discussing what was going on with Vikram. And then we fell asleep. I went to check on appa and make sure his oxygen and all were okay. Then I passed by Vikram's room. I thought I heard snores, but it didn't really sound like someone snoring. It was like an animal snarling. I was scared and I didn't want to open the door. There was a strange smell, like something had died and had started rotting. I held my breath and came to the bedroom and shut the door.' He massaged his forehead absently.

'I told him that we must go to Murthy or someone,' Parvati said, more tears welling in her eyes. 'After that we slept off. I first prayed to all the gods. Then at night, around one I heard groaning. I shook him and told him something was outside the door.'

There was a moment's silence and then they heard mewling, followed by a mix of gibberish and crying.

'There was movement inside,' Gopal said, his breathing now rapid.

'Vikram, I said.' Parvati's tone was hushed and she looked towards Vikram's room, scared that he would walk out if she raised her voice. '"Is that you, kanna?" I asked. There was silence for some time and then I heard, "Amma." It was like a whisper almost.'

'He was outside and he tried opening the door.' Gopal spoke rapidly. 'But it was locked. He tried harder and harder till the door slowly opened. Vikram was standing there.'

Parvati sniffled into her pallu. 'His cheeks were blue blue.

Bits of hair was missing from his head. And he stood so stiff . . . like . . . like a dead body.' She patted her cheeks in contrition as if calling her son dead would render him dead soon. 'What did he do to deserve this?'

Chaturvasi nodded gently. 'And then?'

'By then Arun came to the door,' Gopal said. 'He had come on tour and was sleeping in the hall next to appa. "Dei Vikram," he asked, "what is going on?" But there was no response. He just stood next to our bed and kept rocking back and forth. Arun turned on the light and we saw Vikram's eyes had rolled up and spit was leaking from his mouth.'

'He asked for me,' Parvati said. '"Amma. Amma," he kept saying and I was crying. "I am here, kanna," I said. But he was not inside. That was not my Vikky.'

'He was talking to himself,' Gopal said. 'He had two voices. One was his regular one and the other was someone else's. It was like an angry person's, almost a growl. The angry man was asking Vikram something and Vikram was answering. Sometimes the angry man would punch the wall or lift the bed and then Vikram would come back and speak in a small voice. Arun and I tried to wake up Vikram, but he didn't come out of the sleepwalking. We dragged him back to his bed. He kept fighting us.'

'He bit Arun and scratched him,' Parvati said, pointing at her husband. 'That was when Gopal quickly got behind Vikram and held his neck in a chokehold.' She sobbed and wiped her nose. 'Vikram became faint. His tongue lolled out.'

'Paru and I held him down while Arun tied him up. It was the only way he could be subdued and he has been tied since then. We have been going and retying the knots every few hours. We don't know what else to do.'

Now there was a loud crash as an object smashed against the door. Tony reached for the professor's hand and clasped it. Gopal and Parvati hugged each other. The old man snored peacefully in his oxygen-laced sleep. Chaturvasi's skin prickled and the hair along his spine rose.

Gopal's voice dropped to a whisper. 'He has escaped.'

Chaturvasi caught hold of Ranganathan. 'I'll need your help,' he said.

'What was that?' Ranganathan asked, his voice quivering. There were audible clicks from the room, claws tip-tapping on the floor. Even though he had assisted Chaturvasi in bizarre and sometimes gruesome cases, he had never experienced anything like this. He tried to control his breathing and contort his fingers into mudras but failed out of sheer terror.

'It sounded like,' Tony whimpered, ' . . . sounded . . .'

'Listen to me.' Chaturvasi held the Sanskrit professor's face in both hands. He gazed into his eyes and Ranganathan relaxed. 'Good,' Chaturvasi said. 'You know about this, Ranga. Sound is energy. I need your energy. Bring the verses of the *Tripura Rahasya* into your awareness.'

Ash, his guru had explained, was the material part of light. Clothing oneself in ash was to adorn oneself with stars. When he'd come out after a dip in the icy river and smear his entire body with ash, he'd feel invigorated and bursting with life. Urban living forbade him from daubing himself with ash, and thus Chaturvasi applied it at significant places on his body

– between his eyebrows, at the pit of his throat, on his solar plexus, under his navel, behind his ears and on his abdomen.

This heightened state that suffused his system after applying ash, over the years, led Chaturvasi to regard his body as a mere crane, a collection of bones, muscle and organs. He wasn't the body, but simply operated it from a cranebox, always prepared to jettison the equipment if necessary and suffer none of its physical hardships.

Many temples prepared their vibhuti by burning dried cow-dung cakes mixed with herbs, but any tantric worth his salt knew that only when a vibhuti made from human bone ash was smeared on specific parts of his body would it truly charge it. Getting bone ash was hard in Chennai, but Chaturvasi, with his connections, overcame this hurdle with bribes and, if needed, spells. The custodian of the Besant Nagar crematorium had profound respect for him, which Chaturvasi cashed in on by requesting a small quantity of the ashes to be delivered in an innocuous-looking three-tier steel lunchbox.

He had a crude envelope made of folded newspaper from his bag. He carefully opened it and drew three fresh lines with the ash on Ranganathan's forehead, reinforcing the ones that were already there. He then leaned towards him, cupped his ear and whispered, 'You need to repeat the mantras from the *Tripura Rahasya* when we go in. The chapter on illusion. Which one?'

'Seventh,' Ranganathan replied blankly.

'Good! Let it pour out from your heart.'

Ranganathan, as if in a state of hypnosis, slowly bobbed his head.

'Start now,' Chaturvasi commanded. The Sanskrit professor chanted the mantras, his perfect cadence and diction sounding like a page out of the homams at the temples on auspicious days. Chaturvasi took off his shirt, revealing various amulets and charms tied around his arms. A necklace made from giant rudraksha seeds hung around his neck. With his right ring finger he drew a line between his eyebrows and forehead. He then proceeded to put the vibhuti on his throat, chest and navel. He then asked Parvati, 'Are you on your period?'

'What?' the woman exclaimed, flustered by the unexpected question.

'What do you have in mind?' the voice from behind the door sneered. Now there were slow knocks on the wall, starting at the bottom and moving up. 'You're a dirty man, Chaturvasi.'

'Answer my question,' Chaturvasi said. Gopal nudged his wife.

'No . . . no . . .' Parvati replied.

'Good! Go pour a bottle of water over your head and return at once. Now!' He turned to Tony and said, 'I'll need your presence to temper the spirit when we enter, but it's too dangerous for you to go as is.' He gave his rudraksha necklace to him. 'Wear this. You may get dizzy and feel your body is jerky and acting on its own, but it's okay. Nothing will be able to approach you as long as you have this on.'

Tony wore the rudraksha necklace along with his crucifix. Moments later, he began to sway gently. He closed his eyes as Chaturvasi applied lines of vibhuti on his forehead and throat.

Parvati returned from the kitchen, soaking wet. Ranganathan, meanwhile, chanted the mantras without a pause.

'That's no way to get a woman wet,' the voice screeched from behind the door. A loud cackle followed, its echoes reverberating through the house. A few windows lit up across the street outside.

'Here's a chalk,' Chaturvasi said. 'Draw the swastika on either side of the door.'

Parvati snatched the chalk from his hand and drew the symbols in quick strokes. It came easy to her, given the years of drawing intricate geometric patterns on their yard each morning with rice flour. Now Chaturvasi took out a knife from his pocket. 'Gopal, show me your palm.'

'My palm,' Gopal said, his gaze flitting between the knife and his palm, looking just as frightened as children did when he told them, with a syringe in hand, to roll up their sleeve.

'Your palm,' Chaturvasi yelled. He stepped forward, grabbed Gopal's palm and ran his knife across it. The cut bloomed red. Chaturvasi applied pressure on it until the blood started dripping. 'Extend your right ring finger and dip it in your blood and make four dots inside the swastikas, keeping your fore and middle fingers together.' Gopal obeyed instantly.

Chaturvasi walked to the door with a pile of camphor on his palm. 'The passageway is sanctified. You both can go to the kitchen. Dress his wound,' he told Parvati. 'Ranga, Tony, come closer to me. Keep chanting, Ranga.' Now Chaturvasi closed his eyes. His lips moved rapidly and then stopped. The camphor started burning.

He pushed open the door and they stepped inside to face the madness that had been brought to earth.

11

Ranganathan and Tony followed Chaturvasi into Vikram's room as the fire crackled and hissed on his hand in multicoloured hues. Ranganathan chanted the mantras in an unwavering voice, his lilt and cadence invoking the divine goddess who ruled three of the higher realms.

In a trance, he noticed nothing and merely awaited instructions. Closing the door behind them Chaturvasi stuck his palm out in front of Ranganathan just as he was finishing a sloka. Thin smoke spun up from the camphor fire into a tiny tornado and formed Sanskrit words. The golden letters hung in the air before the loops and squiggles contorted and morphed into glowing orbs and dispersed around the room.

Tony raised a finger at one of the words – rathendram. It wriggled like a caterpillar on his finger before popping into iridescent sparks. When he held the rudraksha beads he experienced a stillness in time and a noticeable distance from his own body. Even though he walked of his own volition, he felt an inexplicable connection to Chaturvasi and a deep sense of devotion to him. He felt like he was inside a cocoon and entered a state of careless abandon.

The room was cold and dark. Chaturvasi felt more than Vikram's presence. An overwhelming stench of rot emanated from the dark, but Chaturvasi held his breath steady. Vikram's face was bereft of any expression as he stared at the tiled floor, rocking on the spot.

Flies buzzed around him. The baby-faced boy in the picture frame was not the same as the ominous creature sitting on the edge of the bed, resting his massive frame on his elbows, his thick dark hair sticking out of his head in oily bunches, though there were visible bald patches on his scalp. He wore a banian and pyjamas which barely fit him. His skin was discoloured in places and mottled with blue-black splotches. Black veins snaked underneath his skin like earthworms scrambling after torrential rain. His face was almost black and leathery and his silhouette revealed protrusions from his temples. His wide back heaved slowly, belying the tempest that whirled inside him.

A large crow, black as Vikram's vacuous irises, sat on his shoulder, its claws digging into his skin.

Whereas the right-hand path of tantra looked for tools within oneself to attain the ultimate, the left-hand path sought help from the world outside. Shortcuts were acceptable and even encouraged. Years of right-hand practices could be cicumvented by left-hand ways with crude assistance from sacrifices and bloody rituals. As a right-hand tantric, he loathed performing these rituals, his days of cavorting with the Aghoris long gone, but time was of the essence now and he did not have the luxury of slipping into the mountains and turning his energies inwards.

The ash came from the femur of a young girl who had passed tragically due to leukaemia. Chaturvasi had been waiting for a body such as hers for a while now and when he received the bone, wrapped in a towel, the only emotion he felt was gratitude. After honouring the girl's soul, he placed the bone in front of Shruti's photo. Then he drilled seven tiny holes along the shaft of the femur. Then he put it on a black cloth, drew intricate yantras with rice flour around it – one for each hole and each one signifying a chakra. He then leaned and whispered sounds before imagining the sounds rising from the lines of flour, transforming into a silver thread of energy and seeping into the hole. After that, he swept the flour away into an empty coconut shell and tossed it into the ocean. Consecrating each chakra took an entire cycle of the moon and after almost seven months the femur was energized precisely the way he wanted it to be.

Ugra had stolen his daughter's skull for his nefarious rituals. He had created his daughter's essence from the physical world. With the same tenderness with which he had cradled Shruti right after her birth, he had carried the femur to the bungalow by the beach. After fetching a bucket of water from the well behind it and dunking it all over himself, he had sat under the new moon, the bone in front of him and an oil lamp hesitantly casting its wan light by the banana grove. None of the neighbours had been around that night and the watchman, Muthu, was nodding off on his wooden seat by the gate, lulled by the siren song of the midnight ocean. But the cries of a little girl and the jangle of her little anklets as she approached Chaturvasi could be distinctly heard. When the sound stopped, the bone crackled and instantly turned bright red. Minutes later it smouldered and disappeared, leaving nothing but dull grey ash and tears on his cheeks.

'Who are you?' Chaturvasi asked now, raising the palm with the burning camphor. The orbs swirled atop his palm like a golden tornado. 'State your name.'

Without looking up, Vikram said, 'Or else what?' His voice was like the growl of a faraway lorry on a dark highway. Shadows danced on his face. He stared down at Tony. 'Tony! Machan!' He grinned. 'Do you know you're going to fail engineering? Sukku is going to ace it, but you won't make it for the finals because of an upset stomach.' He let out a mirthless laugh. It was deep and shook the room. 'The smartest boy in the class, Tony. The fellow who gave up his computer science seat just to study electrons and protons will flunk the finals!'

'Viks . . .' Tony said blankly.

'Ignore him,' Chaturvasi said. 'Simply be here. Don't think.'

Vikram snarled. 'You have no power over . . .'

Chaturvasi, in one fluid move, picked up the envelope of ash with his free hand. He pictured Shruti leaping from it like the goddess Kali from her lion, and flicked it, blowing its contents all over the room.

As soon as the ashes rained on Vikram, he jerked his head up. His eyes were reptilian with narrow yellow slits that opened into soulless inky black pits. In a feline leap he shot up and attached himself to the corner of the ceiling, looking down with his mouth wide open. The raven flew in circles, cawing. The lights outside flickered and went out. A table nearby rose up and moved towards Ranganathan but came crashing down just before it could hit him. Ranganathan's chants rang through the room.

'State your name, you lowly demon,' Chaturvasi commanded, his voice calm despite the chaos. Tony stared at the scene with unblinking eyes as if he had stepped into a circus with the most incredible feats.

Vikram's teeth were like blades of sharp white glass. 'Make the idiot stop,' he screeched, pointing at Ranganathan. 'Make it stop.' The raven tried to attack Chaturvasi, but in one clean swoop, he caught the bird and wrung its neck. He threw the listless bird on the ground and glowered at Vikram. The room reeked of decomposing flesh.

'Tell me who you are,' Chaturvasi repeated. He flung some of the burning camphor at Vikram, chanting spells as he did so. The fragrant flames dispersed before the camphor could reach its target. However, the intent was not to set him on fire. The room was now lit up as if the walls had been painted with glow-in-the-dark paint.

Seconds later, a slow drizzle of glimmering particles like dust motes trapped in a sunbeam filled the room. Tony looked about in fascination and stretched out his palm, but they bored right through it. 'State your name, creature of the lower realms!' Chaturvasi said. 'We are the gates to the netherworld now. I can toss you right through.'

'And take the boy with you?' the creature said. 'I dare you.' Vikram spat. His spittle landed on his bed and instantly started corroding it. Now he laughed. 'Should I pass your regards to your little girl?' His voice turned unguent. 'Maybe she is busy there. You know the types of people that end up there. Young virgins are coveted.'

'Stop!' Chaturvasi was almost pleading the entity now.

'The boy . . . he is ours, tantric. Body, mind, emotion and his energy . . . all of it is ours. If I go, he goes too.' Vikram cackled. 'Go sit naked on a corpse and fondle it. If you want him released, then give yourself to my master.' Vikram turned his head slowly until it was sideways. Chaturvasi heard the bones crack. The boy kept turning his head, his yellow irises not losing contact, until it was at an inhuman angle.

'Stop,' Chaturvasi repeated, but the puppeteer of Vikram's body took no heed. Vikram slowly crawled down from the ceiling like a giant spider with a demented human face. He crept on to his bed on all fours and faced Chaturvasi, rocking sideways all the while.

'Would you like to speak to your daughter? Shruti? She's here with us.' Vikram cackled. 'You think she ascended to heaven? No. No. No. You have a debt to pay and she died because of your carelessness. She's in hell.' Now the voice of a child emerged from Vikram. 'Appa?' Something knocked on the window outside in loud thuds. 'Appa! It's burning here, pa. Help me.'

'Stop!' Chaturvasi roared, holding the camphor fire higher.

But the entity was not deterred. 'The last rites for Shruti were flawed, tantric. Tch! Tch! Tch! Everyone thinks you are a powerful wizard, but you couldn't even send your little girl away in peace. She burnt like a ragdoll.' Vikram crawled towards Chaturvasi, Ranganathan and Tony like a giant scorpion leaving a trail of drool behind that singed whatever it fell on. Tony raised his crucifix in terror. 'You didn't liberate her soul but condemned it to the lower worlds. And my master was able to put her little skull to good use.'

Chaturvasi's nostrils flared, but he reined in his anger, which was thrashing deep down like an eel in a tub. 'Ranga, chant louder,' he commanded and reached into his bag with his free hand. 'Tony, stand behind Ranga.' Chaturvasi's fingers lost no time finding what he was looking for: a firecracker. From the outside it looked like a ladi, a garland of petite red cylindrical firecrackers, each one putting out a little sound and light, but together they sounded like a machine-gun assault by an entire nation. Each petal of the ladi had mantras written all over it and had been consecrated, awakened and empowered by Chaturvasi earlier that day.

Vikram was almost upon them, snarling viciously. 'You could have eased the spirit of your little girl. Now she's preparing to re-enter the world as an insect.' He stepped on the carcass of the raven, its bones crunching under his weight. His banian tore apart, revealing a lithe and chiselled torso and black beetles scuttling across it. A miasma unlike any other filled the room as the temperature dropped sharply. The glowing particles increased in the room and they fell faster. There were groans and creaks as the furniture in the room wobbled, slowly overcame gravity and silently floated inches off the ground.

Chaturvasi gaped in horror as Vikram levitated up too, parallel to the ground like a magician's hovering assistant. As

Vikram's hands reached towards him, Chaturvasi brought the wick of the ladi to the camphor fire still burning on his palm. As soon as the wick caught fire, he flung it at Vikram and slapped the bag containing the yantra.

The ladi began to burst, sputtering at first before turning into a fire. Smoke and animal howls of pain that sprang from the murky depths of the entity filled the room. The levitating objects fell with a crash. Vikram covered his ears and squeezed his eyes shut as the smoke engulfed him.

'Louder, Ranga,' Chaturvasi said and stepped forward. Ranganathan was yelling the mantra at the top of his voice now.

Chaturvasi held out another ladi. 'State your name, you infernal creature.'

'Make it stop,' Vikram yowled from the corner he was now crouching in. 'It hurts.'

'That was not even the main one,' Chaturvasi said. He clapped once, extinguishing the camphor fire. A visible shock wave ran through the room, distorting everything temporarily as if part of a mirage. He drew out a lemon and another ladi. 'What is your name?'

'Hiranyaksha!' came a pained growl.

Chaturvasi tucked the ladi into his veshti and then, closed his eyes and blew the conch. When he opened his eyes, they were bloodshot. 'Hiranyaksha, you nefarious vetal. I command you to leave this mortal body you have possessed and enter this lemon.' He blew the conch again. Vikram covered his ears and clenched his teeth. 'If you don't, I will set off another ladi with the mahamantra.' Saying that he picked up the ladi and dangled it. He hoped that he wouldn't have to use it, for if this didn't do the job, he didn't have anything stronger on him.

'No no no no . . .' Vikram whimpered. With a final resolve he leapt on to his bed and collapsed. And at that instant, Chaturvasi knew he had the vetal trapped inside the lemon. He snapped his fingers at Ranganathan who stopped chanting. He then blew the conch one more time. The lights flickered back on. The floating items fell with a resounding crash. Vikram lay collapsed on his bed, sweating profusely and moaning. Chaturvasi rushed to Vikram, retrieved a pair of scissors from his bag, snipped a few locks of his hair and placed them inside a plastic bag.

'Ranga,' Chaturvasi said, moving to his disciple. 'Let's step out.'

Ranganathan blinked rapidly. 'What . . . what happened?'

'I'll explain to you later. Now walk out backwards and don't let it see your back. Tony, do the same.'

The three stepped back slowly and exited Vikram's room. Parvati and Gopal met them outside with searching expressions.

'Is he okay?' Parvati asked Chaturvasi. 'I heard so many sounds.'

'He's fine. He's sleeping.'

Parvati dashed into Vikram's room and screamed, 'There is a dead crow on the ground!'

'Will he be okay?' Gopal asked, a red dot appearing on his bandaged palm.

'Not yet,' Chaturvasi said. 'He was being held hostage by a

lower order vetal – Hiranyaksha. This means that it was sent by a higher vetal as a placeholder. Vikram is not back to his normal self, though he will be okay for a few hours.'

Gopal's face fell. 'What do we do then?'

Chaturvasi turned grim. 'The situation is dire. A vetal will only seek out a corpse.' Parvati, who had just joined them, gasped. Chaturvasi raised a hand in reassurance. 'He's not dead, but . . . how do I put it . . . he's not himself yet. His soul has been displaced and so his body thinks it's dead. I need to perform an exorcism, an even more powerful one. But it can't be done here.'

He looked around at the house. It was as clean as it could be kept, but there was a lot of unneeded energy. He could see it plain as day – dark clots clumping and growing everywhere like mould. This he had expected. The ladi was meant to keep more of those at bay and neutralize the ones that had already possessed Vikram. Within moments many more appeared, drawn to the intense energies of the demon and the tantric. 'It's not clean.'

'I can ask Shanta . . .'

Chaturvasi silenced him with his hand. 'I didn't mean physically. I have a consecrated space that I use often. It's inside a bungalow in Kalakshetra Colony. He'll be safe there. Safer.'

'When?' Gopal asked urgently. 'Tomorrow?'

'No. We have to wait for the next full moon. The vetal will try to yank the soul out of Vikram's body on that night and completely possess the boy.' He closed his eyes for a second and slightly turned his torso. He didn't want to burden the distraught parents with the truth about Ugra and how the left-hand tantric had used Vikram as a bait to possess him.

Hiranyaksha had conveyed its master's ransom – Chaturvasi had to give himself up in exchange for the boy. Chaturvasi knew Ugra was after his own skull, having exploited Shruti's until it gave him no more powers. Now he allowed himself to relax and sensed the magnetic field coursing through him. 'Next week will be right. I, too, need to prepare. And Vikram needs rest.' He pulled out his prescription pad and scribbled on it. 'Get this medication and give him one tablet every six hours without fail. He will sleep well. Don't worry. No long-term side effects with this sedative.' He pointed at the door. 'Nothing more evil can enter this room through its portal, though it will try. It will try very hard because that is its karma. That is what it was summoned to accomplish.' Outwardly he was optimistic, but in his mind's eye he could see how the events were going to unfold. 'If we keep the portal sealed, the second exorcism will be a cinch. I will send someone who can help. Until then, Parvati ma, please draw a new swastika with rice flour in front of the door before sunrise.'

'More evil means . . .' Parvati began when Chaturvasi said, 'Amma, this is not over. Your son is still' – he looked around – 'he's not here yet. Something else is holding him hostage.'

Gopal studied his bandaged palm. 'Should I . . .'

Chaturvasi placed a hand on his shoulder. 'No need. The dots can be with kumguvam.' He then glanced at his watch.

'I must get going. We'll be in touch.'

And then he left. Ranganathan did the same. Tony was staring at the door when Chaturvasi beckoned him. 'Tony, please come. I need to talk to you both.'

12

Chris was always grateful to Acharya Chaturvasi for having shown him the way out of his imprisonment.

Born and raised a Catholic, Chris never understood the point of the Sunday masses, the confessions thereafter, the Bible studies, the roster of dos and don'ts, and the other gossamers that swung around the church's doctrine. Visiting the San Thome Church each Sunday with his parents and brother in the neatest and crispest of shirts, with polished black leather shoes, smelling of the strong rose perfume, was seared into his mind.

Once, after watching *The Omen*, he believed that he had been possessed by a demon, and the next Sunday, started screaming and thrashing in the car at the sight of the gaunt steeple of the church. His father turned around and slapped him across his cheek, threatening him with more if he didn't stop his raucous antics at God's doorstep. Chris slunk into his crisp shirt, wiping away tears and wanting to punch his grinning brother. Later, after mass, his mother, a devout Malayali Catholic, dragged him by his shirt to the bishop and asked him if a young lad such as Chris had possibly had some sort of allergic reaction to the church, perhaps an exorcism was required. The priest, lost in his flowing robes, inspected Chris from head to toe and shook his head. 'He just needs to pray more,' he said and blessed the young lad.

As he grew older, his queries turned into demands: what was the proof of Heaven and Hell? What was the proof of God or Satan? Why was masturbation a sin? Why were impure thoughts a ticket to purgatory? Why were we born with original sin? Why did Jesus resurrect as a rabbit, hiding colourful eggs all over the garden? These questions boiled and bubbled inside him and when the hormones exploded from the depths of his pubescent body, they acted as a catalyst, causing him one day to lunge at his dad, catch his hand mid-slap and push him back into his chair. 'If anything,' Chris growled with his breaking voice, 'this is sin, appa. Raising your hand' – he glanced at his mother, who was clasping the crucifix around her neck – 'against your own family.'

He took a step forward and towered over his father. 'You think hitting amma and me gets you into the good books of your bloody god?' While his mother wailed, his brother appeared from behind and glared at him. 'Take your hands off appa,' he said, flexing the muscles he had recently sculpted at the local gym. Quivering, his mother stood beside his brother and pleaded. He knew it was hopeless. They were always together, the three of them. He stormed up to his room where he ripped another page from the Bible, burnt it, mixed the ashes with marijuana and smoked the joint.

As time went by, he fell into a miserable existence. He grew his hair out, enrolled himself in the Madras Christian College, purportedly to study literature, but ended up spending most of his days smoking weed with a few friends and pondering about life during weed-induced trances as he lay on his motorbike by the sea. Their favourite spot was the Broken Bridge, an abandoned ruin of a bridge near the Theosophical Society that once spanned the Cooum river.

During hot afternoons, when the tide was in and when other students were busy studying Keats or reading philosophy for an academic essay, Chris and his friends challenged each other to make the nearly fifty-foot jump into the river and climb back up the bridge. Chris almost always won, despite his bleeding fingers and scratches, for there were few purchases up along the crumbling bridge, and his tenacity was legion.

It was on one such day when a man, probably in his late fifties with a ponytail and a flowing white beard, ambled up to Chris and his friends and, without uttering a word, swanned into the waters. For once, Chris felt fear for another's life and yelled as the man disappeared into the swishing green waters. To his astonishment, not only did the man surface, he did so faster than anybody he knew and scurried up the bridge like a langur on a fig tree, grabbing invisible perches and leaping from non-existent footholds. When the man made it to the top, Chris almost fell to his knees and asked, 'How did you do that?'

'Yoga,' the stranger replied, mysteriously almost dry by now. 'I can show you.'

And so began his tutelage under Acharya Chaturvasi. At first, he taught Chris some basic stretches while recommending that he wean himself off alcohol and meat. 'That I cannot do,' Chris said, popping a cigarette in his mouth.

As he lit it, Chaturvasi said. 'Can you give up smoking at least?' Chris shook his head.

'We shall see about that.' Chaturvasi grinned.

'Just show me how to climb the bridge, old man, and we are done.'

'The difference between you and me is that you react. I act. You respond to the situation. I manifest the situation.'

Chris exhaled a big plume and scratched his nose. 'What does that mean?'

Chaturvasi plucked the cigarette out of Chris's hand and tossed it away. When Chris's brows knitted, Chaturvasi stared into his eyes. 'Tomorrow,' Chaturvasi said, 'is ekadasi. You know what that is, hmm? Eleventh day of the lunar cycle. Very important day. Did you know before the British invaded India, we had three days off for ekadasi and another three off for purnima? People here knew the significance of those days. Here is what you do tomorrow.'

'What?'

'Nothing. Simply do nothing. Just be. Just be in your room. Or be here on the beach. But don't do anything. No food. No water. Just be. And at sunset, I'll show you how to take control of your life.'

Strangely drawn to the charisma of the elder man, Chris obeyed him. The next day, he ploughed through without eating a meal, determined to learn the art of manifesting a situation. By sunset he was feeling lighter and springier. He looked up the broken pillar and leapt on to it like a cat. As he climbed, his feet and fingers found perches and holds that he had not seen before. When he reached the top, he knew he had beaten his old record. And this made him thirst for more.

When Chaturvasi asked Chris to start his day with a cup of ash-gourd juice, he did so. When he asked him to eat only two meals, the first at noon and the second at night, he obeyed. When he asked him to give up garlic and onions, he convinced his mother to cook separately for him. When Chaturvasi asked him to fast every ekadasi he did so without question.

A few months later, the acharya introduced him to a set of forty-two rigorous exercises that appeared easy at first but turned out to be hard to master. Chris, determined to impress his teacher, woke up before dawn and practised these exercises on his terrace before drinking his ash-gourd juice mixed with ginger and pepper. Within weeks his body was limber, his need for sleep drastically less and his energy levels surging. When Chaturvasi insisted that he shower before doing these exercises, Chris, frustrated with his damp hair clinging to his face, shaved his locks off and kept a buzz.

Soon, he discovered that he could focus on anything he set his mind to without being distracted and found studying rather easy. He caught up with his college syllabus in no time. A few months after their encounter, Chaturvasi deemed Chris to be ready and initiated him into esoteric practices. 'This,' the acharya said, 'is an ancient set of practices transmitted unbroken from the first yogi himself. It is not given to anyone and everyone. So treat it with respect.' Chris bowed and received the instructions with utmost attention. He kept adding more practices to his daily routine so that at any point of the day he was either physically or mentally engaged in them.

If he wasn't doing hatha yoga, he was concentrating on the nib of his ballpen so hard that the sounds of the classroom and the world outside disappeared. He learnt quickly that this heightened state of clarity could easily take up a few hours and looked forward to retiring to his room for meditation.

Chris left his parents' house, found a government job as a clerk and moved into a small flat. He didn't care about money or the material comforts. What he wanted was control over his body so that hunger, thirst, joint aches and other functions did not interrupt his meditation. In that light, his job allowed him to take time off and journey to remote temples across the country and perform specific rituals that Chaturvasi ordered him to do. His neighbours naturally assumed Chris to be some sort of yogi. Refusing to accept his Christian background they christened him Krish which, to their orthodox ears, was at least a contraction of something more Hindu and tangible, like Krishnan or Krishnaswamy.

Chris excelled at his practices and became Chaturvasi's emissary – meeting up with wandering sadhus and teaching interested acolytes the art of yoga. One day Chaturvasi asked Chris to become a brahmachari, a celibate yogi, and dedicate his life to yoga. Chris agreed without batting an eye. The ritual took place at midnight in the Mylapore tank, a manmade waterbody beside the Kapaleeswaran temple. Chris and a few other young men stood in the tank bare-chested. Oil lamps flickered behind them as Chaturvasi, dressed in a regal black veshti, his hair and beard spread out like a wild mane, applied vermilion on each man's forehead and offered him a red flower.

Chris's spiritual practices and his yogic way of life had tuned his body such that he knew the phase of the moon just by observing his breath. He developed a telepathic connection with Chaturvasi and received messages from him during his deep contemplative states.

One evening, Chris came home from work, shrouded himself in a black cloth and slipped into the deepest recesses of his mind. The message from his acharya this time left him disturbed.

'Appear now,' it said.

~

Chaturvasi opened the door as soon as Chris rang the bell.

'Acharya,' Chris said, bringing his palms together and bowing slightly from the waist.

Chaturvasi placed his palms on Chris's stubbled head and then nodded at Muthu, who had escorted Chris to the door. 'That should be the all of them,' he said. 'Don't let anyone else in.' He tapped Chris's shoulder and said, 'Go on inside. The others are already seated.'

'Acharya,' Chris said, 'I must bathe again. I feel impure.'

Chaturvasi understood what he was going through. As his own practices deepened, he felt a constant urge to wash himself. 'There's a well behind the house. Go quickly and pour a bucket of water over yourself.'

As Chris hurried out, Chaturvasi returned to the living

room. They were in the same beachside bungalow Chaturvasi frequented during his morning walks. He preferred it because of its proximity to the beach and the availability of fresh water on site.

The master studied the group of a dozen brahmacharis and Ranganathan. They sat in a circle, backs straight, eyes closed, palms facing up, lost in a trance. They were dressed in a white veshtis with vibhuti marks on their navels, chests, throats and foreheads. All of them had tonsured heads and wore a rudraksha necklace. They sat in a circle, and he entered it and sat in the middle. Their faces were calm, yet fearsome.

He placed a copper box next to him. It was festooned with geometric symbols outlined with kumguvam. He brought his palms together in reverence. As soon as Chris joined the group, all of them opened their eyes at the same time and placed their palms on their thighs. Chaturvasi nodded and Chris picked up the large conch from the dining table and blew it.

'There's a problem,' Chaturvasi said after the notes of the conch had settled into the room and within them. 'I've communicated it to all of you last night.' The group nodded, all of them expressionless like mannequins in a store. 'The situation grows worse as we speak. Ugra has come out from his twelve-year penance and is after my head. That boy, Vikram, is unfortunately trapped in all this.' He scanned their faces silently. Their breathing was in sync, and if one were to measure it carefully, it was also in sync with the waves outside the house.

'I must act,' he said. 'I have taken care of Hiranyaksha.' He held up a shrivelled lemon. It looked like it had sat in the sun for decades, its skin mouldy and streaked. Despite that, its skin undulated and wriggled as if an insect inside was trying to burst out of it. 'Kakasura remains. He has eviscerated the boy and will soon take over his body. In Ugra's ideal world, I'll surrender to him peacefully and he will have my head. In exchange for that, he'll reward Kakasura with a body with which it can wreak havoc. Now, I know I have not prepared you for something like this, but . . . this wasn't meant to happen. I was going to battle Ugra at a place of my choosing when my energies were ready, but it has come to this . . .'

Despite the gravid words, Chaturvasi's face remained impassive. He sat still, turning his head slowly to scan his brahmacharis. If there was any confusion in his audience's eyes, they didn't show it. 'I must prepare myself for the final exorcism,' he continued. 'And then I must perform it. I'll do it on the next new moon. And I'll need all your help in that.' He tapped the copper box. 'Even this. Each of you has a role to play if we want to stop Ugra.' He turned to his star pupil and clucked. 'Chris, especially you.'

'Acharya,' Chris said, bringing his palms together.

'Perform the purification rituals and prepare yourself over the next few hours. Then head to the boy's house tomorrow by dawn, sit in dhyana in front of the portal. It's weakening and we can't let Kakasura draw from the energy outside.'

'Yes,' Chris said.

'You're stronger than any symbol I can ever draw or any yantra I can consecrate. Your presence will give me the time

I need. Wear orange vestments. If you hear the vetal call out your name, don't respond to it. If you hear the boy cry out in pain, it's a ruse. Don't let the parents in at any rate.'

'Yes, acharya,' Chris said.

'If, and only if, things go bad, reach out to me. I'll enter a period of silence after this and until the exorcism.' Now his voice softened a bit. 'Chris, your transformation has been incredible. Go see your parents tonight.' It was for the first time uncertainty flashed across everyone's faces, but as quickly as it appeared, it melted away.

'Yes, acharya,' Chris said, standing up. 'I leave now.'

'Brahmacharis,' Chaturvasi said, his gaze slowly panning around the room. 'You'll have to prepare yourselves for the exorcism too. Perform bhutashuddhi twice a day before sitting down in contemplation. Start your elemental purification rituals predawn and post-dusk. When the body is clean, perform the mind cleansing practices. When they are both scrubbed clean, wear white clothes and sit facing east. Tie a black band around your right arm for all the days until the exorcism ritual is complete. Afterwards, remove and burn it, and deposit the ashes near a tulsi shrub. Eat only sattvic food for the next few days, only after dusk and only once. Focus on keeping your pitta low and increase your kapha elements until three days before the ritual. The last three days, bring down kapha and increase vata.'

He took a deep breath and hesitated. 'In the event that I don't make through the ritual . . .'

'Acharya!' one of the brahmacharis exclaimed. Ranganathan squirmed in his seat. His shoulders hunched as he leaned forward and clutched his thighs.

Chaturvasi raised his hand and muted him. 'It is a possibility. Kakasura is not an ordinary vetal, he is the lord of that realm. Ugra summoned him for a clear purpose, and I, by myself, don't have the weaponry to take him on. Just like all of you, Ugra has a battalion of helpers feeding the entity. They, too, have been practising for years in their hideout.' He raised both his hands now. 'This must not affect your duties. Remember what I have told you: your body and mind are not yours. Do not let emotions come in the way of your duty. My physical form is of no importance. Even when I am gone, I'll still be with you.'

'Acharya,' they all said in unison and bowed their heads.

'Now,' he said, standing up. 'I'll perform the exorcism right here under the next new moon. Assemble at the shore by sunset and let the waves wash over you twenty-one times before crossing the kolam that will be laid out in front of the house. Pay attention.'

He then proceeded to explain his plan in detail to all of them.

'Ranga,' Chaturvasi said, 'meet me in the living room. Tony should be here.'

Ranganathan got up, adjusted his veshti, brought his palms together and scurried out to the living room.

'Brahmacharis,' Chaturvasi said, 'open your eyes and stand up.' He brought his own palms together and placed them on his chest. One by one they stepped in front of him, knelt and pressed their palms on his feet. When they stood up, he pressed his thumb between their eyebrows and whispered a mantra. When the last of them walked up to him he said, 'I'll always be by your side.'

Tony and Ranganathan sat on the sofa after the brahmacharis had left. Tony fidgeted and looked about nervously, while Ranganathan stared quietly at his teacher.

'Tony,' Chaturvasi said, 'your acumen is razor sharp, and we need your help to assist Vikram.'

Tony glanced at Ranganathan and then back at Chaturvasi. He had returned the rudraksha garland and had felt uncomfortable since, as if he had been ripped out of a comfortable spot. The old teacher's serene gaze calmed him. 'What can I do?'

Chaturvasi picked up an old TTK Atlas from the coffee table and flipped to a bookmarked page. It was a map of Tamil Nadu. 'If I could, I would have done this task myself. Just talking about it is expending valuable energy that I must conserve. But I must prepare for battle and I'm tasking you both for a specific mission.' He lowered his head and stared at them with intensity. 'I'm putting many lives at risk here.'

Tony shrugged. 'What should I' – he glanced at the professor – 'we do?'

Chaturvasi pointed to the map and said, 'Near Kalpakkam' – he pointed to the spot on the page where the Bay of Bengal trickled back in – 'there's a tiny beach. It's hidden and you won't find it even if you went looking for it.' Ranganathan turned his head in puzzlement. 'Yes. The beach will appear . . . well, when it should.'

'Then how will we . . .'

Chaturvasi raised his hand and cut him off. 'You must get

there by passing through a banyan forest. From the highway, it'll barely be visible to people. It'll look like a vacant plot, but if you see a grove of banyans, and you will, then you are close to the beach. If you stand on the beach, you'll spot a tiny island. There's a' – he looked at Ranganathan and then back at Tony – 'there's a shrine on the island used by the most abhorred left-hand tantra sect – the Kapalikas.'

'Left hand?' Tony asked, puzzled.

'Kapalika,' Ranganathan mumbled. 'Kapala . . . skull?'

Chaturvasi nodded and took a deep breath. 'You see, Tony, your body is a miraculous instrument, having had millions of years of evolution to reach this form. Do you remember back in the day when we had to use an antenna to receive TV signal for DD1 and DD2?'

Tony nodded. 'I remember and the programme was for a few hours.'

'Indeed. And do you remember how if you lost signal, you'd have to go to the terrace and adjust the antenna until it caught the signal, and then suddenly, the entire world was in your living room?'

Tony nodded again.

'That's your spinal column, Tony. It's a receiver for the cosmic energy. If you can tune it just the right way, the entire universe can come into you.'

Tony shook his head. 'How?'

'Bring your palms together,' Chaturvasi said. Tony hesitantly obeyed. 'Now rub them vigorously for five seconds . . . go on.' Tony complied. 'Stop. Now keep your palms apart a few centimetres. What do you feel?'

Tony's right brow went up slowly. 'It's like a spring. I feel something moving.'

'That is prana . . . your energy. You just tapped your energy body. A large reservoir of this energy sits at the base of your spinal column. If you learn how to harness it and channel it up your spine, eventually, you can bring it to the top of your head and then . . .' He brought his palms together and slowly closed his eyes. 'You experience the divine. Now, along the way, the energy will hit seven critical points . . .'

'Chakras?' Tony asked sceptically.

'Yes. Chakras. As the energies pass through the seven chakras, you will experience sounds, smells and sights, but you also come into possession of . . . I must be careful here . . . you come into possession of powers.'

'Like what? Levitation?'

'Is one, yes.'

Tony's jaw dropped. 'Can you levitate?'

'Tony, be respectful,' Ranganathan snapped.

'That's not important now, Tony,' Chaturvasi interjected. 'We don't have much time. Listen. When the energies rise to the throat, and if the practitioner can keep it there, he'll be able to manifest much more powerful phenomena. Beings from other worlds will make their appearance and he will be able to commune with them. And if he propitiates them, he can request them to do his bidding. The only problem with this is: it's not easy. It requires decades of penance, of living an ascetic life, of not indulging in worldly affairs, of staying celibate, of discarding material and emotional attachments . . .'

'Are those . . . the men who just walked out . . . are they?'

'Yes, like them, but they aren't out to obtain magical powers. They are doing their practices to take their energies all the way to the top of their heads and be done with the cycle of life permanently. The Kapalikas, however, resort to … uh … interesting rituals to achieve these ends. Shortcuts.'

'Like what?'

'I'll explain later,' Ranganathan said, placing a hand on Tony's shoulder. 'So, Vasi sir, we go to Kalpakkam, cross the banyan thicket to the beach, spot the island, get to it, enter the shrine … and what?' The daunting set of obstacles that lay ahead of them made him dizzy.

'Fetch Ugra's conch from his shrine.'

'Conch-aa?'

Chaturvasi went inside the puja room and returned with a copper box. 'Ranga, nothing will be clear to you because you are still inhabiting your mind and body. Here, take this.'

'But, Vasi sir … this is the yantra. It's your life's work. How …'

Chaturvasi foisted the box into the professor's hands. 'Take it. You'll need it. You're no use to me dead. It has a lock on Vikram's aura. It will guide you to where you need to go.'

Ranganathan held the box with trembling hands. It was a powerful tool, one that Chaturvasi maintained was like plugging one into an explosive energy source. More than once during rituals he had heard the yantra whirr up and wobble before the electricity in the neighbourhood blew out.

During one of their exorcisms, Ranganathan had witnessed the power of a yantra. They were dealing with the seven-foot ghost of a young woman watching them manically from atop a roof as Ranga chanted mantras. Ranganathan's blood ran cold but Chaturvasi remained unfazed. When she swooped down towards them, he tapped the yantra once. A mightier form emerged from it, resplendent in a golden aura, which instantly absorbed the ghost and vanished. Ranganathan had seen Chaturvasi use the yantra many times, but never thought he'd be allowed to touch it.

'We'll be leaving,' Ranganathan said.

Chaturvasi gestured to them to wait. He gave Tony a single jasmine flower which he held tenderly between his thumb and forefinger. 'Keep this carefully and offer it at the shrine of Chinnamalai siddhar. Tony accepted the flower, shooting a befuddled glance at Ranganathan, who simply closed his eyes and nodded once. 'One more thing, Ranga. Both of you wear black. Top and bottom.'

Chaturvasi watched their shadows disappear past the gate and then down the road.

He thought of Shruti and felt a modicum of hope radiate from within. While he hadn't told his wife because she would have erupted into a banshee-like rage and done something impossible to rectify, but, while performing the last rites for Shruti, he felt a strange tugging on his left ring finger, and when he saw his daughter's corpse's toe begin to twitch, he jumped into action.

He blew his conch like a madman as he danced around the funeral pyre. Family members rushed to him, thinking he was grieving, but he shook them off with such force that one man, his cousin, almost fell into the pyre. Chaturvasi hopped on one leg and thrust his arms out, reciting mantras before blowing the conch again. Only when he was certain that he had prevented her life force from being siphoned did he quieten and broke down in an avalanche of tears as his numb wife watched on.

When he regained his focus, he immediately deduced that Ugra was behind the ghastly accident and this morbid post-mortem ritual. At that point he swore to eliminate their filthy clan from the face of the earth and planned for the imminent battle. The brahmacharis were his personal cadre of elite spiritual warriors, trained in the esoteric ways of kriya yoga, well versed with intense ancient yogic practices which turned ordinary men into superbeings. They came to him voluntarily, drawn by an energy that was unlike any other. In some ways it was predestined, for they had spent many lifetimes searching for a teacher. Having been taught ways to dissociate themselves from their physical bodies, they had eventually overcome the fear of dying and were undaunted in their missions.

Now that the brahmacharis were ready and the time to avenge Shruti was at hand, he decided to strike Ugra and his cohort in their hearts by stealing the conch.

13

As a doctor, cleanliness came naturally to Chaturvasi. He scrubbed and donned a fresh pair of latex gloves before probing a patient's mouth and discarded them and scrubbed again before writing out their prescriptions. As a tantric he was aware that keeping the spiritual body clean was even more critical. A fever or an infection could always be remedied with a course of antibiotics, but there was no easy medication for a spiritual infection, save a ritualistic exorcism. And just as doctors had to sanitize themselves before a surgery, Chaturvasi had to cleanse himself before the spiritual operation as well.

As the autorickshaw sped through the city, Chaturvasi reached for the rudraksha necklace and wrapped it around his fingers. He mentally recited the mantra his guru had given him, his fingers deftly moving the beads one by one.

'Saar,' the driver said in an upbeat voice, 'I didn't know I'd find you as my ride again.' It was the same driver, Balu, from the earlier night. 'I'm grateful.'

'Can you do one thing?' Chaturvasi said.

'Anything, saar.'

'Don't talk for the rest of trip.'

The driver was miffed, but he drove steadily, periodically glancing into the rear-view mirror to check on his ride. When they reached Vikram's house, Chaturvasi got out and said, 'Wait here. I'll pay extra.'

The driver slapped his forehead with the back of his hand. 'Of course.'

Parvati came hurrying out of the house, tucking the end of her sari. 'Please come,' she said, her voice hoarse.

'Thank you,' Chaturvasi said. 'But before I enter, I must request you to bring me a bucket of water.'

When Parvati returned, laboriously carrying a plastic bucket, Chaturvasi took it from her and emptied it over his head.

'Shall I bring a towel?' Parvati asked.

'No need.'

The water began to hiss and evaporate from Chaturvasi's body. He removed his shirt and tied it around his waist. He brought his palms together and lifted his left leg so that it was parallel to the ground. He leaned forward and thrust his hands out so that they, too, were parallel to the ground. His posture resembled the letter T, his eyes were clenched and his lips moved rapidly.

Parvati marvelled at the equipoise of the tantric and the way he effortlessly assumed the posture. She held on to the bucket like it was a sacred object and when Chaturvasi brought his palms to his forehead she, too, brought hers to her chest. Chaturvasi returned to both his feet and retrieved a small steel box containing vibhuti from his bag. He dipped his right ring finger into it and applied the ash stripes on his navel, heart, throat and forehead. 'Please,' he said, proffering the container. 'Neck and forehead will do.' Then he marched into the house, leaving his paraphernalia outside.

The house smelled like a temple with the mixture of incense, flowers and the faint aroma of hot sesame oil. Outside Vikram's door Chris was seated on a simple five-pointed kolam that Parvati had drawn per Chaturvasi's directions, surrounded by five oil lamps. Chaturvasi noticed that Chris's eyebrows had flecks of grey and tears leaked from his unblinking eyes.

He stepped closer and peered at his torso and noticed that the skin around Chris's arms was sagging. He stood up, looking worried. He heard unintelligible conversations inside the room. When the speakers paused, he could hear a dull roar like a distant motor. Now there was urgent banging on the door . . . a pause . . . and then a plaintive, 'Amma? Please open.'

Parvati nervously wrung her hands. 'It . . . he's been doing that all the time. Night also.'

Chaturvasi steadied his breathing and imagined a ball of light rising from his heart and swelling outwards. The ball now morphed into a spinning discus, its serrated teeth slicing the inside of his body. Like a Velcro strap slowly coming undone, he now felt his physical body disentangle piece by piece until, within a few moments, he was free of it and was able to step out from it. The world now appeared different – all colourful blobs of pulsating energy.

Chris looked like a gushing volcano with spools of luminous filaments threading his body. And at seven distinct points these filaments coalesced into multihued discs of energy. These discs spun so fast that they created a force field around him. Various amorphous entities hovered around the door. They were translucent and didn't resemble human forms. A couple were over eight feet tall and kept trying to walk into the door. When they couldn't, they got agitated, stretching and contorting like a lump of flour being kneaded.

Chris's energy kept them from entering the portal and anything from coming out through it. Chaturvasi zoomed out of the house in his mind's eye and hovered over it, floating like a jellyfish in calm waters. He scanned the house for aberrations and noticed a glowing black speck near the north-west corner. He spotted a temple nearby. It was evening and its bells were tolling. The sounds washed over the space like gentle waves on a lake shore. Then he assumed his body and animated it. He bowed, joined his palms in front of Chris and then walked out of the house.

'Is everything okay?' Parvati asked, scuttling after him.

Wordlessly he walked the perimeter of the house. 'There is a Vinayagar temple down the street.'

'Ah yes,' Parvati said. 'Vikram used to go there every morning before going to school.'

'Bring a flower from there after the arthi is done and place it in front of the portal.'

'I will . . . but what . . . what are you looking for here?'

Chaturvasi stuck his hand inside a bush and pulled out a lemon. 'This,' he said.

'What is that?' Parvati asked, agog. 'A lemon-aa?'

'Yes,' he said, observing it closely as if it were a rare specimen. He nodded slowly as if communicating with it before finally turning around and walking away. 'I'll take care of it.' When Parvati came after him, he stopped her. 'I'll be in touch. Everything is going according to plan.'

'Vikram . . . hasn't eaten,' Parvati said.

Chaturvasi put on his shirt and picked up his bag. 'He will be fine. His body does not need sustenance for now.' *It's Chris I am worried about.* He got into the autorickshaw. 'Don't worry,' he said. 'Call me if something happens.' He rapped the driver's shoulder. 'Come on, pa, Balu. Take me towards home.'

He stopped at various shops to pick up the things he would need over the next few days. The shopkeepers, aware of his specific needs, always kept what he was looking for hidden from other customers and didn't charge him for his wares, for his charms and amulets always brought them good business. They treated him as they would a holy man.

When he got home, he sought his wife in her room. She sat, wearing a gauzy white sari, embroidering a mandala on to a sheet. Birds hopped on branches and twittered outside. From far below he heard raucous kids playing a game of cricket. A windchime tinkled faintly as the evening breeze blew through the dimly lit room.

He exhaled slowly and held the door. 'I'll need you too to prepare for the ritual,' he said.

She paused and bowed. A tantric practitioner herself, she had helped her husband in many rituals in the past by providing him with material and spiritual support. So harmonious was their coexistence that their neighbours joked that they were the ideal match made in heaven. What appeared to be a seasoned couple's intimate overtures – him fawning over her while she demurely avoided making eye contact for too long – was actually Chaturvasi's anxious effort to ensure that his wife didn't let go of her life's energies and her sanity.

Before the horrible funeral, before the accident, when Shruti was alive, a bright and bubbly child – who came home with her report card filled with pleasant numbers and letters, patiently tied her ribbons into neat knots standing in front of the mirror, skipped on crudely drawn chalk squares under the Gurkha's watchful eyes – his wife had been loving and exuberant, chatty and teasing, filled with love for her family which she expressed in hugs and kisses.

But after Shruti's untimely passing and the mysterious happenings at the funeral pyre, after she saw how her child's tender life had been cruelly taken away, she slipped, slowly at first and then rapidly, into depression. Even though Chaturvasi had trained her, she lost her composure and became inconsolable.

His best efforts at lifting her spirits had been to no avail. She spent months cooped up in their bedroom with the curtains closed, barely eating or sleeping, roaming the tiny flat at night like a ghost. Even though he could have forced her to change with the help of incantations and potent objects, he let her bleed her sorrow in the way she wanted to. It was only when she, just like their daughter, started waking up from her sleep screaming of losing her skull did he realize that they were coming for her next.

He had taken her to a Shiva temple in a village near Rameswaram. It was one of the most potent temples in the south where, after taking a dip in the waters where the three seas meet, and after being doused by water from twenty-two different wells, and after entering the sanctum sanctorum of the temple, he took her to meet the head priest, a good friend of his. As the crowds swarmed around them, the priest sat down with Chaturvasi and his wife, chanted the mantras for the deity before placing the golden crown on her forehead, the one that normally adorned the idol. This was not something offered to the public, but Chaturvasi's clout extended beyond the ordinary even among the world of men. When the priest lifted the crown, she screamed and collapsed into Chaturvasi's arms, where he soothed her as she sobbed their dead child's name.

After they returned to Chennai, he found that her energies had settled. She prostrated at his feet and resumed her practices with extra vigour. She rose predawn and performed the elemental cleansing routines he had taught her. She wore a white sari that had been soaked in a bucket of water containing finely sieved earth so that the sari turned a dull brown. With the elements cleansed, she held yogic postures while watching her breath. When she felt her energies ascend towards her upper torso, she sat down in the lotus posture, closed her eyes, and slipped into a deep state of meditation.

Sometimes, when she was sitting in that state, her eyes not fully closed so that a thin strip of her whites were visible, and her head was tilted downwards ever so slightly, Chaturvasi inspected her aura and studied the patterns of her energetic flow. He noticed that as the days went by she was going into deeper states, and concerned that she might accidentally touch the core of her being and find herself disembodied and unable to get back into her physical self, he advised her to wear a copper ring on her left index finger.

'Fast the next three days,' Chaturvasi told her gently. 'I'll go without food until the ritual is complete.'

She bowed again.

'Please consecrate your space and purify yourself before meditation. I'll advise you when the time is right. I am assuming a period of silence until the exorcism.'

Without being told she gleaned that the time to avenge Shruti's death had arrived. She calmly nodded and resumed her needlework, knowing precisely what her next steps were.

Chaturvasi went into one of the other rooms which was fully equipped for his rituals. Even its vaastu had been perfect to charge the space. He placed a kettle of water to boil on the gas stove. He then assumed the lotus posture on the floor and reached for the familiar presence of his yantra. Discovering that he had given it away, he sighed and closed his eyes. Moments later he imagined his body so magnified that his head was high above the terrace, looking down at the tops of the coconut fronds. In this state the physical world lost sense. Everything was just blobs of energy, like looking through an infrared camera. He saw his own self and his wife as red-hot balls in a sea of blue.

The same five elements that supported the body conspired with each other to destroy it once life had left it. Any tantric who gained mastery over the elements could bend the universe to his liking. And Chaturvasi intended to start the ritual by cleansing the elements in his body, imagining the earth dissolving into water, water into fire, fire into air, air into ether and then ether into higher principles, until everything was dissolved with the universe. He proceeded to repeat his predawn ritual of swallowing cloth and cleaning his innards as he chanted mantras and then applied his practice to dissociate himself from his body. After a few hours, the erstwhile impure Chaturvasi was reborn as a pure being, a worthy vessel for the powerful entity he would have to summon during the exorcism.

When he opened his eyes, a full day had elapsed. Sunbeams pierced the still room, trapping and animating dust motes in them. Outside, a couple of coconut trees waved their slender leaves in the light breeze. A couple of crows sat on them near the nuts, cawing at each other. Chaturvasi ambled up to the window and noticed a retinue of black ants. He placed a few grains of turmeric-laced yellow rice by the trail. With great interest he leaned forward and watched the ants pick up the grains and crawl down the walls of the flat.

Smiling, he stroked his beard and walked to the cupboards where he had kept a box containing doll heads. Always prepared for such situations, he had fashioned and stored a bunch of hollow heads from sawdust and glue using a mould. The mixture took a week to dry and for the facial features to be properly formed. Now he reached for a pouch of chalk that he had ground from shells. The shells he had searched for, studied and picked up from the beach. Once he had enough, he took them to a nearby flour mill, where the operator, a man he had helped purge a curse placed by another tantric, kept a special machine just for Chaturvasi's bizarre requests.

He felt the grains of the chalk between his fingers and nodded. Now he placed a fistful inside a hollowed coconut shell, added water and made a paste. With a paintbrush he carefully painted the eye sockets on the head and affixed glass eyes into them. The faux eyeballs were made specially for him by a prosthetic craftsman, who had suddenly sprouted sores all over his body which an army of doctors could not cure, until Chaturvasi diagnosed the malignant entity that had taken control of his body. The eyes were so realistic that the moment he placed them into the sockets, the doll came alive, gazing soullessly at its maker. Now in another coconut shell he mixed some more of the chalk along with gelatin. He added hot water to the mixture, stirring it well with a neem twig. The result was a thick white slurry which, using a brush, he carefully painted over the doll's face.

With its gaping mouth and wide beady eyes, the doll had earlier looked surprised at its birthing, but the whitewash gave it a serene appearance with pursed lips and closed eyes. Once its skin had dried, using a scalpel, and with surgical precision, he carefully revealed eyes so that now it looked like it was coming out of a meditative trance. With another paintbrush, he added eyebrows and a hairline. Now he chiselled grooves around the hairline. He added the strand of Vikram's hair to a clump of horsehair and brushed the locks with a little plastic comb until they were straight and neatly aligned. He then applied glue to one end of the cluster and pasted it over the groove so that one end of the locks aligned with the painted hairline. With a screwdriver he gently pushed the hair into the groove. He held his handiwork and studied it, checking it for imperfections. Satisfied, he attached the head to a crude torso made from straw and twine.

Now he drew a mandala on the ground and placed the doll within it. He filled a bronze mug with water and then plucked a dried mango leaf from a bunch. Using it as a spoon, he scooped water from the mug and while muttering verses, sprinkled drops of water on the doll.

As an initiated practitioner, Chaturvasi was aware of the minutiae that even the most learned in the city weren't. He knew the purpose and the hidden secrets of temples more than the officious priests who ran them did. He could walk by a temple, study its main gopuram and within seconds assess if it was properly consecrated and built according to the rigid rules laid down by the sthapathis.

Almost always, the temples were not worth their weight, for they were designed by civil engineers and contractors, not by adepts who could place blocks of stone in certain ways and supercharge the space within with the right rituals. 'There's a reason ancient Shiva temples are potent,' he'd tell a sceptic. 'Go to the Tiruvannamalai temple during mahashivratri after fasting for one day . . . just one day skip your nonsense compulsion to eat and go sit for one night with your spine straight at that temple, and tell me if you didn't feel a lightness in your body and thrum in your head.'

There were a few temples in and around the city that he venerated. If he found himself outside those he would make the effort to go in, perform the necessary circumambulations and accept the consecrated prasadam. The Kapaleeswaran temple in Mylapore, the Ashtalakshmi temple in Besant Nagar, the Marundeeswarar temple in Tiruvanmiyur, and the Kamakshi Amman temple in Mangadu were all revered temples, each with its own divine core consecrated by powerful yogis in the past.

While most devotees simply stumbled in, joined their palms in front of the main idol, asked for boons and then circumambulated the sanctum sanctorum, Chaturvasi knew precisely what each temple could offer him to intensify a certain practice. The Kamakshi Amman temple, for example, was the site where the goddess Kamakshi came down to perform her penance to marry and reunite with Lord Shiva, where she rested her left leg over a sacred fire and held a japamala as she meditated on Lord Shiva. When she left the place, the residual heat became too unbearable for life in the vicinity. Animals, birds, worms, even people simply fell sick and died, leaving the place looking like a nuclear contamination zone.

This was before the place was called Madras or Chennai, and much before it became the bustling metropolis it is today. When the great wandering yogi, Adi Shankaracharya, heard of it, he trekked to the abandoned temple ruins, consecrated and installed a chakra in the sanctum to neutralize the fire. Soon life returned to normal around the area and those who knew of it performed their practices in the temple to harness the energy of the chakra.

Chaturvasi was one of them, a habitué. He knew the head priest of the temple, Sri Chandramouli Shastry, intimately.

Shastry was from Andhra Pradesh and hailed from a lineage of priests who had officiated at important temples. He had honoured Chaturvasi's request to allow him and his disciples into the temple on certain nights and meditate around the chakra until the morning arthi. In return, Chaturvasi advised Shastry on the upkeep of the chakra and the temple, and how to ensure its potency for posterity. He even oversaw the monthly cleaning and polishing of the copper chakra, making sure that it glimmered in the array of oil lamps that surrounded it during puja.

They were friends, so when Chaturvasi appeared at the small brick-and-mortar structure beside the temple that served as an office, Shastry put down his thick glasses, slung his angavastram over his torso and hurried out to greet his friend.

'Vasi-garu!' he said, grasping Chaturvasi's palms. 'Randi! Randi! I've not seen you in a while.' In an instant he sensed something was amiss. 'Is everything okay? Come in, I'll get you some sukku tea.' Chandramouli Shastry's sukku tea involved a mixture of pepper and powdered ginger boiled with jaggery.

Chaturvasi smiled and entered the office. It was a sweltering day, but it was a bit cooler inside. Pages from old ledgers fluttered listlessly to the drone of a large stand fan that slowly swivelled on its base. The spartan office looked like a place that time had glossed over with its creaky shelves and antediluvian binders and files. Shastry waddled to the door and then clapped loudly. 'Ai! You . . . yes, you . . . go get two sukku teas.' He returned to his rattan chair, adjusted the deformed pillow behind his back and sank into it. 'What is it, Vasi-garu?'

And so, Chaturvasi narrated the strange case of Vikram's possession, starting from the facts, extending to his hypothesis, then his first contact with the boy's captor, his extraction of Hiranyaksha and his final prognosis of Ugra's intentions. Meanwhile, a wiry, young Brahmin boy entered the room with a couple of tumblers of the spicy concoction that the two sipped on as they chatted.

Finally, Shastry pinched his brows and said, 'This is a very serious case, Vasi-garu. If Ugra allows Kakasura to hold on to the boy's body, then all hope is lost. In Tenali – you know, it's my native village – in Tenali there was a similar case a long time ago. A girl got possessed by Kakasura after a black magician put a curse on her. She killed twenty-five men in her family and nothing could stop her. Nothing! I tried everything to restrain her, but she got too powerful. She disappeared during the day and would only appear on treetops at night. The police were scared of her because they thought she would come for their families next. What to do, Vasi-garu? Tch. Tch. Such a nice girl she was. Charulatha. Ready for marriage she was, but then' – he clapped hard – 'like that. Kakasura! I had no other option.' He lowered his voice and fixed his gaze on something outside the window. 'I had to have her killed.' He tapped his cheeks three times. 'No other chance. I took that karma on me. If I hadn't, more people in the village would have died. You know better than me. If Kakasura possesses even one live body, he will create an army of dead and bring down his vetals from the narakaloka and resurrect them.' He pointed in the direction of the sanctum. 'Our own chakra will be desecrated in no time once those filthy left-hand Kapalikas descend upon it.' He brought his palms together. 'I mean no disrespect to you, but it will be too much for you to repel them on your own once Kakasura has full dominion over the boy.'

'That's true,' Chaturvasi said, exhaling deeply. Typically the vetals only haunted corpses, but Ugra, with his mastery over the occult, had engineered two of them to work as a pair. Hiranyaksha was sent to drain Vikram's life force so that he was practically dead, preparing his body for the more powerful Kakasura to inhabit and take control over.

'What's keeping it in check now?' Shastry asked. 'Is it one of your . . .'

'Chris.'

'That Christian boy-aa? I didn't know he had advanced so much.'

'He's adept,' Chaturvasi said absently. 'And the best I've had and now I fear I might lose him.'

Shastry sat up straight. He placed the tumbler of sukku tea on the desk and leaned forward. 'What can I do? How can I help?'

Chaturvasi slowly rubbed his palms and clapped once. The bulb swinging from the roof flickered and hummed. He then revealed his plan to the senior priest.

Chaturvasi spent the rest of the day visiting the priests of the other temples and chatting with them, outlining his plan and promising to be in touch. He then headed out of the city to Thiruthani. Here was a temple dedicated to Lord Murugan. The unassuming idol of the god with its piercing eyes inside the sanctum sanctorum was potent and people believed it granted boons. The priests were carefully chosen and when the puja was conducted, with sounds of the conch and the cymbals ringing through the temple, one felt the presence of a greater power. The guardians of the temple claimed that Lord Rama himself came to meditate here. Every day scores of people came to worship from afar and for the locals it was a routine stop en route to their schools or offices.

The temple was a simple piece of architecture, its statues and yalis chiselled meticulously by the famous sculptors from Mahabalipuram. The tank abutting the temple contained within its steps a limpid pool. The temple and its surroundings were placidly reflected in its still waters. People claimed that diseases could be cured by simply taking a dip in it on certain days. Most were drawn to the temple due to a strange sense of longing for the ornate and brightly coloured gopuram decked with sculptures from mythological stories.

It was after dark when he exited the temple. He ate the banana the priest had offered him and felt the distinct buzz in his body generated by consecrated food items.

While the crowds flocked to the temple nobody noticed the small inconspicuous structure a couple of streets away. People passed it by assuming it was the lower-caste folks' humble temple, made of brick and painted in gaudy red-and-white stripes. There was no gopuram or ornate architecture. It was more like a box with one side open. Inside were two oblong stone idols with giant copper eyes and tongues, looking like bewildered gods drawn by a kindergartener. Some people thought the stains on the idols were sandal paste. A few wondered if it was blood, but the flowers around them dispelled the thought that anyone would pour blood over an idol in a temple.

Various symbols and designs adorned the whitewashed walls and on one side there were stains which made people wonder if they were from splattered blood, or worse still, paan. Close as it was to a superstar temple, it was largely overlooked by those who didn't know its purpose.

As it should be, mused Chaturvasi, as he laid a jute sack next to the shrine, sat on it and closed his eyes. This was an occult temple, designed by the sthapathis for a specific purpose: to trap the wayward spirits that were drawn, just like the humans, to the Murugan temple.

The laws of karma worked in mysterious ways. This he had figured out many years ago one evening under a mango tree. The connectedness of everything in existence revealed itself with such clarity that he didn't know how many minutes had passed, when, in fact, a few hours had slipped by. A few local villagers had assembled around him with their palms joined. When he opened his eyes, they fell at his feet. That was many years ago, and since then he had lived his life being conscious of his actions.

His guru had told him that it was not the actions, but their intent that mattered in the abstruse arithmetic of karmic equations. The Brahmin who visited the brothel, his guru had said, carried less karmic baggage than the man who was jealous of his friend. Everything was fine until Shruti was snatched from him. Then his equanimity shook briefly.

A master of his mind, body and emotions, Chaturvasi

viewed the incident through a dispassionate lens and attributed Shruti's tender loss to the intricate karmic laws that had been at play for millennia. But as he saw his wife fall into despair and when he discovered that the Kapalikas were coming after her, he abandoned all neutrality and decided to wage war. He undertook a penance that lasted many months during which time he consciously shed layers of his mind and energy to create a human shape.

While the ancient yogis instilled life energy into these forms and roamed with them as companions and guardians, Chaturvasi's goal was to simply use his own god against Ugra and the Kapalikas without accruing any karmic debt himself. It was an intensive process, one that left him drained for weeks, and afterwards at the mercy of his wife as she nursed him back to health by transferring her own energy to him. Too subtle to be noticed, his godly form always walked beside him and kept watch over him.

Ugra had laid his trap based on Chaturvasi's prowess but even he had underestimated what the man was capable of. His god was a secret, hidden from even his brahmacharis and Ranganathan.

Chaturvasi scanned the occult temple with his mind for any trapped spirits. He found one, but was displeased with it, for it was that of a disembodied yogi looking for its final dissolution. He chanted softly under his breath and rubbed the tips of his forefinger and thumb. Seconds later, the spirit was free. A crow fell from a tree nearby, squawking. He exhaled slowly. He had hoped that it wouldn't come to this: having to catch one himself. He sat next to the temple after anointing himself with ash and picked up a human femur. He sank deeper into the folds of his mind until time and space began to meld into a single continuum. Beside him, his god slowly rose like a giant tree emerging from the ground, stretching its amorphous limbs and hovering by his side.

Chaturvasi's lips moved at the sound of an approaching motorcycle. In his mind he saw the drunk riding it, zig-zagging at top speed, honking loudly and swearing. His keen nose detected the noxious mix of country spirits and beer on his breath even from this distance.

His brows knotted in rage. His god turned into a shade of deep red, shot many feet up in the air and looked down.

Here was a useless member of society, a wife- and child-beating man, a regular drunk who gambled away his money, stole from and beat up people at the slightest provocation. Here was an absolute waste of life, Chaturvasi decided. His life was worth nothing. It was one of those men who people wished would drop dead and leave them alone. Chaturvasi raised the bone. The motorcycle was closer now. The man spotted Chaturvasi and started to scream at the sight of the almost naked man with his face and body smeared in ash, holding a human bone, like a ghost out of a bad dream, with a bizarre cloud shimmering above him.

But his screams were cut short when the femur found the front tyre, arrested it and sent the man flying headlong on to the road. Like the offering that he was, his head split open like a cracked coconut a few feet from the temple. With his eyes still shut, Chaturvasi waited. If he had opened his eyes, he would have seen the symbols on the occult temple's walls glow. But he was deep in meditation, his lips moving softly.

The moon moved. The tides turned. And the time was right. He opened his eyes and reached for the doll.

14

When the Ambassador turned into his alley, Ranganathan was ready. He was dressed in a black linen kurta, recently tailored trousers and black leather chappals. A shoulder bag hung on his arm in which he carried Chaturvasi's yantra. He placed a protective hand over it and felt the box through the bag. Recognizing the driver, Ranganathan exclaimed, 'Arre! You-aa? How come? What's your name again?'

'Balu, sir,' the driver said, opening the back door. Ranganathan stepped into the cavernous car, feeling like a VIP about to be shuttled to an important function. 'My friends call me Auto Balu, sir.' An array of pictures and idols adorned the dashboard. Some had LEDs flickering around them like ersatz oil lamps. Balu touched each one of them and then his cheek in obeisance.

The professor leaned back into the luxurious cushions and inhaled the faint aroma of camphor. He stroked the velvety fabric of the seat and marvelled as it faintly turned colour. 'Go to Adyar,' he said. 'We have to pick up someone.'

'Where in Adyar, sir?' Balu asked, adjusting the rear-view mirror. He was an able driver, handling the massive Ambassador with thc same aplomb as he had the autorickshaw.

'Near Aavin Circle,' Ranganathan said, placing his right palm on his left. He kicked off his leather chappals and folded his legs.

Balu glanced at the professor who was cloaked in black, his forehead and throat sporting fresh vibhuti stripes. He saw the man close his eyes, place his palm in front of his nose and his thumb on one of his nostrils. Sensing that he was in the presence of a holy man, he meekly nodded in response.

When Tony joined him, Ranganathan slowly rubbed his palms together and placed them over his eyes. He sat in silence for some time. Tony, unsure what to say, pecked on his phone. He was dressed in a black T-shirt and trackpants. In minutes, they were racing down the Old Mahabalipuram road. The ocean blipped in and out of view from behind lanky coconut trees.

'What's in it?' Tony finally asked, curious. He absently massaged his knee.

'A yantra,' Ranganathan laconically replied. 'Look, Tony, there is so much to explain to you about some of the things you may witness in the next few . . . hours. I hope it's a few hours and not longer.'

Tony's eyebrows rose. 'You said we'd be back by dawn.'

'Yes, that's the plan.' After they had left Chaturvasi's home, Ranganathan began to receive transmission from his teacher. Images flashed and imprinted in his mind: a large skull-shaped structure was the first thing that he suddenly remembered now. Then a glowing yogi dressed in all white with a long flowing beard and a shock of black curly hair. Other images flooded into his head – the moon fully formed and brightly lit, catamarans on a beach, a large banyan tree near the skull. He didn't want to scare the boy. 'We must retrieve the conch before dawn,' he said, 'but we are up against a formidable group of tantrics.' He patted the bag and sighed. 'As long as we have this yantra, we'll be out of trouble.'

The yantra was an harmless-looking object and a casual observer could easily mistake it for a crude toy in a wooden box. It resembled a small black thumb made of granite with coils of copper swirling around it. White threads ran across the box in a specific pattern such that it looked like a black spider sitting in the middle of a white web. However, the black thumb was solid mercury – something an ordinary person would have a hard time believing. But real it was and it took the mastery of an adept like Chaturvasi to transform the vial of liquid mercury, which Ranganathan had himself purchased, into a crystallized mass.

The process had taken place in the dead of night with Chaturvasi, his small coterie of brahmacharis, and Ranganathan in a clearing outside the city next to an old temple dedicated to Kali. As the mercury coalesced and began to steam, the crickets stopped chirping and the air turned deathly quiet as if an eclipse were upon them. Chaturvasi sat straight, chanting mantras, his eyes squeezed shut, his fingers laced in an intricate mudra. They unclasped and quickly assumed another mudra until, finally, he unfurled his palms, as if they were the wings of a bird, and covered the yantra. When he opened his eyes and moved his palms, the mercury had solidified against all rational explanation and perched in the box looking, even in its diminutive stature, like a regal weapon, so perfect were the curves of its shape. As Chaturvasi chanted softly and threaded the twine around the box, the insects and the frogs could be heard again. Ranganathan found tears trickling down his cheeks. Later, many months later, Chaturvasi told Ranganathan, 'A part of me exists in that box, Ranga.'

Ranganathan knew that Chaturvasi always relied on the yantra for protection during exorcisms. His task must be really treacherous for Chaturvasi to have parted with his yantra, but Ranga refused to think about that too much. He stared out of the window for a while, looking at the passing scenery. 'You know, in Ethiopia,' he said slowly, 'they believe that the Ark of the Covenant is kept in one of their ancient churches in a tiny town.'

Tony perked up. His knowledge of world geography and history was extensive. In his quest for vivisecting and inspecting words, he had gleaned cultural minutiae on various parts of the world. 'But, sir, the Ark was just a myth,' he contested, suddenly in his element.

Ranganathan shook his head. 'The Ark is real and it exists. The ancient Ethiopians, one of the earlier followers of Jesus, understood the need to consecrate a place before performing rituals, and that was what the Ark was – a powerful source of energy. Kind of like a radio tower that a receiver can tune into and download its energy.

Tony went silent, mulling over the facts. Ranganathan continued, 'Inside each church in Ethiopia there are two curtains. Behind the first, the priest and a select few people – like the groom and bride, or the parents and the baby about to be baptized – are allowed. Behind that is another curtain. Only the priest is allowed through it, behind which is a miniature replica of the Ark designed to tap into the mother ship, wherever it might be.'

'I don't understand why you're telling me this.'

'Because, Tony,' Ranganathan said, tapping the bag, 'this yantra is something similar. It taps into a powerful source, one that I cannot reveal to you, or even begin to explain.' The yantra against his torso was now causing a thrum in his body. He felt a fervent desire to close his eyes and slip into a state of deep trance, but he fought it. 'As long as we have this with us, we will be safe. Trust me. It's like having Vasi sir with us.'

Auto Balu steered the white hunk of steel deftly around lorries and other vehicles for what seemed like an eternity. He was a colourful chap, giving quick honks at times, or sticking his head out and screaming, 'Have you told your people you won't be returning home?' as he fought truculent drivers. Each time he lost his calm, he turned and apologized to the duo with a sheepish smile.

'Take the next right,' Ranganathan told Balu. 'Yes . . . this one. Next to the tea shop.'

Balu slowed the car and took the turn. The street was narrow and unpaved. A couple of lamps lit the road with their yellow light. A pack of strays that were blocking the road chased the car for a couple of minutes. They passed simple homes painted in bright colours before encountering a patch of green.

'Stop here,' Ranganathan said. 'And make a U-turn and wait. We'll be back in fifteen minutes.'

'Okay sir,' Balu said.

'Where are we?' Tony asked, fading into the dimly lit street in his black attire. Behind them they heard a pack of dogs howl.

'At the shrine of Chinnamalai siddhar,' Ranganathan said, walking briskly. 'Did you bring the flower that Vasi sir gave you?' He froze, sure the boy hadn't brought it. His panic was only momentary because Tony quickly showed it to him. It had a strong skunky smell.

'Whose shrine . . . I mean who is this person?' Tony asked.

They walked to an old peepal tree that stood majestically by the side of the road. Tony noticed a white shrine under it. An oil lamp threw its glow from inside. The walls of the shrine were streaked with mud and dirt. Insects buzzed about and flew towards the lamp.

Something shuffled its wings and adjusted itself atop the tree. Ranganathan reached the shrine and motioned to Tony to hurry. The latter walked up and peered into the shrine. Inside was a life-sized metal statue sitting in a cross-legged posture. The face was that of a yogi with his eyes half open. It sat with a slouch and its topknot and beard were carved with detail and painted in rich blacks. The paint had peeled away in many spots, revealing the dull metal underneath.

'Offer him the flower,' Ranganathan said, his palms together.

Tony looked at him suspiciously but gently placed the flower by the statue's feet. 'Why?'

'Now close your eyes.' Ranganathan closed his eyes and Tony heard his breathing slow down and become deeper. Tony sighed and did the same.

A minute later, Ranganathan said, 'We leave now. One mustn't stay at the shrine for too long after sunset.'

They were back on the road, hurtling down the highway, when Ranganathan said, 'Once there was a great siddhar . . . that is one who has . . . how do I say this . . . one who has complete mastery over the five elements of the body . . . A great yogi. Leave it at that. Chinnamalai . . . no one knew his real name. They knew he lived on a hill and adopted its name as his own. Chinnamalai was a great yogi who decided to undergo the process of self-mummification . . .'

'What? How does one do that? You need to desiccate the body and . . .'

'Correct. He gradually starved himself over the years. He gave up rice and ate only bark, nuts and berries, slowly reducing the quantity so that his fat and internal moisture content diminished over time. He also ate various herbs and sesame seeds to limit bacterial growth. He drank toxic tree sap which acted as insecticide.'

'But why would he do that?' Tony asked incredulously.

'Siddhars do not care much for their physical bodies. They can drop them whenever they please. Sometimes . . . actually very rarely . . . they undertake this process so that others can access the trapped energy in their bodies after their death.'

'And how did he die?'

'After years of adhering to this diet, when he was near death from starvation, he was buried alive next to the tree in an underground chamber. They put a bamboo tube into it for air. He sat in the lotus position and chanted mantras in the darkness. Each day he rang a tiny bell to signify that he was still alive. When the people outside stopped hearing the bell, they removed the air tube and sealed the tomb.'

'And they put him inside the statue after . . . wow!' He leaned back and stared out of the window.

Ranganathan sat cross-legged with his eyes closed. As they drove by the highway signs to Pondicherry, Tony turned on the cabin light, took out the newspaper from his backpack and started mulling over the crossword. The clues were hard today and he tried to push away the memories of Vikram peering over his shoulder, asking him why a certain word was the correct answer, or simply spouting random words that fit the word count.

'Why is that answer *mistaken*?' Ranganathan said, pointing at the grid.

Tony glanced up. 'Oh, it's a cryptic clue, sir.'

'Give it to me,' Ranganathan said, taking the paper from Tony. He squinted and read the clue aloud. 'Confused girl endlessly enamoured. Eight letters.' He put the paper down. 'What type of clue is that?'

Tony retrieved the paper from him and grinned. 'It seems senseless at first, but if you study it for a bit, you will spot the hint. See, girl is miss. Endlessly means take away the last letter.' He wrote MIS on top of the paper. 'Now we have three out of the seven letters of the answer. So, if we can get a five-letter word that means enamoured, we will have the solution.' He looked at Ranganathan with anticipation. The other stared back blankly. Sanskrit was his forte. English was a fool's language, a clumsy hodgepodge of words borrowed from all over the world, cobbled together by an array of masters, each with his own idea of what was correct. The result was a complicated chutney of a language that barely followed any regular rules and boasted of more exceptions than norms. He slowly shook his head. 'I don't . . . I don't know.'

'Taken, sir. Taken!' Tony wrote TAKEN next to MIS. 'Mistaken means confused.'

Ranganathan jerked back. 'That's quite the stretch for a clue. What a crazy way to play with the language.' He chuckled. Sanskrit was a far superior language. Its singular ability to hew words together from root words gave it a much powerful lordship over a language that couldn't. He wished he could share the works of the great Sanskrit poets who had won the hearts of kings by inventing clever verses where alternate syllables revealed a solution to a puzzle. 'But it does require some intellect and command over the language to play this game.'

Tony blushed. 'It's quite hard, yes. Vicks . . . Vikram never understood it. He got frustrated and started shooting random words.'

They passed their time with Tony patiently explaining to the professor the various types of cryptic clues – anagrams, telescopic clues, homonyms and others. Even Balu appeared to have taken his hand off the horn. The Ambassador sliced through the night like a white bolt. Balu's window was rolled down a little and the saline tang of the sea seeped in.

Tony's phone lit up and made a sound. He pressed a button to mute it and took a syringe and a packet of medicine out his backpack.

'What's that for?' Ranganathan asked. 'Insulin?'

Tony shook his head. Injecting himself he said, 'Thyroid issues. I need daily shots.'

Ranganathan drew in a deep breath and let it out. 'Look, Tony,' he said. 'The world is not what it seems to be. You are young and are studying engineering. You think everything must make logical sense, but that's not how it really is.'

'I find that hard to digest.' He balled up the medicine wrapper and stuffed the syringe into his backpack.

'Why do you think Vikram is the way he is?'

Tony squirmed and shaded the corner of the newspaper with the pen. 'I don't know.'

'And I do. So listen to me . . .'

And so he told Tony about the Kapalikas and their nefarious plot to ensnare Chaturvasi.

The Kapalikas were an enigmatic sect of tantrics who led clandestine lives. On the surface they were regular members of society – doctors, engineers, lawyers, accountants – but when they draped their white shawl around their bare torsos and drew a black line on their foreheads, they instantly slipped into their alter egos. Their rituals were esoteric and chilled even the strongest of men. While meat, wine and sex caused the human consciousness to descend into its animal self, the Kapalikas used the same to ascend towards divinity. They did not give in to the bodily pleasures, but merely utilized them to gain more mastery over their bodies.

Joining the Kapalikas was no easy task. One couldn't simply find them in the telephone directory or search for them online. They covered their tracks with bee-like assiduousness. Many rumours floated around Chennai as to how one could cross paths with the sect. Some claimed that one had to post a detailed letter, stamped with a bloody thumbprint, with the return address clearly printed. The rumour went that the Kapalikas had people in the post office who could pick out such a letter from a pile without even looking for it.

Another rumour had it that the Kapalikas performed their nocturnal rituals in the cemeteries around the city and if one knew the venue on a specific night, one could simply walk up to them because they believed that the one who sought hard to become a Kapalika was bound to find his brethren.

While the rumours were endless, the Kapalikas were picky in who they inducted into their clan. Once in, one could never get out of it alive. Their order was too secretive and its goings-on could never be made public. The Kapalikas, like any tantric sect, had adepts: men who were absolute masters of left-hand techniques. And just like Chaturvasi they held the title of acharya. It was the acharya who determined whether an aspirant was suitable or not.

After the initiation ceremony, during which a goat was slaughtered and its blood smeared all over the tyro, the beginner was instructed on a self-abnegating lifestyle. He was expected to remain celibate, keep his mind and body clean, perform the prescribed rituals at the prescribed time, eat sparsely and live a chaste life while in exile. The staunchest among them would banish themselves to a remote village and daily beg for alms from no more than three homes while dressed in the skin of an ass or a dog.

When the time was ripe, the acharya summoned the practitioner who had to bring the corpse of a Brahmin he had murdered himself. This was the point where many of them baulked and tried to quit. They were gently cajoled and, if they still refused, given a grand goodbye and wished the best of luck in their lives. The acharya would apologize for having wasted fourteen years of the practitioner's life, who would feel uncomfortable at the array of blank stares and steely smiles, but take his leave hesitantly, promising to stay in touch.

He would be dead before the next night.

The ones who mustered the courage to lure a Brahmin to one of the temples outside the city and kill him were welcomed into the clan with great fanfare. A weeklong celebration was held in their honour and a comely damsel, young of age, supple in body, was provided to them for their upcoming spiritual practices.

However, the new Kapalika would have to first sever the skull of the corpse, strip off the skin, muscle and tendons, boil it in holy water for hours, place it in a safe place and introduce maggots to it. Weeks later, after every shred of organic matter had been removed from the skull, the Kapalika was expected to use it in all his rituals until his last breath, even drinking from it. The first sip of wine from the skull was a moment that the acharya and the pupil shared and treasured.

After the ritual murder, the initiate was exiled for another twelve years during which he'd have to pursue his practices assiduously. Various rituals were prescribed to the seeker, one of which required him to build a fire and offer eight oblations from his body: hair, skin, blood, flesh, sinews, fat, bones and marrow. This ritual ensured that the Kapalika trainee was performing penance for the worst of all crimes he would have to commit – the killing of a Brahmin. It was said that the true Kapalika, when lost in his rituals and practices, slowly began to transform from an ordinary human to one bestowed with siddhis – magical powers and superhuman abilities.

Most Kapalikas kept to themselves, focusing on their rituals and spending time procuring ingredients for them. If they were zealous and offered oblations of their body parts, they spent days or weeks healing. What took the right-hand tantrics years and decades, the Kapalikas believed could be obtained in a far shorter time frame.

The right-hand tantrics strived to liberate themselves from the eternal cycle of rebirth and in the process they too acquired many siddhis. This, however, they shunned, preferring to keep their practices going in the hope of shedding their mortal shells consciously and merging with the universe. The Kapalikas primarily wanted the siddhis. They believed that with the siddhis in place, they would conquer the realm of the material world, and eventually even transcend it.

And Acharya Ugra was a testament to that. Having offered a couple of his teeth, a strip of flesh from his right thigh, tendons from his abdomen and the entirety of his right foot's little toe, he cut a menacing figure as he limped about, leaning on his glinting trident for support, dressed in a tunic made of donkey hide that was so rank most people gagged when they approached him.

Like all Kapalikas, he had two goals in life: one, to ascend to Kailash with his mortal form and meet Lord Shiva, and two, while on earth acquire the eight siddhis that would make him invincible. Even one of the siddhis would make a person almost godlike among humans, but Ugra was a man of lofty ambitions. He intended to show off his mortal shell, his physical body that he had strived over time to make a vessel for the superhuman powers, to the Lord, and wanted nothing short of the eight siddhis.

He desired the power to shrink in size, the power of levitation, the power of becoming limitlessly large, the power of becoming heavy, absolute control over the body and mind, unshakeable willpower, and control over the five elements.

He had been initiated into the sect decades ago, having murdered a meek Brahmin clerk without batting an eyelid. He watched cold-eyed as the young man's life slipped away. When he was done, the man's neck was blue with dark impressions of Ugra's fingers. His sacred thread had snapped from the struggle. Ugra had choked him despite his acharya's instructions to use a knife. He wanted to experience the prana leaving so that he could harness it for himself. Decades of penance had given him inordinate powers, but he lusted for more. And as per the Kapalika doctrine, the only way to gain a siddhi was to sacrifice either a king or a spiritually advanced man such as a sage or a seer.

'That's possible?' Tony asked, his eyes bulging and his breath so still that Ranganathan thought he had petrified.

Ranganathan pinched the bridge of his nose. 'Yes Tony. Technically, yes. But . . . it's not . . .'

'And Chaturvasi is a . . . what did you call it . . . siddhi?'

'Siddhar. A siddhar is one who has acquired all eight siddhis.'

'Like the Chinnamalai fellow I gave a flower to? And Vasi sir is one?' His tone was plaintive like a child entreating his father at the fair to let him ride the merry-go-round for the second time. 'He can levitate and stuff?'

Ranganathan looked out of the window. The night was slipping by, dragging shapeless trees in big black blobs. A faint mist clung to the road and snaked out on either side into the trees. The boy was smart, smarter than his peers and Ranganathan was loath to give him ideas. Whether Vasi sir was a siddhar or not, he didn't know and he dared not ask. But he knew that he was no mere mortal, having seen him battle ghosts and demons from within a circle drawn with rice flour and his yantra next to him.

He had heard stories of Chaturvasi's time in the Himalayas where he walked barefoot in knee-deep snow. Once he subsisted on nothing but a ball of chilli paste for weeks. Each morning, he stood in a cold running river and, with great control, extracted water through his sphincter until he could bring it out from his mouth. The day he spat clear water, he retreated into a cave for months where he sank into a deep meditative state. At a more human level, he had never seen his teacher yawn. Not even once. The man's body never slacked. He was always on.

So, yes, Chaturvasi was capable of superhuman feats, but he wasn't going to reveal that to an uninitiated boy like Tony.

'That means he can,' Tony said. 'And your silence means you have seen him do stuff.' Tony turned and looked out of the window and silently whispered. 'Wow.'

'Vasi sir's abilities are not . . .'

'What's that?' Tony asked, tapping the window.

Ranganathan tried to look, but the car was going too fast. He turned around instinctively, but the Ambassador's blue-tinted rear window was too opaque.

'It . . . it was like there was a blob of white,' Tony said. 'Like a cloud or something.'

'A cloud?'

'I . . . I am not sure. It looked like smoke or a cloud. Under one of the trees. I just got a glimpse of it. Maybe it was nothing.'

'Yeah,' Ranganathan said, remembering the glowing yogi. He looked out in front through the windshield. The fog had completely covered the road. There was no traffic. In their conversations, they had not noticed the quietness that had settled around the car. 'Balu, is this the right way?'

Balu rocked his head slowly as if listening to an invisible song. Bewildered, Ranganathan caught and shook his shoulder. 'Balu!'

Balu jerked in the seat and the car swerved. 'Sorry, sir,' he said. 'I was focusing and then I lost sense of time.' The car came to a halt. 'I somehow just . . . I don't know how to say it. I felt like I was not in my body any more.'

Ranganathan pinched his chin. 'Are you okay?' He glanced at his watch. 'Let us take a small break.'

'How much further?' Tony asked.

Balu scratched his head and shrugged. 'Swami said that I'd know when we get there once we were on this road.' He opened the door and stepped out. A cool wind slipped in like a wayward moth on a still night. Ranganathan rolled down the window and peered out. It was a quiet night and it revealed nothing. There were no distant lights, wires, or any signs of human habitation, save the road. The mist, now thicker, clung to the ground, making it seem like they were floating on clouds. They could make out the shapes of large banyan tress in the dark. Even though he believed that Chaturvasi knew what he was doing, Ranganathan felt a mild sense of unease. Where were they? And where did they have to go from here?

'Right there,' Tony exclaimed, tapping his windowpane.

'What?' Ranganathan said, leaning towards the window.

Tony opened the door and pointed. 'See that white stuff under that tree there?'

Ranganathan squinted and then suddenly noticed the white blob under a large banyan tree. It glowed and bobbed in the air slowly like a yacht anchored in a marina. As they watched, the blob slowly began to assume a human shape and within moments it resembled a bearded man in flowing orange robes and a head full of dreadlocks. He sat with his arms in his lap as if deep in meditation.

'It's a . . .' Tony started. 'Looks like the Chinnamalai siddhar.'

'It's someone,' Balu said, pointing at the man. His eyes were wide and unblinking.

Tony got out of the car and then his eyes slowly grew bigger. 'Sir!' he said.

'Yes? What is it?'

'Sir, my knee pain is fully gone.' He hopped on the leg and squatted a few times. 'It's . . . it's not there.'

Ranganathan smiled. 'You'll need your body intact for what lies ahead.'

A strange bird's call echoed from the woods. Ranganathan gripped the bag tighter and gingerly stepped out too. 'Be careful,' he said, looking at the bearded man. 'It could be one of Ugra's lookouts.' But, in his heart, he knew it wasn't so.

'Let's ask siddhar where the island is,' Tony said, walking into the woods.

'Stop!' Ranganathan exclaimed. 'He isn't Chinnamalai siddhar. It could be dangerous.'

Tony continued walking, confident that the person was an ally. 'We don't have much time. If we don't know, we must ask.'

Ranganathan didn't know how far Ugra was with regard to appropriating the siddhis, but his years of penance must have borne him some fruit. He didn't think he was capable of manifesting lifelike forms the way he had seen Chaturvasi do, but he wanted to be careful. The yantra was sacred. But he was not fearful of the floating man. At this point in his life, after years of practices, he had tuned his body to be extremely sensitive to malfeasant energies. He didn't have to interact with someone to know if they were angry or jealous. Simply looking or being around them told him a lot about their mental structure and their intent. He didn't feel his antenna tingle. He watched Tony walk towards the man, listening to the sound of gravel crunching under his shoes.

'Hello?' Tony said softly, his voice clearly audible in the still night. The absence of any insect or bird sounds made the thicket even creepier. 'Excuse me, we are lost. We need help.' Tony crept forward. A few more steps and the man gently wafted away from Tony. He stopped and took a step back. The man moved forward. His long beard curled around him like cotton candy in a pool.

Tony once again stepped forward and again the man slid back. His eyes were sealed shut and even though he floated in the air, there was no other movement in his body. Tony hesitated for a moment and then sprinted towards the man, but the figure kept moving away like the horizon. Panting, he turned back and walked towards Ranganathan. 'I don't know . . .'

'Look!' Balu exclaimed. The man lifted his left hand and was pointing. 'Sir, there's a kuccha road ahead,' he said. 'Right through the trees.' While the main road continued to disappear into the lonely night, swallowed by large trees, a kuccha road branched off from it ahead. The kuccha road slipped towards the sea, vanishing as silently as it had appeared into the sepulchral shroud of banyans. 'It goes towards the sea.'

'He could have just said it,' Tony muttered.

'He can't speak,' Ranganathan said with a knowing smile.

'What?' Tony asked.

'Nothing,' Ranganathan said. 'Get in. Balu, take the kuccha path.'

'Yes sir,' Balu said, and hopped into the Ambassador. 'That man looks like a swami, no?'

The road was cut through the banyan grove and it wound about. The Ambassador moved forward gingerly, the gravel crunching under its tyres. Amorphous glowing shapes flew in lazy loops above them, casting eerie shadows on the ground that crawled over the moonlit landscape like startled animals. Balu was driving with trepidation, leaning over the steering wheel and looking up while keeping an eye on the road. After another bend, a beach appeared. Balu stopped the car.

'Can't go any more, sir,' he said. 'Car will get stuck.'

Ranganathan and Tony got out and studied the scene. The beach was idyllic. Unlike Elliot's Beach, this one was devoid of people or their trash. The sand was pristine and appeared to glow softly in the bright moonlight, its intensity waxing and waning with the crashing of the waves. Not far from it was an island covered with large trees, their branches snaking amidst silhouetted rocks. Torchlights flickered in the distance and there was the muffled sound of hand drums being banged in unison. Nearby, the waves crashed gently.

'Okay Balu,' Ranganathan said. 'Stay here.' He took a

deep breath. 'We should be back in a couple of hours.' They were not in the real world any more, but in Ugra's sphere of influence. Time and space were manufactured here by the hyperfocused mind of the Kapalika and he had no idea what a couple of hours would feel like to someone keeping time.

'Don't worry, sir,' Balu said confidently. He tapped the chassis of the Ambassador. 'Vasi sir will take care of you if something happens.'

'Well, I hope nothing happens.' Ranganathan whispered and turned to Tony. 'You ready, Tony?'

Tony picked up his bag and marched behind Ranganathan.

15

As Ranganathan made small talk with Tony, his calm tone belied the terror that rumbled underneath.

Guide me, Vasi,' he muttered under his breath and trudged towards the beach.

As their feet sank into the grains it felt as if millions of tiny hands were reaching up and caressing them. And as the seawater rolled down their pants, it left a faint golden glow like a temporary aura. A few catamarans lay on the sand like the hollowed carcasses of sea giants.

'Looks like there are people,' Tony pointed out with his finger.

Ranganathan discovered a few motorbikes parked next to the boats. For a place so ethereal, the vehicles seemed out of place. If they had managed to arrive here, Ranganathan figured others could too.

'Who would come here?' Tony asked. 'And why?'

Ranganathan gestured to the island. 'Kapaladvipa,' he said.

'Kapaladvipa?'

'Yeah. Kapala means skull. Dvipa is island. Skull Island.'

Tony goggled at the formless pile of rocks surrounded by

lush vegetation. 'The temple of the Kapalikas is there, right? But why is it called Skull Island?'

'You'll see.' Ranganathan adjusted the bag and walked towards the catamarans. 'Now help me with this.'

Before they pushed the boat off, Ranganathan raised his hand. 'Give me some time. I must first prepare myself.'

'Okay,' Tony said. 'I'll be' – he looked around at the mesmerizing colours on the shore – 'I'll be here.'

'Please don't go too far. This place is dangerous. I don't know what to expect and the last thing I want is to have to go looking for you.'

Tony gave him a thumbs up and squatted down on the shore. 'I promise. I'll just watch this blue stuff that's glowing on the shore.' He rested his chin on his palms and poked in the sand.

Ranganathan smiled. He sat down cross-legged and placed the bag beside him. He scanned the beach and then closed his eyes. With Tony engrossed in the glowing sands, Ranga went through the sequence of breathing exercises. Then he focused his attention between his eyebrows and felt the loops of energy around his body converge there. Soon he was removed from his body and the thrumming of the universe came to a soft stop. In this state of abeyance, he experienced fountains of energy gushing around him like erupting geysers.

He opened his eyes and looked at the forlorn island ahead. This place was potent. Ugra was a powerful tantric, and it appeared that he had created many energy sources in this vicinity and wrapped them with substance to create the illusory place. It took a lot of expertise to focus energy into one spot and connect it to the earth so that it became a wellspring, but to do it at many spots, some even in the water, required absolute mastery over the elements.

Ranganathan took a deep breath. He remembered that fateful day on Elliot's Beach when Chaturvasi had torn Ranga's pants and shown him how frail his ego was, before setting him on a path that fortified his spirit. He offered his respects to his teacher, knowing that Chaturvasi was more powerful than Ugra.

When he noticed the professor's eyes were open, Tony rushed to the boat and together they pushed it into the calm sea. The streak the catamaran left in the sand slowly turned blue. Once they were almost in the water, Ranganathan hopped in. 'Push once more and jump in,' he said.

Within moments they were bobbing in the sea. Tony reached for the oars and offered Ranganathan one. 'I don't know how to use this.'

Ranganathan shrugged. 'How hard can it be.'

They fumbled with the positioning and splashed about a bit. Eventually, they found a slow rhythm and the catamaran moved forward. When they had covered a decent distance, Ranganathan paused and turned around. It was a marvellous sight – the beach glowing like an ingot of gold and blue. He spotted Balu leaning against his car, smoking a beedi, gazing up. He looked up too and saw large shapes lazily swimming in the sky as if the clouds had decided to drop their lassitude and animate themselves.

Now they were near the island. The water was choppier here and the catamaran began to bounce.

'Steer to the right,' Ranganathan said. 'See that archway there.' He pointed at the massive rock arch that towered over a narrow canal.

'Yeah.'

'That way.'

As they sailed towards the arch, Tony leaned over the side of the boat and spotted large shapes underwater. At first he thought they were sunken boulders, but the more he stared the more defined they appeared. 'What's that?' he finally asked, pointing down.

'Looks like the gopuram of a temple. I have no idea how Ugra operates,' Ranganathan answered.

They rowed around a bend on the island and headed towards the arch. There was no beach on the island, its shore festooned with sharp rocks. Large bats hung from the arch, cloaking themselves with their wings. When the catamaran neared them, they scattered into the sky and disappeared towards the island. Tony kept rowing, constantly glancing up and down, unsure what the land or the sea kept hidden from them. 'Sir,' he said tremulously. 'What's that . . . below?'

Ranganathan saw bubbles emerging from the sea. A dark shape swam silently deep below under the shimmering reflection of the glowing moon.

'Some animal?' Tony asked, hopefully. He knew all about the marine fauna around Chennai. There were no dolphins, seals, or otters around here. His best bet was an Olive Ridley turtle. The females came ashore to lay their eggs, but neither was this the season, nor would a turtle blow such a constant stream of bubbles.

'Could be Ugra's men,' Ranganathan said softly. 'Could be his creations. Why stop with men when you can create entire landscapes.' The shapes swam along with them like sharks stalking their prey and then as suddenly as they had appeared, faded away into the blackness that yawned just beneath them. 'Keep rowing, Tony. Focus ahead.'

As they got closer to the island, the sounds of the drums grew louder. They were rhythmic and hypnotic, gracefully leaping into the saline air like a herd of gazelles. Interspersed with the drumming were the sounds of trumpets.

'Sounds like some function is going on,' Tony said.

'It's a ritual of some sort. Those are old bronze wind instruments, typically not used any more. Sound is energy, Tony.'

'Yes sir. You mentioned that before.'

'And their sound was used to create specific energy structures within a space to attract beings. I don't know what rituals the Kapalikas indulge in, but they seem to be setting something up.' He glanced at his watch. It was close to three in the world they had left behind. 'And at three-forty in the morning, the earth's position is such that any ritual conducted then will have a lot of impact. Most yogis start their practices at that time.'

'Three in the morning?'

'Three-forty. Brahma muhurtham,' Ranganathan corrected him.

'Brahma muhurtham,' Tony repeated and then almost screamed. 'Look!'

Ahead of them, just beyond the arch rested a massive skull

hewed out of rock. Its eye sockets were pointing towards the sky and its mouth was open as if the owner of the skull had died of shock. The skull was gargantuan and towered over the island's trees. Lights flickered in the eye sockets and the nasal cavity. Even from this distance its teeth were clearly visible. Its chin was a dull shade of red. The space around the skull was filled with bushes and shrubs, the kind they had never seen in Chennai. The leaves were dark red and dripped a thick purple liquid. Long cylindrical multihued flowers shot out from the shrubs and swayed gently. Human shadows flitted about casting ghastly shadows on the off-white rock. Standing atop the skull and resembling pins on a pincushion, were a group of men with spears and tridents in their hands.

'Kapaladvipa,' Tony whispered. He reached for the crucifix and ran his fingers along its reassuring edges.

The air here smelt of charred flesh. Ranga and Tony covered their noses and retched.

Now they both stopped rowing. The catamaran drifted like a languorous croc in a river. 'We must get ashore,' Tony said.

'Yes,' Ranganathan agreed and searched for a spot to pull over. 'There,' he said, pointing to small patch of gravel amidst the rocks. 'Row towards that spot.'

They hopped off the catamaran and dragged it on to the shore, easing the boat a few inches at a time to minimize sounds. Bubbles again appeared near them and faded. Ranganathan held the bag closer to him and stared into the sea.

'There is no rope,' Tony said, looking around.

'Won't need it,' Ranganathan said and took his eyes off the waters. 'The waves here are pretty small. The boat should stay. Come.'

They treaded slowly towards the enormous skull-shaped rock and spotted the drummers in the mouth of the skull. They were bare-chested men with massive drums hanging from their torsos. They sported lamp-black stripes on their foreheads. They beat their drums in syncopated unison, their eyes glazed, their faces serene and their bodies swaying. In the eye sockets of the skull, men whirled on the spot, one hand raised, like gently falling flowers. A steady fire burned in the nasal cavity. From afar, the skull was a hive of sound and movement, chattering merrily in the dead of the night.

Beside the skull was a single banyan tree. It was massive, its canopy spread over a large area. Black winged creatures hopped from branch to branch. The serpentine roots hung from the tree and swung gently like pendulums. A small platform made of stone ran around the girth of the main trunk. A fire smouldered under the tree.

Even from this distance, Ranganathan and Tony figured that it was a burning pyre. The corpse's face had burnt away, revealing a ghastly scorched skull. Its ribs were exposed and its fingers were clenched. Three priests dressed in black vestments stood next to it, holding a cup in one hand and a slender leaf in the other.

Tony gasped and Ranganathan immediately shushed him with a finger.

A small group of people was assembled in front of the skull.

Four men stood in a line, their faces drenched with sweat, their expressions bordering on terror. They wore nothing but trousers. A couple of them sported sacred threads across their torsos. Surrounding them were a group of priests, dressed in white veshtis, their torsos smeared with ash, making them look like a bunch of ghouls that had crawled out from the remains of a cremation. Amidst them a tiny man scurried about, leaning heavily on a metal trident.

'Ugra,' Ranganathan whispered. Unconsciously, his fingers sought each other and entwined themselves in the kurma mudra. Tony crossed himself absently at the sight of the hideous man.

Ugra's face was riddled with scars and looked like it had survived a meat grinder. His forehead had three black lines that started from between his eyes and ran straight up. His skin was dark and scarred. His right leg was visibly shorter than the left and limply dangled below the knee. He couldn't turn his torso; instead, he glanced sideways from the corner of his eye. He leaned on the trident while walking, but he was quick nevertheless. He wore a necklace made of ivory and giant earrings. His long, matted hair was tied up with a jewel nestled in it like a glittering egg.

Ugra hobbled about the group, chanting verses, and blowing ashes from what looked like a bowl made from the top of a human skull. His energy was inhuman. His disability didn't slow him down; he zipped between the four men and the priests with ease. At times, he egged the drummers on like a mad conductor. And at times, he froze, threw his head up and muttered incantations and then uttered, 'swaha', at which the men around the pyre dipped the leaf into the cup and offered some liquid to the flames.

Finally, Ugra raised his arms, and the drumming stopped. The whirling men in the eye sockets slowly came to a halt and sank slowly to the ground like falling autumn leaves. In the sudden silence, only the elements whispered. The fire crackled. The sea swished. And a cool breeze rustled through the vegetation. The flowers stopped swaying and retreated into the shrubs, after which the leaves folded around them like an armadillo balling up.

The crowd was quiet, waiting for their master to speak. The four men stood stiff, their eyes darting about as they nervously wrung their hands. Ranganathan placed a finger on his lips, reminding Tony to remain quiet.

'Today,' Ugra finally spoke. His voice was gruff and came out in guttural spurts. 'Today we have assembled to honour our lord, Shiva . . .'

At the mention of Shiva, the devotees all chanted, 'O Bhairava!' At the same time, the drummers beat their drums and the trumpeters accompanied them. Ugra brought his palms together, his scarred face reduced to a grimace. 'As it is known amongst us Kapalikas that' – he walked to the first man – 'it is known that living the life dictated by the order of Kapalikas will let you go to Kailash with this human form and sport with Shiva.' The man, young and trembling, nodded and brought his palms together.

Ugra clapped him on his shoulder and moved to the next

recruit. 'The life of a Kapalika is not easy.' The second man nodded attentively. 'You've to learn to live in a society that will spurn you . . . be disgusted by you . . . by the deeds you are about to commit.'

He moved to the third man and leaned into his face. 'You'll have to accept them spitting on your face and calling you a murderer.' He laughed now. 'Once, it was easy. You killed your Brahmin, you took his skull and then spent the next twelve years atoning for it. People understood who you were. They feared you and kept their distance, but they revered you in a twisted way and knew that you were on a great path . . . one that they could never dream to get on.'

He moved to the fourth man. 'But now . . . now it's hard. Killing a Brahmin is murder.' He growled, his malicious smile revealing two missing teeth. 'Murder! As if those bastards haven't done enough injustice to the rest of us. Now we have to scavenge burial grounds or medical colleges for our skulls like pariahs.' He limped away from the men and stood facing them. He dug his trident into the ground. Blood oozed and bubbled from the site. It congealed within seconds, turning into small black critters that scattered away, leaving no trace of the blood.

The four men brought their hands together in terror. Ugra beamed with pride. 'Our way of life is not for all, but our way of life bestows powers that mortals can only dream of.' He snapped his fingers. 'You want to levitate? You want to turn into the size of a fly and creep into your enemy's house?' He threw his head back and cackled. 'You'll attain unimaginable powers and live a life of respectability. You will have full control over the five elements.' He swept his arms about as if to show what one could attain by rigorously adhering to the Kapalika way of life. 'You can make your life exactly the way you want it to be.'

The four men, their palms together, stared at the fearsome master with equal parts terror and awe. Ugra walked to the first man and touched him with his trident. 'You, get out.'

'Acharya?' the man said. But before he could say another word, a couple of the priests were dragging him away.

Ugra went to the third man and jerked his head. Two more priests carried him away. Ugra beamed a big smile at the two who remanined. 'I welcome you to the group.'

They laughed nervously and proclaimed, 'Jai Bhairava!'

One was young, barely in his twenties with a thick moustache and a clean-shaven boyish face. He was slender, almost frail, in that very Indian middle-class way, a result of too much rice and as much heat, making the person lose all his life's energies to the greedy city. His trousers were one size too big, making his legs look like a pair of broomsticks. He wore a metal watch and simple leather chappals. Sacred threads hung across his torso. Though he was diminutive and frail, his eyes burned with ferocity. If he had any fears about being around a bona fide murderer – and a group of them at that – they did not show on his face.

'You're a Brahmin?' Ugra asked. He placed the trident on the boy's chest and lifted the three white threads.

'Yes acharya,' the boy said, his voice clear. With one sharp tug he snapped his sacred threads and threw them on the ground. 'That means nothing any more. I'm honoured to join the Kapalikas. I have . . .'

'Have you eaten meat before?'

'I . . .' the boy looked down at his feet briefly. 'No acharya, but I am ready. I'm ready to sacrifice animals and eat their flesh. Lord Shiva was . . .'

'Good,' Ugra cut him off. 'Do you chant slokas? Visit temples?'

'I used to, but that was in the past. I want to be a Kapalika, acharya. I'm a brahmachari and follow the principles of ahimsa, satya . . .'

Ugra raised his hand. 'Good.' He inspected the boy as if he were a cow at a cattle auction. 'All that is good.'

The other man was stout and balding. He constantly licked his lips nervously. He stood with his hands crossed in front of him as if ashamed of his pot belly. When Ugra walked up to him, he brought his palms together and then not knowing what to do, fell at his feet.

'Up,' Ugra said and then studied him. 'Meat and wine?'

'Yes acharya. I . . . I like meat.'

'Hmmm . . . Have you lived the last one year without stealing or accepting more than what you need for sustenance? It doesn't look like it.' Ugra lay his rough hands on the man's belly. 'This wouldn't be there if you were following my instructions.'

The man sucked in his stomach and then exhaled immediately. 'I will. I promise.'

'Hmmm . . .' Ugra fingered one of the scars on his face. Then he limped away. Behind him the burning corpse cracked and collapsed into the now dying embers. The crack sounded like a gunshot. Tony and Ranganathan flinched. Carefully Ugra bent forward and scooped a handful of ash. Then he smeared the ash all over the Brahmin boy's torso, who shivered and looked aghast.

'Don't worry,' Ugra said. 'We didn't kill her. She came dead from the medical college.' Now he proceeded to smear the ash on the fat man. 'Why so much loathing for the dead? Hmm?' He stared at his grey palms and smeared the remnants of the ashes on himself. 'Huh? The dead aren't with us any more. Only their form remains. If we don't use it for our practices, the worms, insects and birds will get to it. We must act out of our need to procure siddhis. Every corpse has potential. Only a fool would let one rot.'

Ugra made a tree stump appear underneath him. Both Tony and the Brahmin lad drew a sharp breath. Ranganathan whacked Tony. Tony cupped his face and watched from behind his fingers like a caged animal.

'When the great sage Shankaracharya,' Ugra said, bringing his palms together, 'was walking by here – not here, out there in the real world – many centuries ago, a Kapalika, like one of us, approached him.' He had everyone's attention. The two initiates, the priests, even the men inside the cavities of the skull knelt to listen. 'What did he ask the great man? He said, "I spent the last hundred years preparing myself with severe penances. And now I'm ready to go to Kailash and meet Lord Shiva with this body." Shankaracharya smiled and asked him why he had come to him to which the Kapalika replied, with deft logic I may add, "You've attained enlightenment and you have no use for your body. But if you offer your body to me, people will speak highly of you. To finish my practices, I need the skull of a king or an omniscient sage. The king, I have no chance of appropriating. Therefore, it is up to you. In offering your head, you will acquire wonderous fame and I'll acquire all the eight siddhis."

Ranganathan jabbed Tony and indicated towards a rock closer to the remains of the charred corpse. The duo stealthily inched forward, blending into the shadows in their dark clothes. The stench of burnt flesh slashed through the stationary air and choked them. Ranganathan muffled a cough with his handkerchief.

Ugra turned his face ever so slightly in their direction and a small smile formed on his lips. He stood up. 'You know what Shankaracharya did?' he thundered.

The Brahmin boy quivered and the stout man shook his head frantically. Ugra grinned. 'He offered his head.' He paced back and forth. 'He offered his head because the Kapalika was right. Shankaracharya had no need for his mortal shell. But just as the great sage was about to enter the state of samadhi and leave his body, his disciples got wind of it and arrived. They chased away the honourable Kapalika.'

Now Ugra limped up to the stout man and in a flash, produced a knife. The man started panicking. Ugra placed a hand on his shoulder. 'I was promised something and then denied it. Now, I plan on acquiring the skull of a sage. His daughter's ashes invigorated me for a good decade and helped me with this' – he swept his arms around – 'but there is more to be had. I intend to acquire all the siddhis as' – he placed the knife in the man's hands – 'as you should too.'

He gave a curt nod and the priests leapt and held the Brahmin boy by his arms. He was startled at first and then realization dawned on him. He began to scream and thrash about but was overpowered.

Ugra nudged the fat man. 'Bhairava is Shiva's most ferocious form and we worship nothing less. By sacrificing a man, you appease him for three thousand years.'

The man's eyes suddenly turned to steel and his breathing calmed. The Brahmin lad screamed louder. 'Badri! We're friends, da. Don't kill me.'

Badri approached his quarry. 'Jai Bhairava!' he said softly at first and then shouted it at the top of his lungs. The priests chanted after him. His lips curled into a snarl. His nostrils flared. He started convulsing and blathering. Ranganathan and Tony held their breaths as Badri plunged the knife under the lad's throat and slit it open.

The boy screeched in agony as warm spurts of thick blood drenched the priests, Ugra and Badri. He struggled, but the priests held on to him, each one linking his hand with the boy's. 'I curse you,' the terrified boy yelled and then blood dribbled from his mouth on to his scrawny chest. He strained against the strongs priests, his screams turning into gurgles.

Badri stood in front of his dying friend with soulless eyes, the promise of siddhis lulling him into a sense of delirium. After a while, the boy went limp like a puppet in the hands of the priests who gently laid him to the ground. Ugra pointed at the boy's head. 'The prana has left the body . . . through the anus. What a sorry way to go.' He took the knife from Badri's hands. 'This is your doing. This is your sin. The skull of this Brahmin is yours to bear for the rest of your life.'

Badri snapped back to reality. Panic began to spread on his face. 'Yes . . . yes, acharya. But the police . . .'

Ugra smacked his cheek with a resounding slap. Badri fell sideways and thudded on to the ground. Then he picked himself up and bowed to his teacher.

'You'll not kill again for another twelve years,' Ugra said. 'You'll now meditate on this corpse and perform the initiation puja. Afterwards, you'll leave this place and live as far from humanity as you can. You will only beg for your food and no more than three times a day. You will eat what you receive.'

'Yes, acharya,' Badri said, his palms together and head bent. His cheek had turned a bright red now.

'When the time is right, we will know. And we will seek you.' His voice dropped. 'We will seek you anyway.'

Tony pulled out his phone, typed on it furiously and then showed the screen to Ranganathan. The latter frowned and then read the contents:

Police?

He took the phone from Tony and then typed a response:

Turn off phone.

Now the drummers slung their drums around their torsos. The trumpeters picked up their massive instruments and then the musicians banged and blew into the night, culminating the sacrifice. The people in the skull slunk away like vapid thoughts leaving one's head. They exited through a door at the back of the skull, after which the skull sealed itself, as if the doorway had never existed.

16

One by one Ugra's men walked to the dead Brahmin boy, touched his feet and then walked to the charred corpse under the large banyan. They scooped a handful of ash and smeared it on themselves, revelling in the powdery ash like elephants in a mud pond. The tree began to shake violently as if it was being buffeted in a storm. The wind howled and raced through the leaves sending them flying everywhere. The pyre, however, continued to burn steadily, sizzling and crackling under the tempest. The black creatures took flight and disappeared into the night. And then, just as suddenly as the storm had started, it died.

A man appeared under the tree. At first he was translucent. Tony and Ranganathan could see the other priests right through him. Within seconds he was fully formed. His beard was matted, his hair tied up in a big beehive, his eyes rolled up, revealing his whites. His face was covered with dark grey ash. His bared teeth made him look like a rabid wild animal. His gaze was skyward, and his lips moved wordlessly. He stood on one leg with the other across his other knee. He clutched a chequered handkerchief with both his hands.

Tony cupped his mouth at that. 'Vikram,' he mouthed silently and mimed a handkerchief. Ranganathan glared and shushed him.

One by one the priests prostrated in front of the standing yogi and then sat down in a circle around him. After chatting with each other for a bit, the men closed their eyes and dipped their heads back slightly as if bathing in an invisible shower.

Ranganathan slowly crouched and then stood up. Ugra and the new initiate sat next to the fresh corpse, talking. Spotting an opening, Ranganathan and Tony duckwalked towards the skull, taking care to stay in the shadows. In front of them, Ranganathan spotted a door in the skull rock. It was shut, with no handle. There was no way to open the door. He pointed at the door and nudged Tony, who studied it carefully. His face went through a series of expressions before his eyes widened. He pulled his phone out and typed:

Can only be opened from inside

Ranganathan pinched his chin and scanned the area. The priests were a good distance away, meditating around the yogi, who sat in the middle, his eyes open. Ugra was near the right cheek of the skull, sitting atop the corpse of the Brahmin boy, his eyes clenched shut. He had lit a camphor fire inside the mouth of the corpse and was offering drops of beer from a Kingfisher bottle. Badri sat at the head of the corpse, his eyes shut and hands on his lap, fingers making an okay gesture.

Ranganathan tapped Tony and shot out from behind the rocks. Tony followed and they stood near where the men had exited the skull. They noticed a thin crack that formed the outline of the door. Both traced their fingers along this hairline crack, looking for an entry point or a secret button that would reveal the contents of the skull to them. Tony tried to pry it open with his fingers, but they kept slipping. He finally shook his head in resignation. Something caught his eye now: letters along the arch on top of the door. They were chiselled into the rock and had accumulated grime and dirt to the point where they were illegible.

'It's Sanskrit,' Ranganathan whispered. He glanced around furtively. A sense of excitement coursed through him. This was his element. 'The words above are in Sanskrit, but I can't make out all of them.'

Tony looked up at the words and traced his fingers along them. 'I can trace the shapes with my finger and draw them on the ground. Maybe you can guess them?'

Ranganathan shook his head. 'It'll take too long. And we may attract attention.'

Now they heard jackals howling and loud cackling. The duo ducked instantly and peered from behind the skull. Badri's torso was bent backwards and convulsing. He muttered incomprehensibly and laughed at random. Ugra sat on the corpse and offered small strips of meat to the camphor fire that still burnt inside the boy's mouth.

'I have an idea,' Tony said and reached for his phone. He took a step back and took a picture of the words. Tapping and pinching his screen, he worked on the image for a few seconds and then smiled. He showed the screen to Ranganathan whose face lit up. The image only had blues and blacks, but the letters were clearly visible:

अत्रि: शिवौच कौमोदकीगद

He stared at them, his mind running like a bird through a forest, dodging and turning, pulling words from deep memory and trying to make sense of them.

After a few moments he pursed his lips. 'It's garbage. I can't make sense of it.'

Tony looked at both sides and then said, 'Garbage? They wouldn't chisel garbage into such an awesome structure. The skull is a work of art. The words must have a meaning.'

Ranganathan nodded. 'But . . .' He studied the text again. 'It says Atri spoke to Shiva: O wielder of mace, Kaumodaki.'

'What? What is Kaumodaki?'

'It's not a what. It's a he, and yeah . . . I told you. It doesn't make sense.'

Tony crept forward and looked around the cheek of the skull. The mouth of the skull was about twenty feet high. If he could figure a way to climb up the side of the chin, and then hop into the mouth, he could reach the doorway from the inside. He tested the stone but found it to be too smooth. If he slipped, he would draw attention.

Tony tried to think of options, but nothing manifested in his head. They couldn't drill their way into it. He couldn't climb up the chin and enter through the jaw. He wondered how the men had gotten up on top. The surface was so smooth that any misstep was certain fall from the top. He glanced at the professor who was studying his phone intently, his brows knitted. He sighed and knocked the side of his head. 'Think, Tony,' he told himself.

Minutes ticked by. The duo agonized over their situation. Ranganathan turned the phone upside down and found that to be useless. He asked Tony to reverse and mirror the text, but even that proved futile. Tony tried to think if he could use fire to somehow cause the crack to widen, but he drew a blank. He slunk back to Ranganathan, dejected. 'It's like a cryptic clue . . . those words,' he said absently.

'What?' Ranganathan asked, looking up, and then an idea formed in his head and washed all over his face. 'What did you say?'

Tony crouched down. 'I said those words are like a cryptic clue. Meaningless at first, but may contain a hidden . . .'

'That's it! Contain!' Ranganathan hissed. He reread the words and then snapped his fingers. 'It does *contain* something. If you pull out *truh . . . shiva . . . gadh*, it means . . .' Unable to contain his excitement, he took a deep calming breath.

'What?' Tony asked and got hushed for the interruption.

Ranganathan tiptoed to the door and said, 'Shiva. Shiva. Shiva.'

A blue light ran along the perimeter of the door. The Sanskrit words pulsed in gold like a child's plaything and with a whisper, the door faded away, revealing a set of stairs. Ranganathan looked around again. The two groups of people were still lost in their trance. He slipped into the skull with Tony in tow.

The stairs inside the skull were made of stone. Imprinted on each step were countless symbols, some familiar – like the swastika – but many others were alien squiggles. The narrow stairway was lit with flickering candles. The air was thick in the narrow passageway and it was hard to breathe. It smelled heavily of fat-based votives. More geometric symbols – nested triangles and fractals – adorned the walls, no doubt chiselled by the same skilled stonemasons that hewed the giant skull out of rock.

Now they reached the first level – the jaws. A dull *aah* sound permeated the entire jaw, cocooning the two. Their breathing slowed down and with each breath, they felt a buzzing sensation at the base of their spine. Tony closed his eyes and started to sway. Ranganathan shook him by his shoulders. 'Don't lose focus,' he whispered.

The ceiling was jagged like the roof of a mouth, made of uncut stone and plastered. Standing on what would have been the tongue, had the skull belonged to a flesh-and-blood human, Ranganathan and Tony looked out from the head. The sight was almost prehistoric, with large banyan groves dotting the landscape as far as the eye could see. There was no sign of city life or even civilization in general. No lamp posts, wires, or roads. The sky was clear and littered with stars. Meteors zipped by connecting the stellar dots. There were no lazy airplanes leaving contrails in their wake. It was unnaturally quiet, save the occasional caw of a crow, and chilly.

Tony inched towards the massive incisors. Gingerly holding on to one of them, he leaned out of the skull. On the left were the group of priests meditating around the yogi who held Vikram's handkerchief. On the right was Ugra on the corpse, slicing a piece of flesh from Badri's forearm, who bit into a piece of cloth. Ugra was giving Badri orders, barely audible. The mouth of the skull was spartan. Two torches lit near the back of the mouth. A well-used leopard skin lay on the floor, its hide mottled with splotches of dried blood. A low wooden table with an indentation down its middle sat in the middle of the room. A channel was cut into the floor and it led to the teeth from the edge of the table. Ranganathan knelt down to sniff it and immediately gagged.

'Blood,' he whispered. 'They sacrifice their victims here and let the blood drain out.'

Tony nodded solemnly. 'Where's the conch?' he asked, looking around.

'Must be higher. Come on.'

They crept to the back of the mouth and spotted an opening which led to another flight of curved stairs. The steps were fewer and took them to a small cavity. Ranganathan and Tony felt woozy. The air smelled bilious and heady. Holding his nose, Ranganathan poked his head into the nasal cavity of the skull. This space with was filled with hypnotic *oo* sound that slowly rose and fell like a wave.

Barring a couple of antelope skins and trumpets leaning against the wall, there was nothing there. The space was tiny and they were already near the edge. They could see outside. 'Stay back,' Ranganathan wheezed. 'It's dangerously narrow.'

Tony stepped back and thrust a finger upwards. They stepped back into the staircase and climbed towards the cranium.

The flickering torches cast oblong shadows that danced their way around the hollow interiors. The space smelled heavily of a nauseating mixture of something metallic and fatty. Now they noticed the dome of the structure and near the top, a couple of doors. Tony began to heave. He put his hand out and leaned against the cold wall. His palm pushed through the wall as if it were velvet.

'Can't,' he gasped. 'Can't think straight.'

Ranganathan looked at the boy with concern. A person who had not practised yoga or taken proper care of his body was bound to be affected by such intense energetic creations, especially those of a crazed, bloodthirsty tantric. He shifted the bag on his shoulder and looked up. 'The conch must be in there,' he said. 'I'll get it and we can escape from here.'

Tony slid down and sat against the wall. His eyes had turned red and his face was sallow. Ranganathan took Tony's palms and brought them together. 'Anjali mudra.'

Tony looked at him with half-open eyes. 'Huh?'

'Keep your palms together and press against your chest just below your ribcage.' Tony weakly complied. Ranganathan patted him on his cheek. 'Hang in there.' And like a medic on a battlefield he instructed him, 'Apply pressure. I'll be back.'

He tried to race up the steps, but by the time he reached the top he too began to feel dizzy. One of the doorways had a red curtain with golden symbols on it. The other led to the eye sockets where a shrill *mm* sound filled the space and from which all he saw was infinite blackness of Ugra's fabricated night. A translucent dragon-like creature hovered in the distance over the trees. With each breath Ranganathan saw it fly towards him with languid flaps of its cavernous wings. He pressed the sides of his head with his thumbs and placed his fingers on his nose. He exhaled slowly, sucked his stomach in, clenched his sphincter and looked down. His chest began to hurt, but he held on.

The pain turned into a spongy blackness that beat against his ribs, the sound drilling into his head. He wanted to open his mouth and gulp in some air. In his mind's eye he could see the dragon in front of the skull, extending its proboscis-like tongue into the eye sockets like a macabre butterfly sucking out nectar. Just as he felt his hair rise, he released his fingers first, inhaled and relaxed his abdomen. The blackness from his heart emerged like a resplendent lotus and wrapped around him. The dragon dissipated into vapour and wafted away, leaving him disoriented.

Tears streamed down his face as he re-experienced past memories. His muscles began to quiver. His mouth dried up and his tongue turned sticky. A great lethargy began to overcome him. He was desperate for a five-minute power nap, after which he could gather enough courage to enter the cranium. But he knew that if he succumbed, he would not leave the skull alive.

He sat down on the crude cut step, folded his legs underneath him so that his left heel dug into his perineum. He kept the yantra beside him, placed his palms one on top of the other and closed his eyes. Fighting the urge to pass out, he gently recited the mantra that Chaturvasi had whispered into his ears many years ago. He repeated it until he began to feel his breath steadying. Now he applied pressure with his thumb to his right nostril and breathed in slowly and deeply and then exhaled through the other. He switched nostrils and repeated the process until his breathing was under control.

As his mind and body unglued themselves, he felt the physical discomfort lessen and dissipate. He imagined himself from an outside perspective, sitting on a step inside the hollow of a large skull amidst a banyan forest. He slowly added clarity and details – the coolness of the walls, the woolly mats on each step, the smell of the passageway – to this mental map and zoomed in until he was inside his head.

Now he imagined a great waterfall of pure white light pouring from above and engulfing him like a towering wave crashing around a lighthouse and cloaking him in a comforting sheath. The light found its way through every pore and into every cell of his body. For a moment he felt detached and weightless. He snapped his eyes open and leapt up.

Reinvigorated and in command of his breath and thoughts, he moved the curtain aside and entered the cranium.

It was a small space covered in thin golden sheets. When Ranganathan hesitantly touched the walls purple ripples ran all along the walls and the curved roof. Idols slowly emerged from them which Ranganathan guessed were the various avatars of Shiva – Bhairava, Rudra, Pashupati. As he stared at one of them – the form of Kala Bhairava – its features began to form. Eyes appeared, a nose formed, and when he leaned in closer, a moustache started to sprout atop its lips.

Even in the absence of light everything was visible. The texture of the wall was so inviting that he placed his palm on it again, but the sight of the gods forming unnerved him. He had the inexplicable urge to strip naked and lie against the wall and let it absorb him, but then he saw the conch perched on a pillow like an emperor in court, and his eyes welled up.

'The conch,' Chaturvasi had told him, 'is not from the sea. Ugra has mastery over fire, earth, water and akash, but he has yet to achieve dominion over the wind. You will find the place windless and still. Eerily still.'

'He has constructed a paradise for himself,' Chaturvasi said. 'It cannot be detected by regular folks and access to it can only be given from the inside.'

'Then how . . .'

Chaturvasi raised his hand. 'It will work out. Now, in his bubble, he has had all the time to prepare. Time does not even make much sense in there. So be careful of any distractions. Every minute could be hours out there.'

'I see,' Ranganathan said, feeling the first pangs of anxiety.

Chaturvasi paced his office and stopped at a photograph of Shruti. It was a black-and-white photo. In it she was beaming, sitting on a tricycle. His wife was bending down next to her, her arms around her daughter, and also smiling. 'What is death, Ranga?'

'Death?' The question came out of nowhere and froze his tongue.

'Death, Ranga, is simply the earth calling in the loan she gave us over our lifetimes. Every atom of your body is gotten from the food you eat, and that came from the earth. When it's time to go, she takes it all back, yes?'

'Yes.'

'Atom for atom, she'll take it, but the soul must go on . . . onwards to its next state where it waits. But between the going and the waiting is the most critical aspect of death

– the point of exit from the mortal shell. For most people, it exits through the anus like a silent fart,' he said with a straight face. 'There are some who are lucky, and the soul may leave from one of the lower chakras – anahata, manipura, or svadhishthana. It is only those who have practised yoga and have full mastery over the chakras that can shepherd the exiting soul through the higher three chakras.' He paced back to his daughter's photo and picked it up. 'Keep up your practices, Ranga. You may be able to control your final few moments.' He chuckled and replaced the photo. 'What Ugra does is that when he sacrifices victims for himself, he performs a ritual and forces the soul to leave through the top of the skull – the sahasrara.'

'But doesn't that result in samadhi?'

'Samadhi is when one channels the kundalini all the way to the sahasrara and out of one's body at will. He will simply keel over and die. It is the most desirable death there is. This is something else. It's like amputating an arm when you have a bruise on it. Sure, it fixed the bruise, but did it really?'

'I see.'

'But when the soul is exiting, he decapitates the person at the precise moment and performs a ritual to trap it in the skull permanently. After many days of . . . practices, he . . .'

'Like what?'

Chaturvasi sighed. 'The building blocks of life are present in the fluids . . . uh . . . emitted and secreted by men and women.'

'I understand that.'

'Ugra indulges in practices in which he collects these fluids and smears them on top of the skull while meditating on the corpse.'

Ranganathan squirmed and made a face.

'I know. You see, even after death there is life. The gross bodily functions may have ceased, and decomposition is under way, but there is still life. And by providing the secretions from the genital organs, he entices the prana to stay rooted to its mortal shell, instead of carrying onwards. After years of diligent rituals, he manages to squeeze the soul into a tiny patch right at the dome of the skull which he breaks off carefully. He has done this for countless years to countless victims, taking a piece of their skull with their souls trapped.'

'And what has he done with all' – Understanding dawned on Ranganathan. 'He has amalgamated them into the shape of a conch. But why conch? Oh! Because it produces the right frequency of sound to resonate with the human body and because it's from human source it's extra powerful and the trapped souls! Oh! They probably do his bidding each time he blows it.' He stood up and then sat down immediately. 'Is he that powerful? How come he has never used that conch? He can achievc whatever he wants.'

Chaturvasi shook his head. 'The material trappings of mankind are useless for yogis. He is out for absolute power . . . dominion over all the elements and the attainment of the eight siddhis. With that he can do more than grab land or rule over people. And he needs just one more skull to perfect the conch.'

'Why the boy?' Ranganathan asked, standing up. 'Why should Tony go with me? It's too dangerous.'

'It is, but he is an umbilical link to Vikram. There are only four things one has in one's control, Ranga: body, mind, emotions and energies. Vikram's mind, body and energies are not in his control any more. Only his emotions remain. When he sees his mother, he does emote, but his body cannot respond. Same thing with Tony. He's his best friend, and his being does want to respond on seeing him, but he cannot act on it. That emotional bond is needed for this mission to work.'

Now Ranganathan pushed himself off the wall and zeroed in on the conch. It didn't look any different from the dozens being sold at Marina Beach's souvenir stands. It had bony spikes and was small enough to fit in one's hand. The surface curved gently, narrowing into a pointed tip. Faint sounds of *am . . . hrim . . . krom* reverberated in the room in an endless loop. Before any more thoughts could distract him, Ranganathan took a deep breath and walked towards the conch.

As per Chaturvasi's instructions, he exhaled until his lungs had wrung empty, then placed his right ring finger on the yantra inside the bag. It was so hot that he wanted to yank his finger out. Cautiously he picked up the conch in his other hand. Instantly his head was assailed by the tormented moans of the lost souls, the final sounds of the departed just before they met their end. Each sound was haunting and he felt a powerful need to listen to them all. His lungs, now burning, reminded him to put the conch in the bag and finally inhale.

The conch began to rattle against the yantra inside the bag. He chanted a mantra meant to be recited during last rites to soothe the spirit and guide it towards the afterworld. A few seconds later, the cranium resonated with his words as the echoes slid off the golden interior and bounced around. While the conch had settled down, he began to worry that the sound might attract attention.

As he exited the cranium with his back to the doorway, a thought blossomed in his head: stealing the conch was too easy. It shouldn't have been this easy to sneak up into a magical island, slip into the skull unnoticed, figure out the magical words to enter it and find the conch. Something didn't add up here, but then he saw Tony slumped by the wall, his palms joined together, his head lolling to one side, looking like a beggar outside a temple on a sweltering day. He ran down to him and shook him. 'Tony,' he whispered. The words of his mantra hummed from the cranium like a song from a distant radio on a calm night. 'Tony,' he said, looking about urgently. 'Get up! Let's get out of here.'

Tony opened his eyes with great difficulty and tapped his head. 'So many words,' he mumbled.

'I know. I know. Come.' Ranganathan slung Tony's arm around his shoulders and hoisted him up. 'You'll be fine once we get out of here.'

They slowly made their way down the cranium. Ranganathan's heart thumped against his chest. All they had to do was slip out the way they had entered, make it to the boat and then head home safely. Tony clasped his shoulder tightly. The boy seemed a little more in his senses now, but he was still breathing hard. When they were passing the nasal cavity, Tony gestured to stop and pointed at his nose.

'Okay,' Ranganathan said. 'Quick break.' The conch was still quiet and he wondered if there was an interplay between it and the yantra, a sort of chemical reaction between the two. He wondered if the best of Chaturvasi was battling the best of Ugra in some proxy battle inside his cloth handbag.

Tony limped to the small nasal cavity. Three steps and he would fall to his death. He leaned against the wall and crouched by one of the trumpets, colour slowly returning to his face. The banyan forest stood silently in the foreground. The group of priests were still lost in their meditation. Badri was now sitting on the corpse with Ugra next to him, his thumb on Badri's forehead. Ranganathan looked at Tony anxiously. He was breathing heavily, his hands on his head. Perhaps it had been a mistake to bring him along, but his quick thinking had already gotten them further along than he would have on his own.

As he evaluated their next actions, two things happened simultaneously. Lightning ripped the dark sky into fragments of blinding white from which a large shadow emerged and swam above like a lazy leviathan in a still pond. And then Tony's alarm went off.

The priests flashed their eyes open at once and pointed at the skull. Their group dissolved into a flurry of activity as they ran helter-skelter, picking up weapons. Ugra looked up with the rage of a man who had been jolted out of a deep slumber. He pointed his trident at them and yelled, 'Catch them!' With ease he sailed up from the corpse and alighted in the mouth cavity of the skull.

Ranganathan grabbed Tony and tried to run, but the moment he heard footsteps coming up the stairs, he collapsed on to the hard floor.

17

It had been a couple of days now since Chaturvasi had installed the strange Christian boy named Chris at Vikram's door. The incident with the lemon had convinced Parvati beyond doubt that a black magician somewhere had decided to wreak havoc on her son's life. Gopal and Arun had gone to Mangadu to procure the items Chaturvasi had ordered. He had promised to return as soon as he could, but she felt terrified being alone in the house.

Her father-in-law had shifted to Arun's house in Kodambakkam so that he could recuperate from his stroke away from the turmoil. Before begrudgingly leaving in an auto, the old man told her, 'When Vikram comes, no, ask him to bring bajjis.'

She asked Shanta, the maid, to take a week off. 'Boy has exams. Best not to disturb,' she said to the befuddled maid who had always swept and cleaned the house through exams, tests, group studies and homework sessions. When a tormented screech exploded from Vikram's room, Parvati shut the main door on her and asked her to return in ten days. 'One week or ten days, ma?' Shanta asked, but she was met with the sound of the door being locked.

'Amma!' Vikram howled.

She rushed to the room. Chris sat outside, not having budged even an inch the past two days. Frankincense cones burnt around him, shrouding him in a blanket of thick aromatic smoke. His hair was a white wig now. Even the hair on his eyebrows and eyelashes was milk-white. His skin had turned wrinkly and was sagging. The vibhuti that adorned his forehead had turned into something resembling lamp black. But for his posture and having seen how he looked a couple of days ago, she would have written him off as her father-in-law's early morning walking buddy. Something rapped on the door from inside Vikram's room. It was urgent and insistent, like a human-sized woodpecker trying to drill through it. Then there was silence, followed by hissing.

'Ammaaaa . . .' The feral wail sounded like Vikram, but did not feel like him. 'Please let me out, amma.' The voice began to crystallize into a human sound. 'Amma?'

'Vikram? Vikky?' Parvati whispered, eyes welling up. She stood by the door and placed a hesitant palm on it. It was thrumming like the surface of a speaker, raising goosebumps along her arm.

'Amma,' Vikram begged. 'Please, ma. Let me out. All kinds of things are happening to me. My head is hurting. And I'm so hungry.'

Parvati sat down next to Chris and stared at him in confusion. He was lost in a trance. His eyes were almost glued shut, but behind his white lashes she noticed his eyeballs darting about. He was so still, she thought he had died and petrified on the spot.

'Swami . . .' she stammered, unsure what to call him. 'Chris?'

There was no reaction. Chris sat unmoved, a rock in a tempestuous sea. The air around him crackled and buzzed, making Parvati's hair stand. She flattened it down and extended her arm towards his shoulder but stopped midway.

'Amma,' Vikram said. 'Don't listen to anyone, ma. I am fine. I just want to eat tasty food and study for my exams.'

Maybe her son was back. Maybe whatever had possessed him had taken flight after Chaturvasi had taken away the lemon from their yard. Just like any medicine, there was a time after which its effect could be felt. She was starting to get buoyed by her theory.

'Amma, I want upma and coffee,' Vikram said, his voice cheery.

'I'll get, kanna,' Parvati said, wiping her tears with her sari. 'But . . .'

'Just open the door, and I can come out. I haven't seen you in so many days. How's appa? Thatha? I forgot to get him bajjis last time. He must have been so upset. Let me go to Murugan's Bajji Palace.'

Weeping, Parvati tentatively took a step forward and placed her hand on the doorknob. She turned towards Chris guiltily. He still sat ramrod straight, his hands on his lap, his fingers folded into strange positions like someone suffering from rheumatoid arthritis. She twisted the knob. But when she tried to open it, she felt a massive resistance, as if something mighty was pulling the door towards her.

Had she paid attention she would have noticed the symbols painted along the door turning black.

'Push harder, ma,' Vikram instructed.

The phone rang somewhere in the background, but she barely heard it. She tried to force it open, using her entire body weight, but even with the lock undone, the door wouldn't open. It moved a bit but snapped right back.

'Vikky, I can't open, kanna.' She wrung her hands and then gently tapped Chris. Getting no response, she shook him. Then she went to the door and spoke into it. 'Are you pushing from inside? I can't open it.'

There was another loud rapping on the other side of the door. And a gnarly hiss. 'Just break it down,' Vikram roared. Parvati jumped back, almost tripping over Chris. 'Sorry, ma,' Vikram said, his voice cheery again. 'Go to the veranda and bring the toolkit appa keeps near the shoe rack. There are some screwdrivers in that.'

'Why?'

'Because . . . because you can remove the screws from the hinge and then it'll be easy.'

She gaped at the door that was cajoling her in her son's voice. A part of her thought that something was still wrong on the other side, and this was affirmed when she saw the white-haired young Chris. But something deeper in her yearned to see Vikram once more and to make sure that he was all right. She brought the screwdrivers.

'I don't know which one,' she said, staring at the tools. She had never handled a screwdriver in her life, the only tools she was adept with being the ones in the kitchen.

'Look at the screws, ma,' Vikram said in annoyance. 'Does it look like a plus sign or a minus sign.'

Parvati studied the screws and said, 'Plus.'

'Then look for a screwdriver with the tip that looks like a plus.'

She found the right tool and tried unscrewing. At first it wouldn't move, but after some effort she managed to remove all the screws in the bottom hinge. She couldn't reach the top hinge and could remove only one screw.

'I can't reach the top, Vikky,' she said apologetically.

'It's okay, ma,' Vikram said. 'Just try to open the door now. I can't wait to eat the upma.'

She placed the screwdriver down and tried to open the door again. It swung open a little but quickly slammed shut as if a giant magnet was pulling it.

'Harder, ma,' Vikram said. 'I'll also pull from my side.'

Parvati once again put her body weight against the door and pushed. The top hinge began to splinter the wood. The door wobbled a few times.

'It's breaking, ma,' Vikram said with a cackle. 'Keep pushing.'

She continued ramming the door with her shoulder until there was a loud crack. The hinge gave way as she felt an enormous force ripping the door apart from the inside. Unable to hold on to it any more, she let go, and suddenly there was a deafening crash as a windowpane shattered. Now she felt a hand on her shoulder. It lifted her and flung her aside like a tennis ball.

Parvati recovered from her shock and opened her eyes. Everything was a blur. She blinked rapidly, trying to focus on what had happened. Vikram's door was smashed. Chris lay curled on the floor in a fetal position, a line of blood trickling from his nose. She sat up in haste.

'Vikky,' she bleated.

The being that wore Vikram as its shell stood there, naked. His muscles were ripped and the hair along his shoulders and chest had grown out even more. His jaw pulsed as he ground and bared his teeth. Saliva leaked from the edge of his lips and hung in threads. He looked more like a werewolf about to shed its human skin.

It threw its head back, stuck its black tongue out and screeched. The sound was so inhuman it couldn't have found a home in a zoo with the wildest of animals. Parvati covered her ears. Tears burst out of her eyes and streamed down her face. She prayed for her husband to return, but she knew Gopal couldn't do anything in this situation. This was out of the realm of humans. She turned her prayers to Chaturvasi.

And Chaturvasi was already there.

He didn't see the point of prayers, for they never worked. If only people knew that their Creator and his creation – them – were the same, they wouldn't direct their prayers outwards, but inwards.

As he sat on the northeast corner of his terrace, cloaked in a linen veshti, tunnelling through hidden recesses in the fabric of reality, he felt a strong tug from the silvery gossamer that connected him to Chris. By simply paying attention to the vibrations on that thread he understood what had happened – the distraught mother had caved in and tried to break down the portal to help her son. And in the process she had disturbed the carefully drawn symbols around the wall and encroached into Chris's energetic space.

Having grasped the severity of the situation, he knew what he had to do.

~

The form that Chaturvasi had painstakingly cultivated over the decades, feeding it his energy, performing the due rituals to keep its system whirring, was meant to be unleashed as his protector during the exorcism. Ugra's conch, if Ranganathan and Tony had succeeded in acquiring it, would unleash havoc, and his form was to be his vanguard, his most powerful weapon to take on the full brunt of Ugra's occult magic.

The exorcism, while dangerous, was still within his purview. It would happen on his terms. He would choose the place and consecrate it, and pick a time to maximize his power. But all that would be pointless if Vikram escaped from his room. Once outside its confines, he could tear apart the charms and amulets he had been festooned with and let loose the evil hiding in him.

The form had to be deployed now.

His breaths became increasingly shallow and rapid, until he was breathing from just the tip of his nostrils. Now he sounded like a well-oiled piston cranking away in a machine, the tremors in his belly the only indication that he was alive. At one point it didn't look like he was breathing at all and soon the air around him started glowing. The veshti burst into flames and turned to ash. The whitewashed walls of the terrace blistered and grew hot. Crows erupted from nearby coconut trees in a raucous frenzy and scattered into the sky. Dogs howled in the distance.

In all this pandemonium life in the city went on, for its denizens were not aware of the hidden dimensions.

Now there was a sudden stillness. There was no sound, but a palpable tension in the space. A trained eye would have seen a lithe human shape gracefully ascend to its full height in front of Chaturvasi. A moment later its limbs formed and its head bore crude facial features. Although human in appearance, it was created out of energy and imbued with intelligence. It was his energetic clone sans a physical body that endowed it with superhuman capabilities. Without a body, it was unencumbered by time and space, able to materialize anywhere it needed to be to discharge its duties. This form was divine, a god. It brought its palms together before its creator and then it was gone.

Chris opened his eyes and drew a deep breath. When he stood up, his joints hurt. Then he took in the carnage in front of him. Parvati lay squealing by the wall, blood streaking down her forehead. He closed his eyes for a moment and understood what had happened. Inside the room, Vikram paced like a caged animal. He bared his teeth and tried to dash out but bounced off the doorway.

'Let me out,' he screamed. He leapt on to the wall like

a giant lizard and turned his head at an impossible angle. His tongue rolled out, thick saliva dribbling from his open maw. The room stank. What Parvati could not see was the god guarding the doorway like a fortress wall, thick and impregnable, filling up the entire space.

Chris lay down on the floor and joined his index fingers and thumbs in a triangle. He placed the triangle in front of the god and then placed his forehead into it, touching the floor. Seconds later, he felt his life force return and his energies rev up. Careful not to draw too much, he stood up.

'Where is the vibhuti?' he asked Parvati.

She pointed to the kitchen.

'Camphor?'

Parvati nodded and continued to point.

Chris entered Vikram's room with the container of vibhuti and a steel cup filled with water. He emptied the vibhuti into the water. His pulse reduced to a flutter. Vikram leapt to another wall, taking a swipe at him, which Chris dodged. Now he flicked droplets of water on Vikram. The boy broke into a feral scream. He pounced from the wall but something arrested him mid-air, his head thrown back, back bent, arms and legs dangling as if he was ascending towards heaven. Chris chanted mantras and sprinkled water. Vikram slowly descended, groaning and writhing. When he landed on the floor he spasmed as if he was having a seizure. With his gaze pinned on Vikram, Chris shouted, 'Arun! Gopal! Help me with the boy.'

The two men had entered the house moments ago and were mute spectators of the circus in Vikram's room. Gopal pulled Arun into the room, and both shuddered as they crossed the threshold, feeling an icy chill run up and down their spines. They stopped, turned and looked at the doorway but saw nothing.

'Quick!' Chris barked. 'Arun, find some coir. Gopal, carry him to the bed.' The men jumped into action. Chris looked down at Vikram and placed his hand on the boy's forehead. A massive resistance coursed through his body. He felt the god rapidly depleting itself as it kept the vetal at bay. 'We don't have much time.'

18

Ugra stood with his eyes closed, wielding his trident in one hand and the other resting on his hip. He had goaded Ranganathan and Tony down to the centre of the mouth cavity. He stood by the teeth, like an angry god defending his domain.

Behind them, a few priests stood in silence, holding sickles and spears, breathing in unison, their eyes glowering with equal parts hate and confusion. The rest were outside, craning their necks up, wondering how the intruders, one of whom looked too young to be a tantric practitioner, managed to not only discover their utopian island but also sneak into their hallowed skull temple and get their hands on the sacred conch. The very thought of that sequence of actions boggled their minds. They had heard of the legendary Chaturvasi whose perfect skull their master Ugra was after, but they were not aware that his disciples were as crafty as the old coot.

Ugra bowed his head and twirled the trident. Now he sneered and slowly lifted his head. The bones in his neck cracked softly. Ranganathan got a closer look at the Kapalika. Ugra was the embodiment of the coarseness of existence. His skin was rough and mottled with scars. He wore a leather loincloth. The hair on his body was thick and wiry. It snaked up his torso like a parasitic vine and thrust out from his face into an unruly shrub of a beard, matted and flecked with blood. His eyes were red, redder than those of the drunks he found lying on the footpath with cheap rum bottles in their hands and filthy words in their mouths.

Whereas Chaturvasi drew people towards him with an inexplicable magnetism, Ugra drew Ranganathan with a certain potency that was at once repulsive. Ranganathan didn't want to look at Ugra's grotesque face, but he couldn't stop staring. Ugra's eyes were closed, but he appeared to be studying the two intently. He glanced at Tony who seemed just as ensnared by Ugra's presence.

One of the priests stepped forward. 'Acharya Ugra! Let me kill them with my bare hands.'

Ugra turned his head without opening his eyes and slapped the priest. 'Fool! Do you mean to tell me what I must do?'

The man hung his head and stood still.

Ugra stepped forward, the trident clinking against the stone floor. Ranganathan and Tony shrank back. They had nowhere to go. Ugra took another step and the duo smelt him. He reeked of death and putrefaction. Tony gagged and covered his nose with his palm. One of the priests growled. Ugra raised his hand. 'It's been a while since our last sacrifice,' he said. Many years. And some of you have forgotten the finer aspects of death.'

There was a murmur amongst the priests. Ranganathan reached for Tony's hand.

Stroking his beard, Ugra said, 'There are five dimensions to the prana.' He held up all the fingers of his left hand. 'Prana vayu. Samanavayu. Apana. Udhana. And Vyana. Prana vayu is responsible for the sensation of touch, thought process and mainly breathing. When someone dies' – he pointed the trident in the direction of the corpse – 'his breath stops instantly, but the prana vayu takes up to one and a half hours to leave the mortal shell. It is during this time that we consecrate the corpse and trap the other four vayus so that we can harness their energies to our benefit.'

He walked towards Ranganathan and then cackled. His laughter rang through the skull and echoed from the banyan forest. 'Why am I telling you my secrets, you must be wondering.' He tapped Ranganathan's head with the end of his trident. 'Your skull is in my skull now. And it's a good one. A Brahmin one. Cultured and cultivated. Sown and vibrant with the sounds of the Vedas and Upanishads. The body that was the nourishment for the skull has been kept in good shape. No meat. No wine.' He lowered his voice. 'No women.' Ranganathan, despite the situation, turned a shade of red. He held on to his bag tightly, feeling the metal of the yantra bite into his palm, hoping Chaturvasi had a plan for them now. In a flash, Ugra slapped Ranganathan across his cheek. The professor shrieked and covered the stinging cheek with his hand.

'Idiot,' Ugra said. 'You're an idiot. Just like your teacher, Chaturvasi. You think I didn't know of your arrival?'

Tony cowered behind Ranganathan, squeezing his hand harder. 'You think,' Ugra continued, 'I didn't know you were in my presence? Tell me, great disciple of Vasi, what is the first aspect of yoga? Since you right-handers seem so prim and prissy about following rules. Tell me, hmm?'

He raised his hand again when Ranganathan spat, 'Yama.'

'And then?'

'Niyama.'

Ugra limped to the back of the jaw. 'And what is the most important rule in them?'

'To . . . be truthful.'

Ugra scratched his calf with the tip of his trident. 'Be truthful. Good. Your teacher has taught you well.' He slammed the metal rod on the floor. 'As have I. How can I not practice something that I preach to my disciples? I must be truthful, yes or no?'

Yes,' Tony squeaked, but Ugra ignored him.

'To kill you, I must have a reason. If I don't, I'll accrue bad karma.' Ugra shrugged. 'Those are the laws of karma. And it'd take me decades to work it out from my system. No. No. No. I cannot afford that at this stage. I'm so close to my goal. I must kill you if you have broken the rules. Fair is fair.'

And then it condensed in Ranganathan's head: Ugra had allowed them into his island, let them sneak into the skull. He had fabricated a clue that would take both to decode so that they were both culpable in the act of breaking in and stealing the skull.

'You started the train,' Ranganathan said. 'You desecrated Shruti's body . . . right at her passing.' He leaned forward, his breathing rapid. 'She was a child. You beheaded a child.'

'I was promised a skull by Shankaracharya,' Ugra calmly said, staring down Ranganathan. 'Once . . .'

'You were that Kapalika? That was . . . hundreds of . . .'

Ugra brushed him off. 'Time means nothing to one who has mastery over it. Once a word is given, it must be honoured. That is the law of karma. Chaturvasi's current form has the karmic baggage from Shankaracharya. He owes it to me.' He tapped Ranganathan's head with his trident again. 'This skull is useful to us. Yes!' He sounded like a chef getting excited over a fresh ingredient. 'It'll add to the potency before the final piece is set into it.' The priests muttered among themselves.

He turned his attention to Tony. 'And this lad? Christian dog.' He spat, noticing his crucifix. He hooked the trident under the chain and yanked it off his neck. 'What religion celebrates the death of their prophet? Bhairava is the only master of the dead!'

'O Bhairava!' the priests shouted three times. Outside, under the tree, the man who had been meditating on one leg started thrashing about and flailing as if he was engulfed by invisible flames.

Now Ugra hobbled back to the priests. 'You've abandoned your duties. Go! Feed your brother. He is distressed.' Everyone hurried out. 'Sen! You come here. Watch them. I must finish the ritual with Badri before time runs out. He laughed at Ranganathan. 'I knew when you left Chennai. I knew when you entered the enchanted zone and when your guru unlocked the portal with his magic box.'

Now Tony looked up with astonishment. Ugra grinned. He

tried to snatch Ranganathan's bag, who held on to it tighter. 'No!' he protested. 'Not this.'

Sen joined the tussle, but Ranganathan put up a good fight until Sen drew a knife from the back of his veshti and in swift strokes cut off the bag's strap. 'The conch always provides what we need,' Ugra said.

Ranganathan squirmed in his spot, his eyes welling up. He had let Chaturvasi down. An immense ball of guilt started weighing him down. His teacher was risking his life to fight a demon controlled by this madman, he had entrusted him with his only protection, and he had failed to accomplish what he was asked to do.

Ugra walked away slowly. 'Your attempt at stealth was laughable. You were barely hidden behind those shrubs. But good skulls are hard to come by and Brahmin skulls almost impossible. When I knew that yantra was coming with you, I couldn't resist. Chaturvasi is not as bright as I thought if he sent you two here, though I must credit him for installing a powerful yogi at the portal in Vikram's house.'

His face softened a bit. 'What has your guru promised you? A life where you will one day feel the distance between your soul and your physical body?'

Ranganathan tensed up. It was one thing to hurt him physically, but another to debase everything that Chaturvasi stood for.

'What else did he teach you?' Ugra continued. 'Hold your breath like this' – he placed one finger on one of his nostrils and sucked up his gut – 'then sit in some asana and wait for your energies to move?' Ugra threw his head back and laughed.

Sen sniggered. 'All that is useless.' He tilted his head. 'You! Christian boy. Definitely useless for you too. What we do here is more powerful. You want proof? This is proof. You are living in my made-up land. If I snapped my fingers, then all this would disappear in an instant, and you'd find yourself in the middle of the Old Mahabalipuram highway. Probably dead in an instant.'

He snapped his fingers and lightning struck nearby. 'This is absolute power.' He clapped and the earth shook. 'This is what everyone must aspire for.' Sen brought his palms together and placed them between his eyebrows. 'If you want it, renounce your teacher and join my sect. Your road to divinity will be faster. After all, I plan on meeting Lord Shiva himself with my own body.'

'No!' Ranganathan said. 'This is not we have come here for.'

'Then for what have you come?' Ugra thundered. 'To steal from me?' He held the bag up as if it were just another skull. 'You will have to pay for this. Sen! Watch them. I must go.'

'Yes acharya!' Sen said.

Ugra paused at the edge of the cavity. 'Don't toy with them. Don't waste your energies on these rats. I need you intact for the final ritual. It is upon us.'

Sen bristled, but bowed his head. 'Yes acharya.'

'Throw them next to the other two and watch over them.' With that, Ugra hopped off the edge and slipped into the night like a bead of sweat down one's spine.

Ranganathan knew precisely what was going on in Kapaladvipa. The events of the past years crystallized into one contiguous flow. And when that happened, he couldn't breathe. He simply held his breath and the state of affairs simmered in his head.

'That which you think is you . . . isn't you,' Chaturvasi had once told him. This was in the early days after he had torn Ranganathan's trousers on the seashore and set him on a spiritual quest. They were seated in a large swing in the backyard of one of Chaturvasi's friends in Kalakshetra Colony. This far from Elliot's beach, there were no visitors or hawkers to disturb the ambience.

Chaturvasi poked Ranganathan. 'That banana you ate earlier . . . where did it go?'

'I ate it,' Ranganathan said. 'I mean . . . it's in my stomach.'

'Indeed. And after that, it'll turn into you. Some part of you.'

Ranganathan's brows furrowed. He had never seen food in that fashion. It was something one ate for sustenance, or if one was in a nice restaurant, for taste.

'And the banana tree, in turn, consumed the earth to make the fruit. Since your conception, you have been accumulating the earth around you and calling it your body. There was a time when you didn't know this . . . as a child. And life was blissful. Because you had no identity. You were a human being. A human that simply was. But then you started making associations with your body. You thought your body was you, and you were only this body. And you believed this lie.'

'I did,' Ranganathan agreed, the germ of Chaturvasi's thesis making sense.

'And then whatever your body experienced, you stored it in what you called your mind. And this mind simply recycled whatever garbage it picked up. It can't make up more experiences, but it's a master at recycling, and soon you believed that thing also was you. Your body was you along with your mind.'

Ranganathan stared at his chappals in silence. Nearby, the bells started tolling from the Temple of Eight Lakshmis. It was the time for the evening arthi.

'But that is the maya . . . the illusion of your existence, Ranga,' Chaturvasi said. 'You are really not this body or this mind. The *you* in you exists deeper, but also everywhere. When you experience it, you will realize that there is no you or I. There is no duality. Everything stems from the same creator. You, me, the birds, the sea, the beach . . . everything. Until then you are trapped in this maya of your own making.'

Ranganathan pursed his lips. Now he was lost. How was he to separate his mind and body from himself. At that point what was left of him?

'I can read your thoughts.' Chaturvasi chuckled. 'That's where the yoga I'm teaching you will come in. One day, you'll experience what I have explained, and then you'll simply know. Only what you experience is real. The rest is not.'

That evening Ranganathan had left more confused than ever, but performed the prescribed practices daily. Months rolled into years, and over time he gradually understood what Chaturvasi had tried to tell him that evening. Many days, in the silence of his tiny flat, locked in his bedroom with the lights off, he'd enter a state of stillness where he felt dissociated from his physical body and mind and slipped out of them like an astronaut dropping his spacesuit.

These episodes were hard to replicate; they happened only when his yoga and meditation happened in perfection, and if he had maintained his diet in that strict way that Chaturvasi had prescribed – no onions, garlic, coffee, eggplant, potatoes, and yes to honey, ginger, ash gourd, peanuts. Chaturvasi's discourses made a lot more sense.

The erstwhile esoteric concepts now felt like emphatic truths, and he watched with great joy as the beginners struggled with them just like he once had. He took it upon himself to tutor them in the ways of tantra, responding to their simple queries – 'Do I have to practise during the Brahma muhurtham?', 'Does fasting on ekadasi involve fruits or no food at all?', 'When I chant the mantra, my voice quavers. Is that okay?' He answered these with gusto, patiently explaining to them what he knew, and directing them to Chaturvasi only if it was something important. During one of these discourses, Chaturvasi ventured into the realm of ghosts.

'Yes, there are ghosts everywhere.' He laughed. 'If you can simply see without any of your karma coming in your way, you'd notice that this beach is crawling with ghosts.' Ranganathan, Chris, and a few others looked around with big eyes. Chaturvasi stroked his beard. 'Not yet. You need to stick to your practices. Do them right. Don't do them so that you can see ghosts.' Then his face turned serious as did his voice. 'You see, when you strip away the mind and the body, what is left is the karmic structure. That is what some call the soul . . . prana . . . whatever. That is the battery for this existence. When a person dies of old age, this prana is subtle. Its vibration is too feeble. But if someone dies prematurely, such as in an accident or a suicide, then this prana is vibrant. However they pass, once the mortal shell is broken, the soul floats about, looking for a new womb to manifest so that it can destroy whatever karmic baggage it still holds on to. This is why, in our tradition, we cremate the body after four hours of death and as soon as possible so as to let the soul find its way out from its confusion.'

They were sitting beside an upturned boat on the beach. It reeked of fish and the sea. Gauzy nets lay in large clumps next to it like the eggs of a strange creature. The waves crashed by them and every now and then they waved away sundal and murukku hawkers, for the topic of the evening was far more interesting than spiced chickpeas or stale fried fritters.

Chaturvasi sighed. 'Anyway, these souls are around us, inhabiting their own dimension that is inaccessible to most of us. So, they don't bother us. Except when they are too vibrant' – he slowly scanned their faces – 'then they can cause much trouble.'

Now, in a moment of clarity, Ranganathan understood what had happened: by reading the verses at the Theosophical Society, Vikram had made himself receptive to a pair of vetals, who had then possessed him. Ugra, who was after Chaturvasi, deduced, rightly, that the latter would be involved in the exorcism because he was the best around. So he got on with the act and figured a way to harness the malevolent entity by means of tantric practices. The Kapalika priest who was standing in the middle of the group with Vikram's handkerchief was feeding the entity and controlling it to manipulate Vikram. Ugra knew Chaturvasi would perform the exorcism, and he would use Vikram to catch Chaturvasi.

Sen had made them sit by the banyan. The remains of the burnt corpse bit into their noses. Sen paced in front of them, fingering a rosary. He had placed the bag with the yantra on the stone platform by the tree. Ranganathan eyed it surreptitiously and wondered if he could run and grab it. And then do what with it? The yantra was a mystical instrument, its workings only known to his teacher.

Nearby, the priests muttered incantations in hushed voices. Ugra and his new apprentice were further away, sawing at the corpse's neck. The sound of the saw against the bone, the stench of human flesh and the weird prickle in the air made Tony retch. He turned around and threw up. Sen stopped and laughed.

'Lightweight!' he said and walked towards them. 'The sight of death fazes you?'

Tony clung to Ranganathan, suddenly questioning the string of decisions that led him to this point. His mother, a devout Catholic, had warned him multiple times not to mix with the Hindus. 'How can they worship so many gods?' she said one day as he prepared to leave for Vikram's. 'Can Vikram confess to his priest? He's a teenager just like you, his life is filled with sin. Without confession, how will he repent and how will his soul ascend to Heaven?' She reached for the rosary atop the fridge and toyed with it. 'Tony, don't get too close with their kind.' Her voice turned stern. 'And stop by the church on the way back and go for confession. You missed it last Sunday.'

Tony dismissed her as orthodox and ignored her concerns. Sitting next to a corpse on a forbidden island, away from civilization and facing his death at the hands of a murderous skull-worshipping sect, he realized his mother had had a point. While Chaturvasi no doubt wielded superhuman powers, Tony still began to regret getting mixed up in this business. He prayed to Jesus that if he got out alive, he'd go to mass regularly and offer confession without fail. His clammy hand instinctively reached for the crucifix that used to resolutely hang around his neck. Ranganathan placed a protective arm around him and said to the priest, 'Death spares no one, Sen. Including you.'

'Aha! You dare speak philosophy in our master's presence?' He marched over and slapped Ranganathan, who keeled over and held his palm to his cheek. Tony helped him sit up. 'I could show you what death tastes like right now,' Sen threatened. He reached for his knife. It glinted in the moonlight.

'Why hasten something that is bound to arrive?' Ranganathan said, his voice bereft of pain or fear. 'You folks meditate on death. What if I showed you what life tastes like?'

Sen growled and kicked Ranganathan in the chest. 'I wouldn't want to be you when Ugra discovers that you have mutilated the physical body that he has been saving for a ritual. Shouldn't Shiva get a pristine sacrifice and not one tainted by your ugly fingers?' Sen was about to strike him again but stopped when the logic of the words seeped in.

With a grunt, Sen stepped back and spat. He replaced the knife and got back to the rosary. 'Be thankful that we are merciful.'

Ranganathan noticed a long scar along Sen's left bicep and how the bulge on that arm was significantly smaller than that on the right. Despite the situation, Ranganathan could not help but pity Sen. He felt an outpouring of sympathy for the man who believed that Ugra, by means of the occult dimension of tantra, would lead him to great powers and eventually liberation itself.

'What are you smiling for?' Sen asked.

'At your plight,' Ranganathan said.

Sen sniggered. 'Look around you, Brahmin. Look! Open your eyes. What do you see? These trees. The waters. The massive stone skull. Nothing is real. Our master, Ugra, could make it all happen by the sheer will of his mind. You are now in his world. Can your master do something this awesome?' His eyes were glistening and his voice took on a softer tinge, as if he was awestruck.

'I'm not here to sing my teacher's praises.'

'Ha! That's because he's nothing in front of mine.'

Chaturvasi had repeatedly stated that only when the mind, body, emotions and energies were in harmony would the true splendour of creation reveal itself to him. And in that light, he had his disciples perform various practices to tamp down the vagaries of the mind and body. Consequently, their emotions and energies were pleasant and more in their control. 'When you realize,' Chaturvasi had said, 'that the source of creation throbs in everyone . . . everything . . . whether it's an ant or a rock or a person . . . even if it's your enemy, then you bow down to it. You don't discriminate.'

Ranganathan decided to gamble on the situation. 'Then do you mind if I pray for him?' Sen's eyebrows climbed up.

'My young friend here is terrified. He is terrified of the place and is terrified of death. He is especially terrified of having to watch me being beheaded and my skull extracted.' Tony held him tighter. 'Could I please offer him some mantras to soothe him . . . so that he is at peace?'

Sen glared at the two of them, his eyes darting like an animal's. He glanced askance at Ugra who was squatting on the torso of the corpse and pulling apart muscles and tissues from the skull as if they were fibres of a coconut. He grunted and walked away. 'Keep it quiet. Don't disturb the rituals.'

'Tony,' Ranganathan said, shaking the boy by his shoulders. 'Are you okay?'

'We're going to die,' Tony cried. 'They are going to kill us.' He brought his palms together and started praying. 'Our Father, who art in Heaven . . .'

Ranganathan waited for Tony to finish. Then he clasped his hand. 'Listen, Tony, Listen!' Ranganathan dropped his voice. 'I'm going to get us out of here. You have to listen to me.'

'How?' The word almost came out in a petulant cry. 'There are dead bodies around here. They just killed a man in front of us.' He pointed in Ugra's direction. 'He's cutting the head off there. How can you get out of this?' He beat Ranganathan's shoulder feebly. 'I shouldn't have agreed to this trip. Vikram is fucked. I'm now dead too.' He looked up with tears in his eyes. 'Right?'

'Tony, look, we don't have much time. Do you trust Chaturvasi?'

Tony didn't say a word but stared at the earth glumly. He had been sceptical, yes, for the man spoke about energies and chakras that made no sense. But after he had proffered the jasmine flower at the shrine of Chinnamalai siddhar the pain in his knee had simply vanished. After months of dogging him, it disappeared without a trace. He begrudgingly attributed this to something beyond logical comprehension. 'I do, but what good is that? He's somewhere.' He looked around. 'Where the hell are we?' He looked up and noticed the absolute emptiness of the sky now. Such a place shouldn't exist.'

'Will you do this one thing for me?' Ranganathan said softly. 'I'll teach you a mantra. It's two lines. Repeat it after me.'

'Why?'

'Think of it like a psychic hotline to Chaturvasi.'

'How can he hear us from here? My phone' – he remembered how it had betrayed them and flung it down – 'it has no signal here. We're in some bubble.'

'Just trust me, okay?'

Tony sniffled.

'Now', Ranganathan began. 'Sit cross-legged like this. Good! Now bring the fingertips of both your hands together. Good! Now move them counterclockwise by one finger . . . right forefinger touches the opposite thumb, right middle touches the left fore . . . yes! Like that. That's called a mudra. See! You are on your way to becoming a yogi.'

'How can you be so cheery in a place like this?' Tony held up the ball he had made with his fingers and despite the situation, smiled.

'That's because what hasn't happened hasn't happened yet. It's in your mind. Don't suffer what's not real! Now pay attention to my words. Close your eyes and imagine Chaturvasi's form.

'Form?'

'His . . . his body . . . image. Whatever you remember of how he looks. Bring that into your mind and try to hold it.'

Tony closed his eyes.

'Now repeat after me.' Ranganathan slowly and carefully enunciated the words of a sloka.

Tony repeated the words haltingly.

'Good,' Ranganathan said, crossing his legs. 'We'll chant this together twenty-one times. Okay?'

'Why twenty-one?' He looked at Ranganathan and then immediately said, 'Sorry. Okay. And then?'

'And then we'll get up and simply walk out of here.'

Tony laughed. 'Just like that?'

'Just like that. Now close your eyes and chant. And pay attention to every syllable.'

The Sanskrit teacher and the engineering student sat with their eyes closed and chanted the mantra slowly, chewing on each syllable. They felt the gaze of Sen from afar but paid no attention. After the twenty-first iteration, they stopped. Ranganathan brought his palms together. Tony followed and looked at him expectantly. Ranganathan stood up and gestured to the other to do the same. Sen stopped pacing and seized the bag.

They stared walking towards him. Sen adjusted the bag and came racing. 'Where do you think you're going?'

'Home. It's time.' Ranganathan raised a finger. 'And by the way, I'd like my bag back, please.'

Sen stared at them agog. He raised his arm to slap him when a knife found its mark precisely along the scar on his left arm. Sen yelped and dropped to the ground. Now they heard the familiar cluck. Tony's jaw dropped and his eyebrows rose, for he knew he was in the presence of Chaturvasi. But standing behind Sen was Auto Balu.

Sen was about to scream when Balu instantly fashioned another knife from the mud beneath them. Flipping it deftly in his hand once, he flung it at Sen. It found the back of Sen's mouth. He sank like a stone in a pond. Ranganathan snatched the bag.

'The boat is tied,' Balu said, but in Chaturvasi's tone. 'The keys are in the car. You know how to drive?'

'I do,' Tony said. 'I can drive.'

'Good,' Balu said. 'Hurry and get out.'

'What about you?' Ranganathan asked. 'We can wait . . .'

'No. It's already late. The exorcism has begun. I'm going to stall for time here and see how much I can damage. You go!' Behind them there was a commotion amongst the priests. Their chants had stopped and the priest in the middle of the circle, his eyes still closed, Vikram's handkerchief stuffed in his mouth, had a long bony arm pointing in their direction.

'But . . .' Ranganathan said, 'Then Balu . . .'

'Don't worry,' Balu said. 'I'll take care of it.'

And right away Ranganathan knew that Balu would not make it back. However, Chaturvasi was going to make his last few moments as pleasant as possible, allowing him to leave his body with awareness. Ranganathan hugged Balu and held his hands between his.

'Come, Tony,' he said. 'Sprint!'

19

It was the eve of the exorcism and Chaturvasi's body thrummed like the air inside a flute. He hadn't eaten in days, but he barely felt any discomfort from the fast. If anything, his body felt light and malleable. He heard the pom-pom air horn from below and rushed to the balcony.

The versatile driver, Balu, was out on a mission with Ranganathan and Tony. He didn't feel anything for what was going to be Balu's fate. Something deep inside him sensed that the driver would not be returning from the adventure, and he was okay with it. He would be sacrificing himself for a greater cause, for if he hadn't gone on the trip he would have died in a devastating accident. This, Chaturvasi knew. After all this was over, he'd go and meet the widow and take care of Balu's family's needs.

The severity of the issue at hand was not evident to anyone save Chaturvasi. Ugra's methodical plans had taken years to hatch and now that they were coming to fruition, he had to act immediately. When he saw Ranganathan, Tony and Balu drive away the night before, he felt nothing. No tinge of any emotion. They had to do their jobs to prevent a major catastrophe.

If Ugra was successful in obtaining his skull, his powers would blossom and cement, turning him into the most powerful man alive. Getting into politics, becoming the chief minister, or even the prime minister, was nothing compared to what he could do with the eight siddhis under his control. No, he felt nothing, not even for the trio on his mission. He may have sent them to their deaths and that was fine. But he had parted with his yantra, which concerned him the most, for if Ugra got his hands on it, the tables would turn on him.

He had already deployed his god to trap Vikram back again in his room. That had deprived him of another one of his most potent weapons. Now the exorcism would have to be conducted with the god significantly weakened or probably disabled. That didn't faze him. He had a duty – to stop Ugra – and he would execute it with all the intensity and focus he could muster. The god had weakened significantly, for not only did it thwart the vetal, it also supplied Chris with the life force needed to stay alive. It would be months before he would recover, and years before the form could be re-energized to its full intensity, but Chaturvasi didn't let those things cloud his mind now.

He had asked Balu to recommend another trusty driver to ferry him to Vikram's house and wherever else he may need to go after that. Balu had immediately set him up with his friend, Guna.

Now Guna stepped out and waved at Chaturvasi who

acknowledged him, gesturing that he would join him shortly. The sun was about to set. He felt the subtle surge in energy from the earth extend its serpentine coils within him. It rose from his spine in a helical fashion, swarming and energizing his system as it exited through his head. In this state of fasting, his body was like a powerful radio antenna, tuning itself to vibrations from the cosmic radio stations.

Before leaving he peeked through the slightly ajar door of his bedroom. His wife, wearing a white sari and large crimson dot on her forehead, sat cross-legged with her eyes closed. He picked up a flower from a heap nearby and carefully placed it in front of her and brought his palms together. She was a key player in the events that were about to unfold. Just as every electrical circuit ought to have a ground to channel any surges away from the main components, she was his ground. She waded through life selflessly, unable to feel anything. Mental health experts would have classified her as clinically depressed, but she really was in a state of emotional abeyance, unable to feel love, sadness, greed, or anger any more. She went through her daily practices and yoga phlegmatically and each minute was spent scrubbing her emotions clear. Her stoic nature was not by choice, but a result of her practices. She had evolved significantly from that day when she had requested that he teach her the esoteric ways of tantra. Then she had been an emotional mess, unable to reconcile with her grief and wallowed in it. Now she was a focused yogi, stripped of material and emotional wants. When the time came and he needed to disperse any surge of negative energy, there was nobody he could turn to save her.

Chaturvasi hopped into the autorickshaw. Guna turned back and smiled. 'That Vikram boy's house-aa?' he asked.

'Yes,' Chaturvasi said, closing his eyes. 'And don't make any conversation.'

Guna's smile vanished. He was curious about the boy. Balu had told him that he was possessed by a demon and that he had witnessed strange things happening at the house the other night. He wanted to know if the lights really went out in the neighbourhood, if crows started swarming and cawing over the house, if there were demonic screams coming from the house, among many other questions, but Chaturvasi's stern red eyes, his pursed lips and flared nostrils shut him up. He started the autorickshaw and drove.

Earlier in the day, Chaturvasi had instructed Gopal to move his son to the bungalow by the beach in Kalakshetra Colony. Urging him not to waste any time, Chaturvasi had asked him to take Arun and Chris along for help, leaving out the fact that his god would cocoon Vikram the entire time and render the demon inside him impotent.

'It has been consecrated many times by powerful rituals,' he told the anxious father. 'A lingam made of solid mercury sits at the bottom of the well behind the house, shrouding the area with its protection. Don't worry. I'm going to rid Vikram of this demon. But you'll have to shift him to that house. It is important that people he recognizes are in proximity to him. He must be grounded.'

Just before hanging up, Chaturvasi had added, 'One more thing, Gopal. When you take Vikram out of the room, the seals will be broken. It may appear that he's having a seizure, but it's normal and will die down once sunlight hits his skin and you reach the safe house. Tie the red threads I sent you on your right wrist before noon. Did you get the other materials for the exorcism? Good. Ask Parvati to tie her thread on her left wrist. And, if possible, tie one on Vikram's right wrist. I'll be there by dusk.'

In the afternoon, he had received a message from Arun saying that Vikram was bound to the bed, but moaning and talking in his sleep. 'Good,' Chaturvasi had replied and said, 'Buy three mirrors. At least five feet tall.'

Chaturvasi felt at peace as the auto arrived at the bungalow. This was his turf, his haunt, his choice of battleground. He stepped out of the vehicle and savoured the tang in the breeze. The sun was setting on the other coast, but the Bay of Bengal was awash with warm colours. He hoped to be there to see the sun poke its head again precisely twelve hours and sixteen minutes later.

The watchman, Muthu, saluted him and pushed the wrought iron gate that creaked and sang open. Chaturvasi stepped in and observed the intricate kolam on the ground in front of the parked Mercedes. It was a yantra, a geometrical representation of the divine.

'Fresh-aa?' Chaturvasi asked. The maid, whom Muthu had roped in to draw it, knew nothing about the power of yantras, but decades of drawing them had made her lines and angles perfect. The kolam swirled and slashed, spiralling its hypnotic tendrils in and out of itself, mesmerizing anyone who set their eyes on it. It was, in a way, its own occult temple, repelling things that needn't approach Chaturvasi while he consecrated the exorcism site.

'Yes sir,' Muthu said. 'I had the maid draw your design fifteen minutes before sunset as you ordered.'

'Good.'

The watchman, who had witnessed Chaturvasi perform exorcisms before, beamed, happy to have been of some use.

Chaturvasi approached the veranda and noticed Chris sitting with his eyes closed. He sat next to him in vajrasana and closed his eyes. He gauged that Chris didn't have much energy left in him, but Chaturvasi needed him nevertheless. The boy was his safety net if the exorcism were to go awry. He transmitted specific instructions and stood up.

Chaturvasi stopped at the threshold, tucked the loose strands of his hair into his ponytail, and said a prayer. As soon as he stepped in, he felt like he had been socked by a bag of bricks. He closed his eyes and let the feeling subside, commanding his god to stand by him.

He was greeted by a small, but nervous, crowd. Gopal ran up to grab his hand. Parvati stood behind, clutching her pallu. Two other men stepped forward and greeted Chaturvasi. He set his bag down and greeted each one of them. He was dressed in a T-shirt and linen pants. His hair was drawn into a ponytail that stuck out from the base of his neck. Had he carried his stethoscope he would have resembled a doctor on a house call.

'I'm Arun,' one of them said, 'Vikram's uncle. And this is Mahesh.'

'My cousin,' Gopal said wearily.

Mahesh stepped forward holding the mirrors. 'Mirrors, sir, like you asked.'

Chaturvasi told him to put them down and looked around the room. The air was thick with diaphanous amoebic blobs. Most were black while a few were scarlet red. Chaturvasi noticed that they were swarming and moving in a slow vortex through the ceiling. No doubt they led to the possessed boy. From the room above, he heard faint, distressed moans.

'We . . . we tied him,' Mahesh said, his voice loaded with guilt.

Chaturvasi raised his hands. 'It'll be fine. Don't worry.' He looked at Parvati. 'I can only imagine your pain as a mother.' He brought his palms together. 'Your son will be fine. I have done this ritual before,' mentally adding, 'but not on such a high order demon.'

He felt his energy form weaken as Kakasura gnawed at it. His vision exploded with bright blots. Without the yantra, he couldn't keep the form energized. The exorcism depended on several things working out. He wasn't one to take a chance, but the pace of Ugra's machinations left him no choice. Now he rubbed his fingertips together and went quiet. His eyes darted across the room and the hair on his body stood up. 'It's here,' he said. A faint howl came from the top floor, filled with pain and laced with terror.

Chaturvasi snapped out of his haze. 'We must hurry. All of you take a bath in chilly water. There are three bathrooms.' He turned to Gopal. 'Did you tie him up like I asked you to? The loops in the knots must go clockwise? Right hand first?'

Parvati sobbed. Gopal placed a hand on her. Arun stepped forward and said, 'Yes . . . sir. We did. We used thick coir that was covered in vibhuti.'

'Good.' He handed Gopal a small cloth bag. 'Please take a head bath. When you're done, switch off all the lights, light a lamp, sit in front of it and compose yourselves. Now listen to me carefully. I want you to imagine Lord Narasimha in any way you can.' He scanned the distressed faces. 'You know who he is, right? Good. When you sit down, think of him and bring him to the front of your consciousness. Place his image between your eyes.' Then he started walking away.

'Where are you going?' Paravati asked, concerned.

'I need to cleanse myself too.' He pointed at the main door. 'In the ocean.' Before stepping out he paused and turned around. 'Mahesh,' he said, 'please come out with me for a minute.'

He left with such sure-footedness that the fancy crystal glasses entombed inside fancier showcases trembled. Mahesh darted after Chaturvasi. Above them Vikram moaned. The rest quickly dispersed to the bathrooms.

Chaturvasi held him by his shoulders. 'Mahesh,' he said, 'take out your phone and type out these two messages.'

One of them was a single word: help.

The other was also a single word: now.

Both addressed to different numbers.

'Send them . . . hear me carefully . . . send the messages if you see my left ring finger turning black at any time. The nadi running through that finger is the way a possession happens.'

Mahesh took a deep breath and nodded quickly. He was a

big man, Mahesh, with broad shoulders and beefy forearms. He was instrumental in restraining Vikram during the transfer to the bungalow, but his might quickly fizzled out when he was given this responsibility. Why was he talking about possession? Wasn't Vikram already possessed? He figured Chaturvasi was referring to himself being possessed and he felt weak. He stuffed his phone into his pocket, then took it out, opened the message and imagined hitting send – as if rehearsing a complex procedure so as not to go wrong at the final moment. 'Only when the ring finger turns black,' he repeated. 'I can do that.'

When Chaturvasi got back almost an hour later, his transformation took everyone by surprise. He had left looking like a mild-mannered dentist and returned looking like a banshee with his white hair loose and thick kohl around his eyes. He walked to the unused well. Where regular men saw a placid moon swimming in the inky water, Chaturvasi saw a blinding pillar of white light, stretching like a lighthouse beam to the centre of the universe. Muthu, who had quickly flung the gate open for Chaturvasi lest he should barrel right through it, turned around and saw him jump into the well. When he dashed over to check, there were only ripples in the water.

The fires of the oil lamps sat unmoving on their wicks, soaking sesame oil and casting a hazy light. In that crepuscular light, Chaturvasi entered the house, wearing a black veshti and a thin black cloth covering his shoulders, holding a bucket of water. Tucked into the veshti was a pouch. His milky white hair floated around him like a frizzy halo. Large bronze earrings dangled from his ears.

If the group had assumed that he was a Brahmin, they did not see the sacred threads across his torso. Instead, he wore a garland of giant rudraksha seeds so large that it resembled the charred spinal cord of an animal. More beads and necklaces hung from his neck and amulets were tied around his arms. There was a thick brass anklet on his right leg. His eyes were electric and his gaze intense. He looked like a fierce tribal shaman capable of reducing someone to ashes by mere sight.

Though he looked terrifying, his energies were so pleasant and intense that instinctively they all brought their palms together, aware that they were in the presence of a higher being.

'The moon ascends,' Chaturvasi said, putting down the bucket. His voice had a deeper tone and a sharper edge. It didn't appear like he was speaking as much as commanding. If he had ordered the sun to rise, it would have meekly appeared in the sky at that moment. He clapped once. It was a thunderous clap, sending a shiver down their spines. At the same moment, a scream erupted from the floor above.

'Untie me, you bastards,' Vikram shouted. They heard grunts and groans punctuated by silence. In these pauses, the air was filled with breath of the sea and the loud gasping of air by Vikram.

Chaturvasi walked to one of the corners facing the sea and arranged the three mirrors so that two were along the wall and the third one straddled the corner. He adjusted them carefully until they touched each other at right angles so that they created a three-sided box. With Arun and Mahesh's help he laid out a black cloth atop the mirrors, forming a small tent. He then took out a coconut shell and removed the thin plastic it was covered with.

'Parvati,' he said, 'please draw a kolam under the cloth.'

Quickly, Parvati drew a simple geometric kolam with the rice flour, which felt more powdery than what she was used to. When she was done she noticed her fingertips had turned deep red. Chaturvasi lit and placed oil lamps around the kolam.

Five pots, arranged in a pentagram formation, sat in front of the mirrors. He pulled out a ball of twine dyed in turmeric from the pouch and unravelled it. He muttered mantras as he tied the twine around the mouths of the pots. He went from pot to pot like a spider weaving its web until the pots were connected and he was in the middle. He poured water into the first pot and brought his palms together between his eyes. He repeated this with the other pots, emptying a bag of mud into one, blowing into one and covering it with a lid, emptying a bunch of camphor into the third and setting it alight, and simply covering the last one. He stood in the middle and raised his right leg until it was parallel to the ground. He stretched out his arms and brought his palms together. He stood that way for a few moments before sitting down.

When he sat down under the black cloth, it was as if infinite Chaturvasis had entered the space and simultaneously sat down in front of millions of lamps. When the real one brought his palms together, his army of clones mirrored him. Whatever he uttered, they followed. The others stared in amazement at the scene and sat down silently. If they had had any doubt about the efficacy of the ritual, this was the assurance they needed.

Now Chaturvasi placed in front him a wooden container filled with frankincense granules. With a deft strike of a match stick, he lit the granules. Soon, thick smoke billowed out from under the cloth and spread into the room.

He walked up to the edge of the twine perimeter and handed the container to Parvati. 'Bring up Narasimha's image in your mind and walk around the room clockwise with this.' She took the smoking container and started circumambulating. 'All of you do it.'

He returned to his perch under the cloth, retrieved a tiny brass bell from his bag and tinkled it while chanting mantras. The millions of Chaturvasis followed suit, filling the air with unending smoke and millions of bells. A portal had opened in that bungalow's off-white walls and an army of tantrics were revealed, each assiduously chanting mantras.

The mellifluous sound of the bells was compensated by the tortured groans from above. Arun gently placed the pot of frankincense inside the perimeter.

Vikram's voice had turned nasal. Parvati and Gopal cast pained glances at each other and their relatives. Arun and Mahesh patted the beleaguered parents' palms, equally terrified by the entity threatening to descend from above. They stood huddled next to one of the pots. 'Narasimha,' Mahesh reminded them and closed his eyes. The others followed suit.

Every now and then Chaturvasi stopped to pick up a camphor cube or some frankincense. He placed it between his eyes and muttered something before offering it to the small fire in the container. Every time he made the oblation, the moaning heightened from above.

The room turned into a dreamy world. The sparse furniture floated like rocks in a still predawn sea. The oil lamps, despite the evil in their vicinity, burned like the distant twinkling lights of ships on the horizon, a narrow string of hope in the darkness ahead. He stopped the incantations and put down the bell. Only Vikram's groans filled the house. With a calm voice, Chaturvasi said, 'The consecration is now complete. I will now summon the vetal that has taken possession of the boy. All of you step inside the perimeter.'

The group held each other's hands so tight that their palms turned colour. Gingerly, they stepped over the threads and stood within the consecrated perimeter. They toyed with the red threads on their wrists and whispered amongst themselves – 'What if Vikram doesn't recognize me?' 'What if the demon jumps from him into me?' 'Will he ever be normal?' 'Will he remember after all this is over? Will it ever be over?' They spoke softly, their words seeking each other out for comfort. Fingers intertwined for support and breaths synchronized subconsciously.

All this time, the infinite exorcists sat under the makeshift tent in their respective worlds, their backs ramrod straight, their eyes sewn shut, their lips barely moving as they chanted magical mantras.

Now Chaturvasi stood up and chanted the mantras into a coconut. When he placed it down, it cracked open on the tiled floor, laying bare its innards and splattering its water everywhere, extinguishing one of the lamps. He stopped next to the pot with the camphor fire, and after baring his feet to the flames, he stepped out of the pentagon. He raised his finger and the group stopped chatting. 'It is important,' Chaturvasi said, his voice deep and sombre, 'that you do not address the vetal when it approaches.' The oil fires slowly turned to the left and burnt at an unnatural angle. Parvati made a motion to turn towards the stairs that were behind them, but Chaturvasi yelled at her. 'Don't! Don't turn and look.'

'Why?' Parvati said, her voice trembling. 'Is he okay?'

Chaturvasi didn't respond, but the flicker in his eyes indicated that Vikram was now standing behind them. He felt his god rev up to full intensity. A sharp shooting pain erupted near his spleen. He knew his form was on its last legs. Ignoring the pain, and with his eyes on his quarry, Chaturvasi slowly said, 'It can't physically harm you as long as I am present.'

Vikram stood at the base of the stairs a few feet away, with his back towards them. His head was down, his thick locks sprawling all over his shoulders. In the dim light he cut a fearsome figure, like a demented being from an unearthly world. He swayed back and forth on the spot, wheezing softly like an animal gasping. Parvati cried. Gopal pursed his lips. Arun clenched his fists. Mahesh put his fingers into his ears.

Chaturvasi adjusted the black cloth around his shoulders and stepped forward. His fingers were in motion, constantly rubbing against each other as if he were feeling the texture of an invisible cloth. With every step he felt his energies bleeding away. Images began to flash in his mind – scenes from Shruti's accident, his wife's mania – and he shook his head to dismiss them. He had weapons at his disposal, yes, but this entity was drawing from a deeper source and overpowering him. Ugra, it would appear, was more powerful than he had thought.

'Vikram,' he commanded. 'Are you in there, son?'

Vikram rocked sideways and then his torso spun on its axis, his hair swishing about like a mop. He took another step. Chaturvasi felt pain shoot up his legs. Bumps the size of lemons started popping on his calves. The negative energies from Vikram were shooting into his system in a sniper-like attack. Chaturvasi took another step forward and winced. The pain began to spread from his legs. He hadn't expected this so early, but he quickly distanced himself from his body, just as he had been preaching to Ranganathan and others for years.

Now he became a mere observer of his body, controlling its motions like a puppet master. Decades of practice had ensured that even though his body felt pain, it was devoid of suffering. This worked wonders for him, but he knew that if the pain became too strong he'd have to let go of his body permanently and dissolve into the cosmos. And that would abort the exorcism.

Vikram turned and snarled. His shrivelled face was laced with deep scratches. There were dark circles under his eyes which had rolled up. His lips were parched and gashed as if someone had put a razor blade to them. The same rank odour followed him as Chaturvasi let his god loose and appear beside him. Parvati and the others held their noses, too shocked to breathe.

'Vikram?' Chaturvasi repeated.

'The boy is ours,' a chorus of voices came from Vikram. 'You could have given yourself up, but you didn't. Your ego was too big. We will now get you and the boy.'

Gopal looked at Parvati and then at Chaturvasi, worried. Chaturvasi raised his hand. 'Leave the boy out of this,' he said calmly. He inched forward.

Vikram did the same. 'Everything has a beginning. Mine is here.' He looked up and around as his bones cracked and sinews squeaked. He pointed a finger at Muthu who was staring in through the window. 'This is an orchard with fruits ready to be plucked.' His grin stretched from ear to ear. 'Muthu . . .' he rasped and then ran his finger across his throat. Blood, thick as molasses and as dark, gushed from the cut.

Muthu shrieked and ran away. There were more screams as Vikram's family backed up against the wall.

'Ma?' Vikram said.

Parvati had been stunned into silence.

'Appa,' Vikram continued, his voice barely above a whisper, but deep and guttural. 'When you and amma had me, when you gave life to me, did you ever think that I would die one day?'

'Dei Vikky . . .' Gopal said softly.

'The surest way to kill me was to have me? How does it feel knowing you and ma conspired to kill me?'

Tears streamed down Gopal's face. 'Vikky . . .' he whispered and the words died out.

'Don't listen to it,' Chaturvasi said. 'That's not your son . . .'

'But . . .' Parvati mumbled, wiping her tears.

'That's not your son!'

He held the doll out. Vikram hissed and stepped back but not before taking a swipe at it.

'In this doll is a vibrant soul. Trapped,' Chaturvasi said. Mahesh's face contorted to ask a question, but he caught himself and remained quiet. 'Kakasura! Kakasura! Possess the life force in this doll. It has the essence of a human. Turn in the boy. You'll have an escape,' Chaturvasi ordered.

Now Vikram suddenly jerked back and forth from his waist, tossing his wild hair. He shook violently, his mouth frothing.

'What's happening?' Gopal asked, concerned. 'Vikram?'

'Kakasura!' Chaturvasi continued, his voice steady and commanding. 'You have underestimated me.' He started chanting mantras. Vikram covered his ears and screamed in rage. He took a step back. 'Your umbilical link to Ugra's minion won't last long. He will be dead soon.'

The doll twitched in Chaturvasi's hands as if struggling to escape his vice-like grip. He brought it to his forehead and held it there while he muttered incantations. Now he dropped it on the mosaic floor. He retrieved a plastic packet filled with the seashell chalk from his bag. With quick strokes he started drawing lines around the doll. Behind him, his army of Chaturvasi reflectionss repeated the same. At first, they seemed random, but his practised hands moved fast, looping, slashing and sprinkling, until there was a detailed yantra around the doll. It lay in the centre, immobilized like a fly trapped in the most intricate spider web ever spun.

Vikram began to whine like a wounded animal. Chaturvasi spoke, keeping his eyes locked on his target. 'Vikram invoked Kakasura when he read the verses. The demon was fed by another . . . source, someone who is out to get me.'

'You-aa?' Parvati exclaimed. 'How is it connected?'

'No time for that,' Chaturvasi said. 'We need to get rid of this demon before it gains full possession of your son.' He quickly placed oil lamps at the perimeter of the yantra and closed his nostrils alternately while breathing rhythmically. Vikram collapsed into a ball on the floor and sucked his thumb. After a couple of minutes, Chaturvasi touched his heart with his right hand and uttered, 'Om hrimkrom.'

Gopal hugged his wife. Arun and Mahesh linked fingers.

'Om hrimkrom!' Chaturvasi said, louder now. The doll twitched.

Chaturvasi repeated the mantra. 'Om hrimkrom!'

Parvati screamed. Arun yelped. Everyone cupped their mouths with their palms as they watched the doll slowly rise and stand up in the middle of the yantra, gazing at the participants with a childlike curiosity. Parvati's eyes searched for Vikram but he was no longer there.

'Vikram?' Gopal asked, his tone quavering.

Chaturvasi raised his palm. 'Your son is not alone.'

Parvati looked anguished.

Chaturvasi continued chanting, his intonation sounding much like a wedding or a gruhapravesham ritual. The doll slowly spun in a circle, making eye-contact with each one of them. After many twirls, its eyes rolled up, revealing only their painted chalk whites. Chaturvasi now dipped a leaf into a bronze pot and placed droplets of water around the perimeter of the yantra. When he placed the last drop, the entire design began to glow with a pulsing light.

'Amma?' the doll said, its voice plaintive and scared, but distinctly Vikram's.

'Vikram is safe in there,' the tantric said. 'Kakasura wouldn't take it, so I brought Vikram over.'

Like the audience at a dimly lit magic show, the crowd gasped. Parvati keeled over. Gopal caught her absently, his eyes riveted at the floating doll. The oil lamps swayed rhythmically, making their shadows dance on the walls. But from no angle could they spot the shadow of the doll. Thuds and knocks rose to a crescendo around the house and Chaturvasi matched it with his chanting. The group looked around the room for Kakasura but couldn't find him.

When Chaturvasi stopped chanting, silence reigned. The only sound was that of the ocean. The moon was a slit in the jugular of the sky and the night came pouring out. Moonlight filled the room, its wan milky light dusting over them like morning fog creeping through woods. The air was so still that even the lamp fires seemed too scared to flicker.

Now they heard a faraway siren. It came in bursts and slowly grew louder. Mahesh shot panicked glances at Arun and Gopal. 'What was that?' he asked, fingering the bronze serpent-shaped ring on his finger.

'I don't know,' Gopal said, equally terrified. He glanced at

Chaturvasi who was now sitting with his spine straight, eyes tightly shut, body shivering as if shocked by a sudden onset of winter. As quickly as the siren sounds came, they faded away into a palpable silence. 'It's coming from up.'

Now there were moans, as if they were suddenly in a mental hospital. Interspersed between the human groans were the howls of jackals. Windows rattled as the sounds grew louder. Lights came on, sputtered and went off. A TV came alive somewhere upstairs playing film songs before it went silent. Furniture creaked and groaned as it lifted off the ground.

Muthu, whose curiosity had got the better of his fear was back to peering through the frosted windows. Now he hurried back to his perch and pressed the amulet that Chaturvasi had given him a long time ago. First the bedroom on the top floor lit up with a flash of light, which slowly moved down the house towards the tantric.

Parvati clung to Gopal. 'What is happening, Gopal?' she said. She glanced at the doll, still serenely floating in the air. 'Vikram? Are you . . .' Chaturvasi held up a finger and silenced her. A sudden chill swept the room as if a powerful air-conditioner had been turned on. Their breaths started fogging in front of them. Chaturvasi rubbed his hands together. The others crossed their arms as their teeth chattered.

'I don't . . .', Gopal started and froze. He pointed at the ceiling.

'Vikram!' Parvati screamed at her son who hung upside down from the ceiling, rocking back and forth.

'That is not your son,' Chaturvasi thundered. 'Your child is safe. Don't address the demon by its shell's name.'

It was human in form, but inhuman in nature. Its eyes smouldered red and its hair squirmed like a clump of snakes. Ridged horns radiated from its temples and two gauzy wings protruded from its back. Its mottled skin was bruised and covered with bluish-purple spots, like a cadaver's. Its purple tongue stuck out like a bruised thumb. It hung without a shred of cloth on its body. Things moved underneath its skin like tadpoles in an egg. Outside, the moonlight was blotted by a swathe of shadows as a murder of crows cawed and flew in circles.

'The demon has assumed its full form,' Chaturvasi said softly. 'It must manifest fully or else the exorcism won't be successful.'

Chaturvasi started chanting again. He shook a bronze bell fervently, filling the room with its shrill notes. The doll levitated higher. The creature screeched and the clangour of the bell was matched with the tortured screams of invisible sufferers.

'Let go of the boy,' Chaturvasi bellowed and sat down in vajrasana. His words condensed into a plume of vapour and dissipated. He closed his eyes, joined his thumbs and forefingers in a ring and placed his palms near his kneecaps facing up. He struck the pose of a meditating yogi, his back straight, his milky hair cascading around his shoulders, his beard pouring down his chest and his eyes serene even though closed.

Above them, the demon mimicked Chaturvasi's posture, upside down. Its eyes were open and its head cocked. As the group looked on, it opened its mouth so wide it resembled a boa constrictor trying to stuff a large prey into its maw. Chaturvasi grew quiet and still. The demon spat obscenities in a raspy voice.

Parvati tried to move, but Gopal and Mahesh pulled her back. 'Stay,' Gopal hissed. 'But Vikky,' Parvati complained and Mahesh patted her hand. Caught in the axis of evil and redemption, the four of them glanced up and down, equal parts terrified and hopeful. A few minutes later, a boil appeared on Chaturvasi's back and grew like a bubble as they looked on. Another one bloomed a few inches down his spine.

'What's going on?' Arun asked, stroking his stubble. He then rubbed his hands to generate heat. 'It's been a few minutes.'

From above, Kakasura cackled. 'I shall get what I came for.'

Now Mahesh snapped out of his daze and whipped around towards Chaturvasi whose head was bent and shoulders loose. His left ring finger was turning black. 'Shit!' he exclaimed and reached for his phone. 'Sorry, sorry,' he muttered and fumbled with the phone but managed to send the two messages.

20

'Hurry!' Ranganathan said, leaping from the catamaran. He tripped as he landed, but quickly rolled over to his side and shielded the bag.

Tony stumbled right behind him. 'The keys, sir. Where are the keys?'

Ranganathan lunged into the rear seat of the Ambassador. 'It must be here.'

Tony sat in the driver's seat and reached for the ignition slot. The keys were there. He jiggled the steering wheel. It barely moved. It was an old car and didn't come with a power steering. That meant he'd have to use all his strength to steer.

'What's the problem?' Ranganathan asked turning back and squinting through the blue-tinted rear window. 'Let's get out of here.'

Tony's hands were quivering when he turned the ignition. The car roared. He looked around and discovered that the gear was behind the steering wheel, not on the floor like he was used to.

'Get going!' Ranganathan yelled. There were shapes forming in the waters behind.

'I am,' Tony said, pulling the gear towards him and engaging it. 'I think this is first.' The car lurched and stopped. Tony restarted it and this time the car began to move.

'Faster,' Ranganathan said, tapping on the window.

Tony quickly figured out the gears and they were speeding down the gravel road. The wind howled through the banyan forest, sending the swinging roots into knots as if an army of invisible apes were swinging through them. The leaves shook and began to tear apart from the branches. As they drove, the ground on either side began to dry up as if it had been exposed to an awfully long drought. Cracks began to form on it, small ones at first that connected and formed larger ones. Soon chunks of the earth fell apart, revealing inky blackness.

'What's happening, sir?' Tony asked nervously, swerving around potholes. Now he spotted the main road. It was an effort to commandeer the steering wheel and stay on the road. The trees whistled louder now and began to shed their leaves as if it were autumn.

'Ugra's world is peeling away,' Ranganathan said, 'starting from the core and gradually moving outwards.'

Ranganathan had employed the guru mantra to summon Chaturvasi and he had immediately responded, albeit in Balu's form. Ranganathan knew this wasn't the time to distract his teacher when all his energies had to be concentrated on destroying the demon. They had been outsmarted by Ugra and he had no choice but to reach out. After all, Chaturvasi had promised to come to his rescue whenever he needed him. Ranganathan still felt a lingering connection to Chaturvasi as they were driving away.

Calming his breath and focusing inwards, he guessed what must have transpired on the island since their escape: Balu stumbling towards the group, the priests shouting, Balu picking fistfuls of dirt and fashioning it into a bow and arrow, the priests running towards him, Balu placing the arrowhead to his lips and whispering incantations, one of the priests pulling out a knife, Balu drawing the arrow, the priest leaping at him, Balu letting go of the arrow, the priest stabbing him, the arrow finding the spot between the eyes of the priest who stood on one leg.

He felt a pang of grief thinking about Balu, but put that emotion aside. In this convoluted game of chess, some pieces had to be sacrificed.

Balu, or Chaturvasi in his skin, had destroyed the puppeteer who was controlling the demon in Vikram, but Ugra was still out there. And he simply had to look out of the window to deduce what the tantric was up to.

'Ugra is closing the gates to his paradise,' Ranganathan said. 'Drive fast, Tony. Drive like your life depends on it.'

Tony tore down the lonely dark highway. He struggled with the car as it was buffeted by the winds. Once, he braked as a large branch flew across the road. The primitive steering wheel was no help. Now he spotted thc glowing yogi from earlier.

'Sir!' he exclaimed, keeping his eyes on the road ahead. 'Look!'

The rishi was pointing his hand, but the other way this time, in the direction they were driving.

'I know the route,' Ranganathan mumbled. 'We just need to get out of Ugra's aura.'

The trees outside were barren and desiccated now, standing like giant ancient skeletons on a scorched earth. The ground continued to fly away. Tornadoes formed around them, hurtling stones and dust. Tony messed with the controls and the windshield wipers started smearing dust all over it. The car hit another pothole. Ranganathan touched the bag and winced, drawing comfort from the yantra within.

'Sir,' Tony said, his voice uncertain, 'I can barely see ahead and the road is cracking up.' He glanced back once and then said, 'Sir! You have a beard.' He touched his chin. 'I have a beard! How long have we been gone?'

'Focus, Tony. The portal can't be too far,' Ranganathan said. 'Just keep going straight.'

'Sir,' Tony said now. 'There is a glow coming from the right side. It's getting stronger.'

Ranganathan pulled out his handkerchief and took a deep breath. He rolled down the window partially, stuck his hand out to wipe the pane clean and rolled it back up. He did a double take when he saw the yogi running beside them on all fours like a lithe animal. He kept pace with the car, so Ranganathan was able to look at him closely. His matted hair held in place as was his long beard, the hairs barely even moving. It was incredible to see such a scrawny and almost malnourished man bound so effortlessly next to the speeding car. He didn't look at the car, his gaze fixed ahead. He showed no signs of exertion, neither breathing through his mouth, nor flaring his nostrils. The professor noticed that they were clocking over a hundred kilometres per hour. In a heartbeat, the yogi disappeared under the car.

As Ranganathan pressed his face against the window, the Ambassador hit a stone and was airborne. Tony saw a small chasm ahead and his eyes widened. The car was not going to make it. He gripped the steering wheel hard. He closed his eyes and held his breath, bracing for the impact . . . but nothing happened.

The car was cruising like a jetliner. When he opened his eyes all he saw was dust and stones whizzing by him at an insane speed. He couldn't move or speak. He sat transfixed, simply noting that the car was in fourth gear and his right foot was pressing down on the accelerator. He didn't feel the familiar friction of the road or the resistance in the steering wheel when he jiggled it. He looked to the right into the maelstrom and saw nothing. When he turned around, Ranganathan was smiling.

'Sir . . . I . . .' he began.

'It's all taken care of, Tony,' Ranganathan said. 'Keep your eyes on the road. Any moment now we'll be amid traffic.'

21

'We are deeply intertwined with the dance of the moon,' Chaturvasi's guru told him one afternoon after a morning of intense yogic practices. The three disciples, including Chaturvasi, all dressed in orange loincloths, sat beside the teacher under a shady peepal tree. Far from civilization, the only sounds were those of birds twittering and the gentle murmur of a nearby brook. It was customary for their guru, a practice that Chaturvasi would also adopt, to have regular question-and-answer sessions to clarify the myriad doubts that arose in his disciples' minds. Chaturvasi was all ears, consuming his guru's every word.

'When she draws,' the guru said, 'don't the oceans rise up towards her?' The disciples nodded solemnly. 'And when she pushes, don't the tides go down?' He looked at the eager faces. 'Then what are we but mere specks on this vast planet? What are we made up of if not the same water that flows right there?' He pointed in the direction of the brook, and its chatter seemed to become noisier. 'And when oceans rise to the pull of the moon, so do we.' He looked at each one of their faces. 'Remember that. The dance of the sun, earth and the moon intricately determines our lives. If you can divine what they're up to, you will know it all.'

As his practices deepened over the months and years, Chaturvasi felt like a new sense organ had evolved within him, one that knew precisely where the moon was in its rotation and its revolution around the earth. He had spent many months simply sitting and observing the natural surging and dampening of his energies during the day. And he had seen for himself that precisely an hour and thirty-six minutes before dawn, during the brahma muhurtham, his energies reached their most vibrant state and subsided forty-eight minutes before dawn.

Now, in Chennai, the brahma muhurtham was approaching. Soon the sun would rise from behind the horizon and start grilling the city. In a distant dimension of his existence, Chaturvasi felt it happen. But he was unable to respond to the grandeur of that sacred window. He was repelling Kakasura with every ounce of his energy, much of which had dissipated. His energy form had been destroyed and torn to shreds. Pieces of it lay in pink throbbing blobs splattered across the bungalow.

Kakasura was a powerful vetal by itself and Ugra's machinations had made it omnipotent. Even with its link to Ugra severed, it was still formidable. If it had been just the demon he would have managed to best it, but the constant attack from all sides had weakened him. With his energy form neutered and his yantra not at hand, he was too feeble against its force.

Outwardly, he painted a picture of a meditating Buddha

– calm, composed, with his eyes gently closed, hands in his lap – but in his mind and his energy body there was a battle to resist the infection that was threatening to rip him apart. If he couldn't stay strong, the demon would leap into him and his body would be a massive upgrade from that of a gangly teenage body.

The breath was connected to the prana and marshalling one's breath in certain precise ways could channel one's energy to circulate through the body. In this, Chaturvasi was an adept and could direct his energies to specific points in his body, pool and concentrate them, before unleashing them towards a certain goal. Now he collected his energies and forced them to the base of his throat, giving him an extra few minutes to resist the demon, which was now bleeding him dry.

Around three-thirty in the morning, Sri Chandramouli Shastry's old Nokia phone buzzed with a message from Chaturvasi. He had been dozing lightly, knowing that his friend was performing the exorcism. Without even reading the message, he leapt out of his cot and threw a thin cotton cloth over his shoulders. He dashed out of his tiny quarters by the temple, yelling, 'Ring the bells! Ring the bells! Balaji! Chandrasekar! Get out and ring the bells!' A couple of lights came on in the adjacent quarters. The apprentice priests had been told to stay on high alert for precisely this scenario. Two young men stumbled out of their quarters, hurriedly tying their veshtis.

Shastry reached for the bunch of keys tucked into his veshti. With practised moves he opened the massive padlock. 'Hurry!' he urged the two priests. 'There's no time to be lost.'

'What pattern?' Chandrasekar asked.

'First untie the rope!' Shastry ordered. Balaji quickly disassembled the knot from the coir rope and wound it around his palm.

'Ring like the typhoon. Ring the pattern to awaken the gods.' Shastry clapped and set the rhythm. '*Tung. Tung. Tung. Tung-tung. Tung-tung* . . . come on!' Balaji jumped and yanked the rope towards him. The sonorous bell above tolled. Even though the bell was outside, its sound filled the temple with its deep notes. Within seconds he had it pealing continuously.

Meanwhile, Chandrasekar reached for the smaller bell that was inside the temple. Shastry nodded. 'Same pattern. Quicker.' He began to ring the bell. This one made a tinnier sound, but it was more rapid. The head priest opened the door to the sanctum sanctorum and stared at the oil lamp. Behind him the bells briefly paused, for the priest also looked agog at the purple flame bent to the right. In his years of apprenticeship, the oil lamp had never turned colour, forget bending.

'Keep ringing, you fool,' Shastry thundered and pecked on his cell phone. The bells pealed. Lights flickered in the homes around the temple, with people confused why the temple bells were ringing in the dead of night. Now the flame dipped left and a beam of light shot out from the deity.

Shastry held his hand up. The bells stopped. Moments later, the flame tilted right again and the head priest gave the signal. The bells now pealed in a distinct rhythm much to the puzzlement of the ringers and the people around the temple.

Second by second, across the city, other venerable temples came alive and their bells began to peal in the same rhythm so that an observer standing atop St Thomas Mount would have wondered if there was something special going on in the city.

At the bungalow, Vikram's family watched Chaturvasi with trepidation. The tantric sported bumps on his forehead. Bruises appeared on his arms, ripping away the amulets. Each one fell, leaving scratch marks in its place. Parvati's fingers trembled in fear. Instinctively, she tried to reach for the doll, but it hovered just out of reach. Kakasura stood in a corner, staring unblinkingly at the tantric and swaying on the spot. She was desperate to look at her son, but his terrifying visage kept her from doing so. She brought up the image of Lord Narasimha and prayed hard to him. Mahesh raised his finger. 'What's that?'

'Sounds like bells,' Arun said, cupping his ear. He got up to check but the moment he locked eyes with his nephew, he was transfixed. Even though every cell in his body shuddered at the gruesome sight – the vacant stare, the silent grin, the protrusions on his head, the leathery skin tattooed with blue spidery veins, saliva smeared on his face and dripping slowly on to the floor – Arun couldn't tear his gaze away from this embodiment of evil.

Gopal tugged Arun's hand. 'Don't look at it. It may jump into you.'

With great difficulty Arun turned and walked to the window. They could hear the bells very clearly.

'The Temple of Eight Lakshmis,' Parvati said, tears in her eyes. 'Vishnu will save Vikky.'

'He did ask us to pray to Narasimha,' Gopal said.

'Something is happening,' Arun said, pressing his face against the windowpane. Muthu opened the gate and a line of men streamed in. They were tonsured and wore white shirts and veshtis with orange sashes around their waists. Their movements were lithe and careful. Without uttering a word, they bowed to Chris, spread out around the house and sat down on the ground.

'Appa,' Kakasura spoke in a childlike voice. It sounded so real that the four of them looked around in confusion. 'Appa,' the demon said from its corner. 'It's burning, pa.'

'Who is that?' Gopal asked, his hands scrambling for Parvati' and Mahesh's. He looked at the doll, but it was silent, its eyes closed.

'Appa,' the girl repeated, her voice shaking. 'Everything is hot here, pa. Please help me. I don't want to die.'

Chaturvasi slowly leaned forward. A tear ran down his cheek, the only sign that he was still alive.

'Pa, I can't feel anything, pa. Pa, please, pa. Everything hurts.' Now she screamed a little girl's scream. It was shrill and high-pitched. The four of them covered their ears and wondered if the ghost of that little girl had entered Vikram's body.

'Vikram, kanna,' Parvati said. 'Please fight these things inside you.'

'I'm here, ma,' the doll said.

'Pa, someone's cutting my head off, pa,' Kakasura shrieked. 'The knife is sharp. I'm not even dead yet. Pa, it hurts. Please do something. Pa, please wake up.'

'What's going on?' Mahesh asked, standing up. He was filled with nervous energy and he felt like he was losing control of his limbs. He glanced at Chaturvasi who seemed to have stopped breathing. He sat with his head slumped as did his myriad clones in the world of mirrors around him. The frankincense container was almost empty. The black cloth that he had laid on top of the mirrors slipped and fell on him like a dark shroud.

Mahesh wanted to shake the tantric and see if he was okay, but he figured it was best not to disturb him, considering he had already almost forgotten to notice the blackness of his finger earlier. 'Gopal . . . is . . . is he okay?'

'I don't know, pa,' Gopal said, his tone worrisome. 'He hasn't opened his eyes or said a word in a while.'

'I can't see him breathe,' Mahesh said.

'He knows best,' Parvati said. 'Don't disturb him.'

'They are forming a perimeter,' Arun informed them. Outside, Chris tossed a ball of white yarn to the man next to him and urged him to pass it on. When one received it, he threaded the yarn around his fingers and hands before tossing it to the adjacent person. Now they brought their hands forward in sync and touched their foreheads. They then placed their hands in their laps and began chanting.

The words were syncopated and hypnotic, rising and falling like a steady rain on an autumn evening. Behind them the bells tolled in the same rhythm. Now the bungalow began to tremble ever so slightly. In this cocoon of sounds, a tiny bell began to tinkle.

'Vasi sir!' Parvati exclaimed as Chaturvasi lifted his head. He tossed the cloth aside and stood up, wincing as he did so.

He held a small bell in one hand which he tinkled in rhythm with the temple bells outside. The lumps along his spine began to pulsate, but at the same time a few of them slipped back into his skin like a bubble disappearing into a pond. Chaturvasi rose like the phoenix, his energies revving slowly but surely about him, moving in precisely the way he needed. He held the doll in his other hand.

'Kakasura,' Chaturvasi said in a low rumble. The windows rattled. The demon snarled, making Vikram's muscles bulge as he smacked the wall.

Chaturvasi approached him warily, tinkling the bell with each step. 'Gopal, Arun, Mahesh, come with me,' he said. They followed the tantric with hesitant steps. 'Hold the boy.'

'But . . .' Gopal said.

'Do it!' Chaturvasi roared. The men moved in on him, but the demon paid them no heed, his distant gaze glued on the tantric.

'Don't stare into his eyes,' Chaturvasi warned them. They carefully held Vikram, but the papery skin and sulphurous smell made their stomachs lurch. It was like diving into a septic tank. Now they adjusted their grip so that Gopal held his son from behind, and Mahesh and Arun held his arms from either side. He struggled like a chained animal.

'I command you to leave the boy,' Chaturvasi said, tinkling the bell. He raised his palm up and the doll descended into it.

'No!' the demon hissed, sticking Vikram's tongue out and roaring.

Chaturvasi approached him and placed a finger on his forehead between the eyes. Vikram began to have a seizure. Parvati whimpered from behind. 'Please . . .' she wept.

'I'll give you one last chance. Set the boy free and take this.' He thrust the doll forward.

Thick vapour leaked from Vikram's nostrils and wafted up towards the ceiling and disappeared. The room was filled with translucent snow-like particles that drifted up from the ground around Vikram, like a slowly forming tornado. To the backdrop of the temple bells, jackals howled from within the bungalow accompanied by the tormented wails of the dead. And the hisses made it seem like they had stepped into a nest of vipers. 'Never,' the vetal said and with a herculean pull, freed himself of his human chains. The men huddled together behind the demon. Parvati and Gopal sought them out and they clasped each other's hands.

The maelstrom of particles swarmed and rushed across the room, dislodging the bell from Chaturvasi's hand. Vikram tried to reach for the hovering doll, but Chaturvasi snapped his fingers and the vetal snarled and retreated. He wrapped his arms around his chest. 'This body is mine. Ours.' Then he stared at Parvati, slowly breaking into a perverse smile. 'You did well in making this. Did you enjoy it?'

A glow began to envelop Chaturvasi. At first it appeared as if his skin was turning blue, but slowly the air around him began to shimmer a pale blue. Vikram's body shuffled forward. Cawing erupted in the room. Outside, there was a screeching of tyres.

The earth and the moon moved. The tides changed a tiny bit. And everything was just right. Chaturvasi closed his eyes and brought his palms together with his thumbs folded in. Now he made a fist with his left hand and then stuck his right thumb into it. He started chanting and his palms melded into each other, forming intricate mudras, briefly stopping every few seconds as if he were conjuring shadow puppets for his audience. Now they heard footsteps outside and then Ranganathan chiding, 'Tony, don't cross the sacred perimeter.' Watching Kakasura with full awareness, he reached out to the only deity who could annihilate the vetal, the one he paid obeisance to each morning on his trek to his meditation spot, the only one who had the essence of both man and beast. He was an omnipotent creature who, during his brief period on the mortal plane, had once terrified and mesmerized humans when he rid them of a terrible demon king. He reached out to the deity with a leonine face and eight arms – Narasimha.

There was a loud caw and a sharp thud as a crow smashed against the window. The thud came again, and a second later, it sounded as if there was a hailstorm outside. Within seconds, the bungalow was surrounded by crows from all sides. Everyone except Chaturvasi fell to the ground and put their heads to the down and covered their ears.

'*Aim hreem kleem kreem shreem treem streem hleem Kakasura*,' Chaturvasi chanted, forming the final mudra. His middle fingers formed an intricate steeple while the other fingers were enmeshed intricately.

At that moment, Ranganathan stepped in with Ugra's conch. Chaturvasi gave him a nod and Ranganathan brought the conch to his lips and blew into it. Instantly, something blue and translucent emerged from Chaturvasi's body. His head began to throb. Ranganathan inhaled and blew again. The form assumed a vaguely human shape. Moments later its head morphed into a lion's with a flowing mane. Eight arms grew from the torso. Narasimha stood in front of Ranganathan, waiting to be birthed fully. He opened and clenched his palms until claws shot out of them. He lowered his head, set his sight on Kakasura and growled.

Outside, the brahmacharis placed their thumbs into their ears, their fingers along their forehead and held an *mmm* sound. The bells tolled incessantly around them. Blood trickled down Ranganathan's nose as he breathed in. Chaturvasi's back arched, his head parallel to the ground, his hands dangling when Narasimha leapt and ploughed through the room. There was a sudden explosion as the blue god darted towards Kakasura. At the same instant, Vikram shrieked and pounced, grabbed the doll and landed on Chaturvasi. The family members screamed as Chaturvasi collapsed under Vikram's body.

Arun rushed and hesitantly pulled Vikram off the tantric. He turned him over. The widened shoulders, reptilian skin and the horns had all gone, revealing the boy's prosaic college-going, rice-eating figure. 'He's back,' he exclaimed. 'Vik is back.'

Parvati swooped down and cradled her son. She brushed his damp hair aside and stroked his cracked lips. 'Go get water,' she ordered. Gopal got up and shot out of the room, turning on the lights on the way to the kitchen.

'Vikram,' she cooed. 'It's amma. You're okay, pa.' She rocked him gently. 'It's all over.'

Gopal returned with a cold bottle of Bisleri and clumsily offered sips to Vikram. The boy, his eyes still closed, moaned. 'Everything hurts,' he whispered.

'I know, kanna,' Parvati said. 'I know. It's all over.'

Arun wiped the tears from his face. 'Don't worry, Vik. We are here for you.'

'Vasi!' Ranganathan exclaimed, wiping the blood from under his nose with the back of his hand. 'Vasi sir!'

Arun got up. 'What happened?'

'He's not breathing,' Ranganathan said in panic. Outside, the bells stopped pealing and there were only the monotonous chants from the brahmacharis. 'Vasi sir is not breathing.' He slapped Chaturvasi's cheeks. His eyeballs had rolled up. 'Give me some water.'

Gopal tossed the bottle to Ranganathan who sprinkled some on the tantric's face. But there was no reaction. 'Aiyo!' he exclaimed. 'Someone call the ambulance.' Arun reached for his cell phone. Ranganathan made a fist. 'No need. There is a car outside. Tony can drive. Go!' He kept shaking his friend. 'Vasi sir! Please get up!'

With tears welling in his own eyes, Ranganathan held on to his teacher and guide. He chanted verses from the *Ayushhomam* as he grasped at straws, figuring that the mantras to bestow longevity would somehow work. He invoked the nine planets and sang Sanskrit paeans to all the gods he knew and entreated Narasimha to reappear. He beat his palms helplessly, unable to recreate the complex mudra he had witnessed earlier. He tried to blow the conch again but couldn't make a sound. He pulled the yantra out and placed it next to Chaturvasi's limp form, hoping that something would magically happen. He endlessly begged his friend to wake up, but to no avail. Mahesh and Arun had moved Vikram into the car. They returned and tried to lift Chaturvasi, but Ranganathan clung to him.

'Let go,' Mahesh said. 'Let us take him to the hospital. It's urgent.'

'I'm also coming,' Parvati said and dashed out. 'Don't leave me without my son.'

'I'll come,' Ranganathan said.

'No space, sir,' Mahesh said as he gently cradled Chaturvasi's head in his lap and shut the door. 'Take an auto. There is a stand down the road.'

Tony and the rest of them crammed into the commodious car. Ranganathan watched in despair as Tony fumbled with the gear for a bit before the car tore away from the bungalow, leaving the place suddenly quiet and peaceful as if a demon had not been terrorizing them only moments ago.

'Is . . . is sami okay?' Muthu asked. It was after dawn now and the light hurt Ranganathan's eyes. He shook his head slowly and went back into the bungalow. Thoughts mobbed his mind. Chaturvasi hadn't breathed for minutes. Any ordinary human was certain to be dead by now, but Chaturvasi wasn't any ordinary human. Ranganathan refused to accept that his friend had passed away. Not only did a gut instinct tell him that, but he had seen the tantric's eyeballs dart back and forth even when the rest of him lay still.

He noticed the doll in the corner. He got up and approached it. It was still a magnificent work of fine art, even though its face had turned black and its hair had been singed. He was scared to pick it up. It looked like a miniature demon itself. When he turned to leave, he heard a familiar voice. 'Ranga?' Ranganathan spun around and stared at the doll.

'Va . . . Vasi?'

'Ranga, give this doll to my wife. She'll know what to do.'

Ranganathan looked around and found a plastic bag in a corner. He tenderly picked up the doll. 'Are you okay?' he asked.

'Hurry,' the doll said. 'The moon is on its way out.'

Chaturvasi's scheme made sense now. He had secured Vikram's soul in the doll to free it of Kakasura's clutches. Then he invited Kaksura into his own body so that Narasimha could destroy the vetal. As soon as this happened, he had brought Vikram back to his body and transferred his own consciousness into the doll. However, the tantric would require some assistance getting back into his body. Ranganathan placed the doll in the bag and ran out, tears of joy streaming down his face.

22

Dr Shetty replaced the stethoscope around his neck and stood up. 'Vikram is fine,' he said with a smile, revealing his paan-stained teeth. Vikram was on the hospital bed, an IV in his arm. He looked frail and tired with dark circles under his eyes and scraggy facial hair. Despite his physical condition, his eyes glinted with life. 'He has made a miraculous recovery, I must say, from the last time I looked at him.'

Gopal took the doctor's hand in his. 'Are you sure? No life-threatening' – he glanced at his son – 'or permanent changes? Did you check his skin?'

Shetty guffawed and scratched his bald head. 'Arre Gopal! You are the doctor or me? Huh?' He patted his friend on his shoulder. 'He's fine.' He leaned over and inspected the skin under Vikram's eyes. 'If you want, I'll get the dermatologist to look. But what is there to take a look at? Some mild discoloration. Fatigue. Patchy skin. Dehydration. He has been indoors for so long, no? He'll be fine once he gets out in the sun and goes about. What, Vikram? You have to go to college soon, okay?'

Parvati, still holding Vikram's hand, stroked her son's hair. 'How are you feeling, kanna?' she asked.

Struggling to keep his eyes open, Vikram said, 'Thatha?' It was barely a whisper.

She hugged him and wailed. 'He's fine, kanna. Thatha is doing better than all of us. Here!' she said, reaching for the plastic cup next to the table. 'Have some Glucon-D. It'll give you energy.'

Vikram smiled and tried to raise a finger, but Parvati gently pressed his hand down. 'Look, your friend Tony is here too.'

Tony raised his palm, unsure what to think and unable to speak. The happenings of the past few days were slowly coming home to roost in his head, and he was reeling from them. He still couldn't figure out how one night in Ugra's world had been a few days in this world. Each moment he discounted that it happened, he stroked his face and felt the week-long beard. He sighed. 'I . . . I didn't go to college too, man.' Vikram nodded weakly and smiled.

Now there was a scream and the sound of commotion. Dr Shetty's brows furrowed. 'What's going on?' he asked to no one in particular.

A stretcher slowly wheeled itself across the hospital door, its squeaky wheels making it go haywire. Shetty and the men gingerly walked out. Parvati lay a protective arm over her son.

'I must see the boy,' Chaturvasi said, barging into the room and pushing Shetty aside.

'He rose from the dead,' Mahesh screamed from behind him, running out of the elevator.

Arun tailed him, looking frazzled. He looked at Gopal

and shook his head. 'It can't be. I was in the ambulance . . . I . . . I . . .'

A nurse and a couple of ward boys dressed in whites followed Mahesh and Arun, looking equally shocked. 'He . . . he was . . .' the nurse started and then stood mute as the wild-haired dentist rushed to the barely conscious lad on the bed. He was still dressed in the black veshti from the night before, but had put on a T-shirt.

'Who's this?' Shetty asked, disoriented. He moved to place a hand on Chaturvasi when Gopal intercepted it.

'He's a friend,' Gopal said.

Chaturvasi sighed and smoothed his hair. He preened his beard, twirled the tips of his moustache and clucked his tongue. It sounded like a knock on the door. Everyone nervously looked around, the events from the previous night still fresh in their minds. Parvati stood up. 'More than a friend.' She knelt and reached for Chaturvasi's feet, but the tantric shuffled back. Ignoring the talk around him, he placed one palm on Vikram's forehead and closed his eyes. A few moments later he bent his head forward. He stayed that way for a while.

Dr Shetty checked his watch and announced that he had to do his rounds. He patted Mahesh. 'How can he be dead when he's clearly alive? Tired must be. Just like Vikram.' They heard the doctor admonishing the nurse and ward boys as he walked down the hallway. 'Must I teach you how to check for pulse?'

With Chaturvasi's hands on him, Vikram closed his eyes, though his eyeballs flitted underneath his lids. After a while, Chaturvasi opened his eyes. Vikram opened his too. They both smiled at once. The mischievous spark returned in Chaturvasi's eyes as he visibly relaxed. 'He's going to be fine,' he said, standing up. He walked slowly, wincing with each step. 'Kakasura had drained his prana. Give him a few days to recover.' He looked at Parvati. 'Feed him a diet rich in sattvic food, especially ash gourd.'

'But what happened?' Gopal asked. He looked tired with bags under his eyes. His shirt was torn in places.

Chaturvasi took a breath. In an instance the whole saga flashed before his eyes: Ugra orchestrating the accident many years ago, beheading Shruti and laying the trap to ensnare Vikram so that Chaturvasi could be roped in. Why? Because Ugra, despite his malevolence, believed in adhering to the karmic laws of nature. Ugra had been denied Shankaracharya's skull and waited centuries for another skull of equal value – Chaturvasi's. And in that pursuit, he had started a battle in which Vikram was merely a bait.

No, he couldn't tell the boy's family any of this. He couldn't tell them about Ugra's utopian island, Kapaladvipa, nor could he tell them about Ranganathan and Tony's close shave with death there. Or the death of the innocent driver, Balu. Or the magical conch that was so potent with life energy that it could summon a god. He exhaled slowly. No, none of them was ready for this. In fact, all that they had experienced needed to be effaced from their consciousness, for their understanding of the world beyond their five senses was minimal.

'Gopal,' Chaturvasi said, placing a hand on his shoulder. 'Life is not what it sometimes appears to be. Vikram read the verses under the banyan tree and summoned Hiranyaksha which came along with Kakasura.' Tony glanced at Vikram, who winced and closed his eyes. Parvati caressed his head.

'But what happened?' Vikram asked hoarsely. Even the act of speaking tired him. He lay back and closed his eyes.

'I'll tell you later,' Tony volunteered. 'Long story.'

'Vetals are a terrifying class of demons,' Chaturvasi said. 'They haunt corpses that have not been treated properly after death but can be commanded to haunt the living if one is capable enough. A pair could take over a living person. One would slowly drain the life energies of the person while the other takes over. Eventually, the possessed person will be essentially dead, his memory gone, his body under the thumb of the vetal.'

'But who was that little girl?' Arun asked, his brows knitted. 'She . . . she was in pain and it came from Vikram.' Vikram slowly raised his eyebrows and then looked at his mother.

Chaturvasi said nothing. He stroked his beard. If he tried to make a logical case, he'd go down a rabbit hole. It was time for them to let the events go and focus on healing. From the pouch tucked in his veshti he retrieved a black bundle of cloth. He unfolded it and revealed a bunch of copper rings, each shaped like a serpent. 'Each of you,' he said, dropping a ring on their palms, 'wear this ring on your left ring finger.' He looked at Tony and then smiled. 'Don't ever take it off for at least twelve years.'

'Twelve years-aa?' Mahesh said, adjusting the ring on his finger.

'It's for your good. You are all vulnerable to other spirits and demons. This is to protect you. Think of it as a vaccine.'

Mahesh walked up and said, 'Are you okay, sir? We thought we had lost you.'

Chaturvasi laughed. 'Kakasura underestimated his opponent. And its opponent wasn't me, but' – he brought his palms together and raised them to his forehead – 'Lord Narasimha himself. Nothing can survive when his presence is solicited.' He dusted imaginary lint off his shoulder and grinned. 'Clearly, even me!' He raised his palm and smiled. 'I'm fine.' He approached Parvati. 'When Vikram has recovered – should be fine in a few days – take him on a tour of the panchabhootasthalam.'

She bent down and touched his feet again. Chaturvasi stepped back. 'I don't mean to be rude, but please don't touch me right now. It's not good for me or you.'

Parvati trembled and clasped her hands. Chaturvasi raised his palm. 'It's okay. It's okay. No need to be scared. It's just that the energies are not settled.'

'There are five powerful temples in the south, very sacred and consecrated by tantrics centuries ago, one for each element. Four of them have a lingam that is kept in a specific way by the priests of the temple. I'll tell you the order to visit, but before you go to each one, you must prepare him for at least eleven days by doing appropriate practices and following a strict diet. Spend at least three days in each temple. When you go to the next temple, apply the vibhuti from the previous ones first. He should always apply vibhuti after prayer. Never leave home without it. Do you know how?'

Parvati slowly shook her head, knowing that she had probably been doing it wrong all her life. Vikram shook his head too.

'Right index finger . . . like this . . . dip and apply. Where? Between eyebrows. Base of the throat. Just beneath the rib cage. Under the navel.'

'Yes, Vasi sir,' Gopal said. 'Whatever you say. Where are these temples?'

Chaturvasi looked around the room. 'Any guesses?'

'I know a couple,' Arun said. 'The Arunachaleswara Kovil in Thiruvanamalai and one in Kanchi . . . oh! And that one in Chidambaram?'

'That's good. Yes. There are a couple more. One near Trichy and the other in Kalahasti. Take him there last. The lingam there was consecrated for the air element. I'll tell you the dates when to go. His visits should end here on a lunar eclipse. The temple will be kept open. In fact, it's the only temple that'll be open. When he's done with that temple, he will be properly vaccinated for the rest of his life.'

'What if it comes again?' Gopal asked.

The exorcist stopped on his way out and clucked. He rubbed his hands slowly and clapped. Everyone in the room shuddered. Vikram yelped and sat up, suddenly alive. 'It won't. It cannot. It has been destroyed. In a way it has been liberated from the eternal cycle of birth and death.' Chaturvasi turned, brought his palms together and raised them to his forehead. 'It's you lot that are still trapped here.'

Acknowledgements

A big thanks to Sivapriya for commissioning me to write this horror story. She is the one who reached out to me with the idea. Right when I was feeling good about the first draft, Chiki Sarkar gently suggested that though we had 'something amazing here', it needed work. And that took another year or so of rewriting. The book couldn't have emerged from its muck without her. A tonne of thanks to Keshava Guha, who read the second draft and guided me through the next round of edits with his encouraging words and an axe-sized scalpel. And to Arushi Singh, who had the patience to study it carefully and point out all the inaccuracies in the book. And, finally, thank you to all the people who helped shape the book in its different stages, such as cover design, typesetting and marketing.

A Note on the Author

Ashwin Mudigonda is a roboticist and travel photographer. He spent his childhood in Madras (not Chennai) and now lives in Oakland, California. This is his first novel.

CRAFTED FOR MOBILE READING

Thought you would never read a book on mobile? Let us prove you wrong.

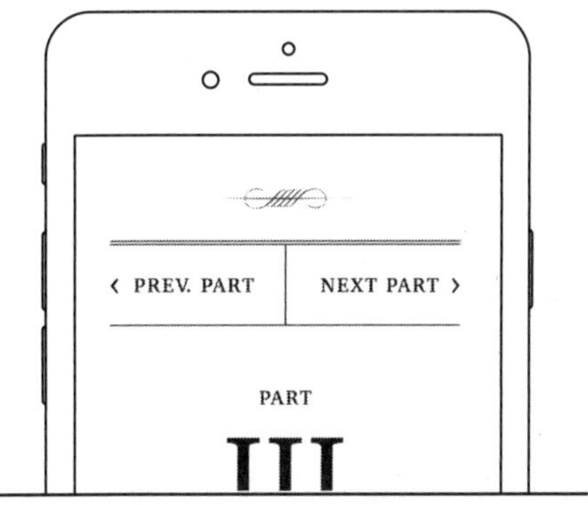

Beautiful Typography

The quality of print transferred to your mobile. Forget ugly PDFs.

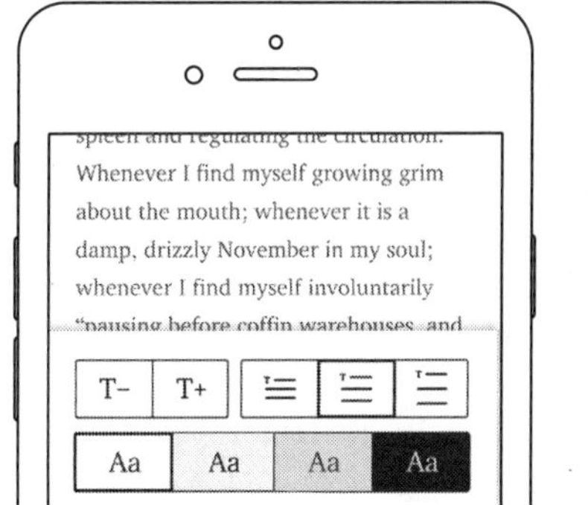

Customizable Reading

Read in the font size, spacing and background of your liking.

juggernaut.in

AN EXTENSIVE LIBRARY

Including fresh, new, original Juggernaut books from the likes of Sunny Leone, Praveen Swami, Husain Haqqani, Umera Ahmed, Rujuta Diwekar and lots more. Plus, books from partner publishers and loads of free classics. Whichever genre you like, there's a book waiting for you.

CRUCIBLES OF SIN
HITESHA
Can a Geek ever find Love?
Finding Juliet
Toffee
Mary Shelley
Frankenstein
A FAROOQ BSHI INVESTIGATION
COLD FLAKE
PRAVEEN SWAMI
A Psychiatrist's Guide To Heartbreak
How to Heal Your Broken Heart
DR SHYAM BHAT
MOIN and THE MONSTER
ANUSHKA RAVISHANKAR
Mafia Queens of Mumbai
stories of women from the ganglands
S. Hussain Zaidi
with Jane Borges
Foreword by Vishal Bharadwaj
UMERA AHMED
Nowhere Girl
A Story of Love & Forgiveness
THE BEHEADING
This Is How He Will Bless Her
ABHEEK BARUA
THE Peshwa
The Lion and the Stallion
THE INVISIBLE WOMAN
SAURBH KATYAL
ANGRY BIRDS FAN? READ THE BOOK!
ANGRY BIRDS TOONS
TOONS TALES
ARCHANA SABOO
ADIKOOL
in
#AfricanAdventures
i am not a bimbette
Tarana Khan
DON'T FALL IN LOVE
Vandana Shankar
KHUSHWANT SINGH
WE INDIANS

DON'T JUST READ; INTERACT

We're changing the reading experience from passive to active.

Ask authors questions

Get all your answers from the horse's mouth. Juggernaut authors actually reply to every question they can.

Rate and review

Let everyone know of your favourite reads or critique the finer points of a book – you will be heard in a community of like-minded readers.

Gift books to friends

For a book-lover, there's no nicer gift than a book personally picked. You can even do it anonymously if you like.

Enjoy new book formats

Discover serials released in parts over time, picture books including comics, and story-bundles at discounted rates. And coming soon, audiobooks.

juggernaut.in

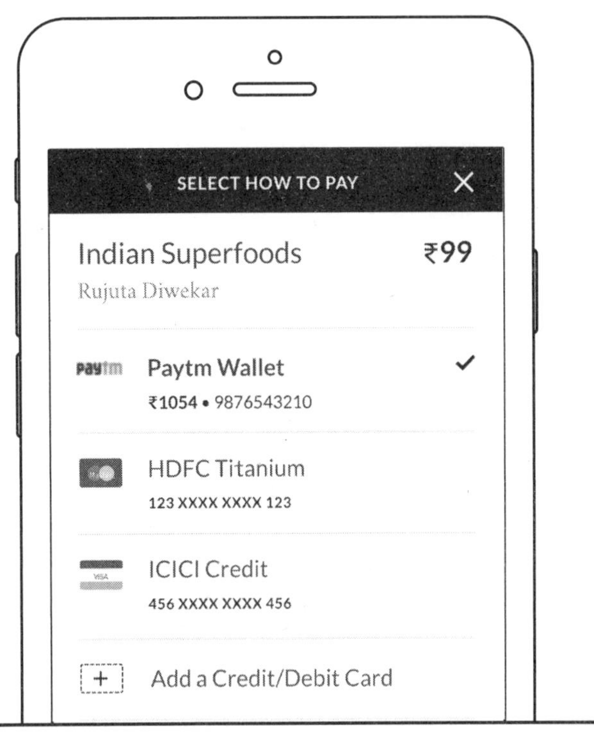

Paytm Wallet, Cards & Apple Payments

On Android, just add a Paytm Wallet once and buy any book with one tap. On iOS, pay with one tap with your iTunes-linked debit/credit card.

To download the app scan the QR Code with a QR scanner app